FIERCE
CREATURES

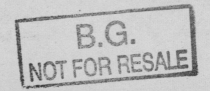

FIERCE CREATURES

A novel by
Iain Johnstone
based on the screenplay
written by
John Cleese and Iain Johnstone

BOULEVARD BOOKS, NEW YORK

FIERCE CREATURES

A Boulevard Book / published by arrangement with
Kensington Television Limited

PRINTING HISTORY
Boulevard edition / January 1997

All rights reserved.
Copyright © 1997 by Kensington Television Limited.
This book may not be reproduced in whole
or in part, by mimeograph or any other means,
without permission. For information address:
The Berkley Publishing Group, 200 Madison Avenue,
New York, New York 10016.

The Putnam Berkley World Wide Web site address is
http://www.berkley.com/berkley

ISBN: 1-57297-196-7

BOULEVARD
Boulevard Books are published by The Berkley Publishing Group,
200 Madison Avenue, New York, New York 10016.
BOULEVARD and its logo are trademarks
belonging to Berkley Publishing Corporation.

PRINTED IN THE UNITED STATES OF AMERICA

10   9   8   7   6   5   4   3   2

FIERCE
CREATURES

CHAPTER
1

Director: Archibald Leach LI.B. (Hons) Cantab

> Missão Wanda,
> Fazenda da Esperança,
> Tijuca,
> Rio de Janeiro

8th April 1996

Dear Rollo,

Crikey! You could have knocked me over with a quill pen when I got your letter. Truthfully I had given up all hope of ever hearing from you again.

I did try to track you down about five years ago but some fellow in the Hong Kong police personnel department told me you had changed your name from Leach to Lee. When I pressed him on this, he said your apparent thinking had been that politically it might have helped your chances of promotion if they thought you had some Chinese ancestry. Pretty sniffy he sounded, too. Said you'd left the force but refused to reveal where you'd gone. He probably didn't know—but he wasn't prepared to reveal that, either.

Do you have any idea how many Lees there are in the Hong Kong telephone directory? I wonder why they bother putting their bloody names in—unless it's with the express purpose of confusing people. So I simply gave up. And—let's be frank—I did harbour the suspicion that you might be avoiding me. I was aware that the Hong Kong police are not in the habit of giving positions of responsibility to men whose brothers are maliciously accused of having done a bunk with a jewel robber, even though they may have been a Queen's Counsel and damn nearly got a First at Cambridge.

Sorry about all that. More about me in a moment. But how about you? Octopus Inc., eh? We get the odd copy of the *New York Times* or *Wall Street Journal* down here when some passing philanthropist pays us a visit so I have a pretty fair picture of Rod McCain, king of Octopus and the Seven Seas and anything in between he can get his mitts on. Not an award-winning philanthropist himself, I suspect. (I do hope someone else doesn't open your mail—I have put "personal" on the envelope.) I suppose you can't be too choosey about who you work for in the world today. Even Albert Speer had to put up with an employer he didn't greatly care for. But McCain seems to me to have hit the bottom of the cesspit of capitalism. I mean, what's his master plan? How does somebody in their sixties spend five billion dollars or whatever during what's left of this mortal coil?

I used to play tennis at Queen's with a chap called Leonardo from some Italian bank—Monte dei Paschi di Sienna, I think it was—and they would get deposits from various international fat cats because it was said to be the only bank in the world where, after you died, you could pick up

2

your money on the other side. I remember asking Leonardo if it was true and he just smiled an enigmatic smile and said they'd never had any complaints from deceased customers; on the other hand, neither had they had any communication of any kind from them. But the myth persists.

Anyway, it was a good idea for you to get out of uniform and have a go at making your way in the real world and I suppose Octopus TV Hong Kong is a decent start even if, as you say, all they show are kung-fu movies and women wrestling with each other. I gather that's how Rod makes his millions—bringing culture to the masses. And I wouldn't be too worried about firing people if I were you: it's as certain as not that you're going to get fired yourself sooner or later. That's the way these operations work—on fear. And it tends to be the fearless who stay the course the longest. Besides, what's the worry in looking for another job compared to having some drugged-out Triad holding a knife to your throat? Beats me how you stuck the HK force so long.

(Much later . . . the children are asleep now. Well, most of them.)

You asked about me and Wanda. We're certainly together, very much so, although I still don't quite understand her. But that was the problem with me and Wendy: I did understand her—only too well. Wanda loves having children. She says giving birth is the ultimate high. So we seem to have had one every year—except in 1990 when we had the triplets. It's a fairly natural state of affairs out here but when Portia came to stay I couldn't bring myself to tell her she had ten stepbrothers and sisters so I pretended half of them were little lepers. She didn't seem that interested, anyway. She insisted that I had—her words—"fucked up" her childhood and caused her to steal credit cards and do a lot of drugs. Apparently the psychiatrist her mother sent her to told her that

3

she had an hereditary gene with inherent criminal tendencies which she got from me! Trick cyclists, we used to call them, and rightly so. What a load of bollocks. I've never done anything criminal in my life. Well, not intentionally. What the press failed to understand at the time was that Wanda and the jewels were inseparable. Literally so, as it transpired. I tried to persuade her to send them back but she said that they would do more good helping our lepers than ending up in various safe-deposit boxes where even the people who owned them weren't able to enjoy them. There is a certain moral logic in her argument but not one, I fear, that she is able to share with Scotland Yard. I can't go back to Britain, either. Nor do I want to. The prospect of a spell in prison is a minor irritant compared to the thought of being visited by Wendy.

It's rather fun out here; you should come and visit. The worst thing is that people keep introducing me to Ronnie Biggs at dinner parties as if we had a lot in common. Well, common is what he assuredly is: the man can't even hold his knife and fork correctly. And if I hear him putting on a mock posh voice to tell that BBC announcer joke—"Here is the latest news about the great train robbery: the great train is still missing"—once more, I'm likely to end up on an assault and battery charge.

Talking of which, we had friend Otto through a couple of years ago. Not the most welcome of guests; in fact a wholly uninvited one. Evidently South Africa under Mandela was not exactly to his liking so he appears to have been roaming the world looking for some National Socialist Party where, he said, he can find like-minded individuals. I would have suggested he start one himself but, knowing his potential for irrational outbursts of violence, I kept my counsel.

He had tried to catch up with Ken Pile in London on his way over but Pile, who is now master of ceremonies or something at Sea World, evidently had him thrown out by the security guards, claiming he was a danger to the fish. "They've cured the stammer but not the paranoia" was Otto's observation.

Thankfully he only stayed for three days as he said he was on his way to some secret reunion in Argentina of retired high-ranking officers. I've rarely met a more odious individual. After one dinner with him I made an excuse and went up to visit another mission in the mountains where we send recuperating patients to try and recuperate myself from my encounters with him—I didn't fancy hanging upside down again from a fifth-floor window as a result of his paranoia. When I returned Wanda seemed happy to see the back of him, too, although she did fall into the habit of reciting recipes in Italian for several days. She's stopped now, but the children keep sticking their french fries up each other's noses—some trick the thug taught them at a fast-food restaurant.

Rollo, I have to tell you that I've found a happiness that I just didn't know existed before and it's all due to Wanda. Her mystery gives her an undying allure (getting a bit poetic here, aren't we?). She disappears from time to time on unannounced trips into the rain forest to visit the Indians but she never fails to come back with some gold or other valuables to keep the colony going for another year. Every Christmas she joins a samba class and disappears again for nights on end during the Lent carnival. But I know she will always return and that knowledge is like a constant fire within me, warming the spirit and making it feel good to be alive.

I'll write longer later. But take this advice to heart. I know you've always had difficulties with women and when we were young we blamed it on the old British public school thing and the fact that our parents were too formal with us. But it's there. It's inside you, too. And if the right woman comes along, give up everything and go with her.

When I think of those wasted years I spent on the commuter train to Waterloo . . .

God Bless.

Affectionately yours,

Archie

Rollo Lee gazed again at the meticulously neat handwriting of his brother. It was the kind you only ever saw on end-of-term reports as a schoolboy.

And then he gazed out of the twenty-fourth-floor window of the Octopus Building, which dominated the Wing West Road, and watched the tawdry green Star ferries crisscrossing Victoria Harbour from Tsim Sha Tsui to Hong Kong Island. He had arrived on one at eight-thirty that morning, and at six-thirty that evening, unless a crisis blew up at the station, he, too, would be part of that crowded human cargo as he returned to his neat apartment in the New Territories. Was this his Waterloo?

For nearly four years now he had been on the corporate treadmill at Octopus TV and for nearly four years, he conceded to himself, he had loathed the place. It had none of the camaraderie or sense of purpose he had enjoyed in his two decades in the Hong Kong police. Yes, it paid him more money, but just when he thought he was getting on top of the job in personnel some new managing director would be shipped in from Sydney or Singapore or Seattle with a directive to expand the output and reduce the staff. Usually it was a bull-necked Australian or cocky Londoner who had been wrenched from editing a local tabloid newspaper or a twelve-year-old from Octopus headquarters in Atlanta, but whichever type came along the one thing they would have in common was their complete lack of culture and their de-

6

termination to prove to Rod McCain that they were "hard-nosed." Making other people redundant was evidently a way of showing their strength.

Inevitably it fell to Rollo to inform people that their jobs had became "nonessential in the restructuring." He felt himself a coward. As opposed to resigning, he would resign himself to the task, justifying his role by the fact that at least he could carry it out as humanely as possible and obtain the best redundancy terms for the unfortunate individuals whom he had to fire. But Archie, as usual, was right: one day he would be summoned to the thirtieth floor and informed that his own services were surplus to requirements.

In his mind he had planned for that eventuality. He had saved enough money to stay in Hong Kong until June 30 next year, when the Chinese would, without justification in his opinion, take over the territory. It had been ceded to Britain by the Treaty of Nanking, which had brought the Opium War to an end. At the time Lord Palmerston, the foreign secretary, had described it as "a barren island with hardly a house upon it." What was being handed over next year was the last jewel of the British Empire—a flourishing commercial community where the rule of law and the fundamental right to freedom had enabled two races to live together in remarkable harmony. Rollo intended to put on his officer's uniform and stand sentinel by Government House to greet the arriving Chinese mainlanders and, by drawing himself up to an erect six foot five inches, remind them of a system that had worked for nearly a hundred and fifty years.

And then? Well, the obvious place to go was England. But he had no emotional home in his own homeland. His parents were both dead and his brother was in permanent exile, so he had no real idea how to form a way of life there. It would be like a stranger arriving in a foreign country with a nagging sense of déjà vu that once he had been there before. No, he intended to head south. Several of his colleagues from the force had gone to Queensland and opened bars or small ranches with their savings. Rollo wasn't much into that sort of thing but thought he might get a job as assistant secretary at a golf club or bursar at a boys' prep school—if they had such things. He had always been fairly adept at fitting into an existing hierarchial structure and helping to run it, having an innate love of order and discipline.

They were at the forefront of the reasons he had come to the Crown Colony in the first place. He had never been in the A-stream at school, nor indeed the B-stream. Thoughtless masters would belittle his academic abilities by comparing them with the golden pathway his elder brother had cut through the institution. An open scholarship to Gonville and Caius College Cambridge had never been likely to be his culminating glory.

But Rollo, as those neatly written reports inevitably informed his parents, had always had a strong sense of duty, something that had found its home in the Hong Kong force. They were never likely to clean up all the crime in the territory, but somehow the sight of an English officer in a military uniform proved a more effective presence in breaking up gangs, Rollo thought, than those American cops with their sunglasses and motorcycles and chewing gum whom he watched on TV. He was always wary of Americans: they gave too much, too soon. On aeroplanes they would tell you their life story before takeoff.

And after that, what? The marketing department in Octopus TV consisted of a dozen of the pushiest Americans he had ever met in his life, always talking about concepts and ideas and campaigns and never, as far as he could see, actually doing anything except plastering the company logo over everything in sight.

He glanced at the bank of television sets on the wall opposite the window. They had their sound turned down but he could see on the screens the appalling low-budget gangster and kung-fu movies that Rod was broadcasting to the Chinese. Culture for the masses, he thought disdainfully as he put his feet up on the desk and yawned; what a crock of garbage.

His relaxation was short-lived. A sharp knock came at the door, causing Rollo swiftly to remove his feet and tuck his long legs under the desk. He picked up a pencil and his diary and assumed the assiduous pretence of ticking off items in it.

"Come in," he snapped, in the tone of a busy man slightly irritated by the interruption.

It was Miss Po, the secretary he shared, a slender Hong Kong girl with close-cropped black hair and wide thin-rimmed glasses.

"Good morning, Mr. Lee," she said respectfully. "You got in early today."

"You know how it is," he replied with a sigh. "Work piling up, overseas calls, decisions, decisions."

Rollo looked every inch a British civil servant as he sat there in his cream colonial suit, white shirt, and regimental tie, his hair neatly parted and his moustache still trimmed to regulation police guidelines.

He put down his pencil and rubbed his hands together, a familiar habit. "What's on the agenda today, Sandra?"

She handed him a sheet of paper. She had already memorised the contents; it wasn't hard. "You have a scheduling meeting at eleven A.M. and the finance committee at two."

He took it from her with an expression of exasperation on his face, as if such work was an interruption. Miss Po smiled. She understood Rollo and rather liked him.

9

"Anything else?" he demanded, wondering why she was still lingering in his office.

She dropped her voice. "Don't forget—you have to fire Elvis Ho at six."

With that she turned and made a dainty exit. Rollo sighed, yet again. A look of terminal boredom spread across his face. No, he hadn't forgotten. He had even rehearsed in his mind all the usual bullshit about "reengineering" or "downsizing," when the bald fact was that if the station could be run with one salary less, then that amount of money went straight to swell Big Rod's coffers.

Rollo glanced again at his brother's letter and smiled to himself. He had lied to him. He hadn't changed his name to Lee in order to get promotion in the force: it was when the fourth UK visitor to his club had asked, half-joking, whether he was related to that lawyer Leach who let down his chambers rather badly by doing a bunk with that American moll who had masterminded a jewel robbery. He had always been in awe of Archie. He and Wendy had seemed to have the perfect life: good golf club, house in Surrey, horse for the child, Jaguar, weekly dinner parties at which people complained about school fees. All the things you were supposed to aspire to in middle-class England. Rollo had been the outsider, the younger son who had gone off to make a life in the colonies.

And now the roles were reversed. Archie was the black sheep of the family—lucky their parents were dead—and Rollo had a respectable position in an international conglomerate. It had been both a shock and a consolation to learn that Archie's previous lifestyle had been such a sham.

Yet, still he envied him. He envied him Wanda. From the moment he had seen her picture in the *South China Morning Post,* before even he had read that his very own brother had fled the country with her, he had been smitten by those

10

Lorelei eyes and the teasing confidence of her smile. Women had always been a bit of a problem for Rollo. In truth, he didn't understand them. The few relationships he had had with British women in the colony—divorcées mainly—had inevitably come to grief when they began, sooner or later, to try to change him. How could they genuinely be attracted to him, he reasoned, if their secret agenda was eventually to turn him into someone else? He had worked out an ordered lifestyle and he was buggered if anyone else was going to come along and alter it.

He was snapped back into the present from his reverie by the sound of the bell of St. John's Cathedral in Battery Park ringing as if to signal poor Elvis Ho's doom like the last act of *Tosca*. Rollo made a pistol with his hand and pointed its barrel into his right ear. At that very moment Don Bennetts, a beer-bellied Australian who was his immediate superior, strode into the room. He hadn't bothered to knock, but there again he never did. For the second time in ten minutes Rollo felt like a schoolboy who had been caught. He hastily stood up, pretending to bite a broken fingernail.

"I've been talking to Atlanta." Don always dispensed with the formality of any kind of greeting; to him it was time-wasting. "There's a big deal going through. You're being transferred."

He handed Rollo a fax but, before Rollo had time to glance at it, continued with more than a hint of a sneer: "You're going to run a zoo. In England."

Rollo surveyed the fax with incredulity. "Run a zoo?" he repeated.

Don rarely bothered to disguise his distaste for Rollo. The man was a walking rule-book and he was relieved to be rid of him. "Oh, cheer up, you miserable Pommie bastard," he enjoined him as he left. "It's a promotion."

Rollo said nothing. He merely looked down and read the piece of paper in his hand. It was like one of those military commands in a Shakespeare play. "Get thee to England, hence!" He had always known that one day he would return to his native heath, for however short a time, in some capacity. But in this capacity? It bordered on the risible.

And yet . . . and yet maybe not. Here was a chance to helm his own command. And to get away from Don and his like, people who had made his last years in Hong Kong less than tolerable. After his being an officer in the Hong Kong police, a bunch of British zookeepers would undoubtedly present him with very few problems. Here was a second chance at life, when he least expected it.

A broad smile spread over his face as he looked up at Rod McCain's obligatory picture on his office wall.

"Sorry to disappoint you, Rod," said Rollo, "but you've just made somebody very happy."

CHAPTER
2

No, it was a bit premature for the Prada outfit. Too much, too soon. Save that for her introductory meeting with other departmental heads or, yes, better still, her first major corporate presentation.

Besides, Willa Weston thought as she glanced out of her apartment window at the sun-streaked Atlanta dawn, there wasn't a cloud in the sky and a dinky black raincoat, even a Prada, might seem inappropriate on such a summer day.

She swiftly removed the black outfit, then cast it casually onto a chair—Aida was due in later today—and returned to her step-in wardrobe. Yes, why not? The Barbara Bui jacket worn with nothing underneath it except a bra. Excited, she slipped it on, admiring her long legs with their recent Caribbean tan in the full-length mirror inside the door. Girlfriends had warned her that her workout program might make them muscled; on the contrary, Willa noted with self-appreciation, it had merely accentuated the contours of her calves in a rather enticing fashion.

13

But no, Barbara Bui was not for today either. Again the signal it was sending out was overridingly strong. Too much flesh and a little too flash. The jacket was accordingly consigned to the pile for Aida to hang up. If necessary she would iron them first. There was no need to leave a note for her; Portuguese maids had an innate sense of tidiness and decorum.

She glanced at the bathroom television to see what time it was. Just after seven. She would need to leave in ten minutes. Willa had noted from the day she went for her interview that most executives tended to arrive between a quarter to eight and five to eight, and she needed to hit the peak period for maximum impact. Besides, her appointment was for eight. She paused for a moment to look at Bryant Gumbel—was that his real name?—and the woman sitting next to him whose name she didn't even know. Perhaps she was a newscaster drafted in as a summer replacement. Willa had always fancied herself on the NBC couch sitting beside Bryant and swapping jokes with Willard but, even as a younger woman, she could never stoop to the position of having to audition for anyone. Besides, she reasoned, those types all started out as beauty queens or weather girls, and that was strictly for the bozos.

By allowing her usually concentrated mind to go into free-flow the answer to her clothing conundrum presented itself as if by instinct. There is was—the black Thierry Mugler suit with the voile semi-see-through waist that left men in no doubt as to precisely what shape she might have cut on the beach at the Half Moon Club in Jamaica. And the shoes to match. She scrambled into the outfit while grabbing the internal phone from beside the door.

"Raymond, can you have the XJS ready in seven minutes."

"Do it in six, Miss Weston." The doorman chuckled at the familiar request. "You want the lid off, ma'am? It's going to be a gorgeous day."

"Good idea . . . ," she began. But then, catching sight of her strawberry-blonde locks immaculately sculpted round her neck, she changed her mind. "No, leave it up."

"The old hair, eh?" came back the knowingly impudent reply. "Got to look good on your first day with the big Octopus."

The traffic on the 1-20 West was already building up as she joined the freeway. This city has never been the same since the goddam Olympic business began, she thought, irritated, and then cleared her mind to itemize in her head the probable formalities of her first day in the organisation. To begin with she had the long-awaited meeting with Rod McCain—although that probably wouldn't last long. Then she would make a brief address to the senior staff at WOCT—the Octopus radio group—promising to hold one-to-one meetings with them individually later in the week. Most important, she had to talk to the design people about her office, make sure she had a male secretary, and then take meetings with personnel to discuss conditions of service and even pensions, for heaven's sake! She felt confident and optimistic. She was more than ready for the off. What was it Shakespeare said? A greyhound in the slips.

Willa had grown up in Atlanta—her father had been a pilot with Delta Airlines—and ever since she had graduated from college she had always had a hunch that one day she would work for Rod McCain. The man intrigued her beyond measure. Nobody ever got behind the mask. Whereas Ted Turner was from the South and expanded his father's family billboard business into a television empire by the simple expedient of buying space on a satellite and transmitting his entertaining channel, WTBS, across America and thereby funding CNN, McCain was an altogether more complex character. For a start he was an alien, a New Zealander who, like some conqueror of old, Hannibal or Alexander, had fought his way across the globe, from Auckland to Sydney to Hong Kong to London to New York to Atlanta, setting his sights on undervalued media assets and then joining battle with the entrenched local owners of newspapers and radio and television stations and usually leaving blood in his wake. And he had had the nerve to set the corporate headquarters of Octopus Inc. opposite the CNN HQ in Atlanta, two skyscraping giants glaring at each other in the centre of the city.

Willa admired the fact that McCain was a warrior. Although she had never met him, she hoped that he might sense the same determination in her. Here was someone who had breathed the heady intoxicant of global media domination and was prepared to gamble his all to achieve it. For what purpose? The answer was glaringly obvious to her— for the sake of winning, to demonstrate his superiority over mere mortals. McCain knew that the modern world would no longer be controlled by politicians or generals; it was the man who could capture people's hearts and minds with his newspapers and television and radio stations that could spread a gospel as incisively pervasive as communism. Deep down she wanted to be part of that great crusade. Too many of her contemporaries were married to losers or sat on their butts and watched the world go by. Willa wanted to *make* it go by.

Having left the car in the executives' car park—a status symbol she had never been accorded at Coca-Cola (although the man at the gate had no record of her but simply assumed that anybody driving a Jag XJS must be an executive)—she took the steps up to the outside entrance to savour the moment of entering the mighty edifice from the sidewalk for the first time as a member of staff.

She glanced at her watch as she went through the swinging doors. She was six minutes early for her meeting with McCain. Mustn't seem too eager. She paused by the vast list of companies the man owned that were posted like victories on triumphant oak panels just inside the entrance.

OCTOPUS, SA. ARGENTINA

OCTOCORP, LTD. AUSTRALIA

OCTOPUS, NV. BELGIUM

OCTOPUS, SA. BRAZIL

OCTOPUS, WU CO LTD. CHINA

L'OCTOPUS FRANCAIS. SA. FRANCE

OCTOSCHNELLEN. GMB. H. GERMANY . . .

. . . and on and on. Was there any major territory on the planet where McCain had not left his giant footprint? A slight shiver went down her spine: the sight intimidated her.

She snuck another glance at her slimline Panther Cartier watch. Four minutes to eight. Time for her approach. She purposefully strode the twenty yards or so across the atrium towards the central reception desk. As she did so every male head, and not a few female, turned in her direction. Willa was the sort of woman who turned heads, especially in the outfit she was wearing today.

Three uniformed security guards manned the desk and Willa confidently walked up to the burly one in the middle. He was older than the two men on either side and seemed to exude more authority.

She gave him a brief smile. "I'm here to see Rod McCain. Willa Weston."

The name McCain caused the man to straighten up; the revered word seemed to trigger off this automatic reaction.

17

At the same time he eyed Willa with a hint of suspicion. "Do you have an appointment?" he inquired.

"Gee, you need appointments?" Willa replied with feigned innocence. "I just wandered in off the street in case he felt like a cup of coffee."

"What?" The man was completely taken aback; it was a little early for irony.

Willa leant across the desk and indicated the well-thumbed signing-in book with her forefinger. "I have an appointment with him at eight A.M."

The guard, still eyeing her warily, lifted his phone and dialled a number.

Willa stepped back and nonchalantly looked at the portrait of McCain that dominated the fairly austere reception area. It was surrounded by clocks giving the time in other business centres—London, Sydney, Frankfurt, and Hong Kong. Heads continued to turn in her direction; one young man actually walked into a pillar, so absorbed was he in this striking-looking woman. Also watching, but, so far, unharmed by any columns, was a dashing man in his mid-forties, who looked as if he might have stepped from the pages of a fashion magazine, his dark blue Armani suit offset by a louche silk scarf.

"The line's busy—you'll have to wait." The security guard was still unsure of Willa.

Her patience was being tested. She indicated the clipboard beside the signing-in book. "Am I not on the list?"

"Can I help?" The man with the silk scarf surfaced beside her.

"I really don't think so, thank you." Willa hardly bothered to turn her head to take him in. But she did bother to address the guard, as he was beginning to annoy her. "Listen, you are trying Mr. McCain's assistant, right?"

The man nodded.

18

"Well, can you try again." Willa's irritation was ill-concealed. "I suspect she has more than one line."

"Are you sure I can't help?" The male model with the scarf was evidently not someone who was put off easily.

This time Willa did take him in. "Look, Mr. . . . ?"

He stepped back a little and gave a pert smile. "Vince McCain."

Willa's attitude changed abruptly. She returned his smile—in spades. "I'm sure you can help, Mr. McCain."

"Vince," he insisted.

She held out a hand. "Willa Weston. I'm starting work here today. I'm running WOCT. You're vice president marketing, right?"

"I'm impressed by your knowledge," he replied flatteringly, and then added: "But mainly I wait for my father to die."

Willa acknowledged the joke but didn't choose to participate in it. "I hope it's a long wait, Vince. I'm so excited to be working with him. There's no glass ceiling with Rod McCain. It's just about talent."

She now noticed that a lot of men were appraising her and suddenly became self-conscious about it. "Why are those men staring at me?" she demanded. "I'm a businesswoman, for God's sake."

Vince nodded affirmatively and then leant across to the security guard, who was still unable to get through to his father's office.

"Bill, I'm taking this lady up," Vince told him confidently. "She's from the White House. She's arranging a meeting with the President."

The man hastily put down the phone, embarrassed. "Oh, sorry, Mr. McCain. Sorry."

As Vince guided her by the arm towards the elevators, she wasn't sure she could quite believe what she had just heard.

"What was that about the White House?" she inquired delicately.

Vince clapped his hands together and gave a vapid grin. "I was just changing his perception of the situation. First law of marketing."

Willa glanced to see if he was joking and was somewhat discomfited to observe that he seemed to have a look of triumph on his face. She was about to say something, but they had reached the bank of six elevators which whisked people up into the various executive offices of Octopus Inc. A tall young man, probably fresh from business school, walked past them and greeted Vince with a respectful: "How ya doing?"

"Never better" came that smile again.

Three groomed executives in their Brooks Brothers suits were there ahead of them, waiting for the elevator. Vince obviously knew them.

"Hey, Joe," he greeted one, removing the man's postal edition of the *Wall Street Journal* from under his arm. He then used it to hit the other on the back of his legs, demanding: "Ed, what did you shoot Saturday?"

"Seventy-nine." The man was evidently as pleased with his round of golf as he was displeased by Vince's surprise gesture.

"Beat you," Vince announced, elbowing his way past him into the elevator. The other two men waited graciously for Willa to enter before them. She nodded her appreciation and took up a position in the corner.

Vince, meanwhile, greeted a bubbly blonde secretary already in the elevator with an overfamiliar squeeze.

"Hi, Lisa," he said with that smile.

"Hello, Mr. McCain."

"Vince, please," he insisted. She flushed slightly with pleasure at this offer of equality, but it was a short-lived joy.

20

"Lisa . . . posture." He put his hand on her shoulders. "Take the hips back. Relax the shoulders. Let the neck grow. There's a column of energy coming right out of the top of your head. You have beautiful breasts—don't be ashamed of them."

The sense of embarrassment among the other men was palpable. Is this for my benefit, Willa wondered, or does he do this every day? She permitted a half smile to be signalled from her lips, just in case he caught sight of her.

The girl was grateful to get out of the elevator at its next stop, whether it was hers or not. "Thank you, Mr. McCain," she said pointedly.

Nothing daunted, Vince stuck his head out after her. "Don't mention it. I'll give you the name of a guy."

Willa first examined her briefcase and then looked at her watch, so unanxious was she to catch Vince's eye. But once again her attention was drawn to his insensitive behaviour. In the corner of the elevator opposite to hers stood a tall, distinguished man in his early sixties with a military moustache, identifiably a visitor by the tag on his lapel and probably a high-ranking executive in another company. Vince casually lifted the man's tie and inspected it.

"Oh. Could have sworn it was silk," he pronounced to the visitor's astonishment as the man absorbed the reactions of the elevator's other occupants.

Willa didn't have time to be astonished. Vince had taken her arm as the doors opened at the chairman's floor to reveal a large portrait of Rod McCain on the wall.

"Rod Almighty," Vince observed proprietorially. "You want to meet Dad?"

"Yes, I do. Most certainly. I have an appointment." Willa's joy at this stroke of serendipity was only tempered by the fact she was dealing with one off-the-wall son. What the hell, she thought.

21

"Come on," urged Vince, almost dancing before her down the corridor. "He's the most powerful man in the world."

When they reached Rod's two secretaries, whose desks formed a definite bastion preventing all entry to their master's den save for the summoned few, Vince waltzed over to the one who looked less like a bulldog. Nevertheless she greeted him with an admonitory warning that seemed to indicate no entry. "Er, Mr. McCain . . ."

"He called me, Gina," Vince countered airily as he maneuvered past her desk and threw open the door to the office.

Willa peered in eagerly, hoping for her first sighting of the great man. What she saw was a nearly empty boardroom, coldly furnished in anonymous grey, with a stocky man in a suit as shiny as his nose quickly bearing down on Vince, a grimace of irritation on his florid features. Vince seemed oblivious to this, as indeed he did, Willa had already noted in a very short time, to many things.

"Hi, Neville." He gave the man, who either wore a fringed dark brown wig or had a barber who wanted people to think he wore one, a friendly slap on the shoulder. "How's it going?"

"Rod's busy," came the stoney-faced retort.

"That's the way he likes it," Vince smiled as he slipped past him, almost breaking into a jig. "Busy, busy, busy."

Neville turned in fury and, in an Australian accent as thick as his neck, began to warn menacingly: "Vince, he said—"

But both of them were frozen to the spot, as indeed were Willa and the two secretaries outside, by the noise that came from behind the double doors off the boardroom which led, presumably, into Rod's holy of holies.

"Yes, oh yes, oh yes!" It began, thought Willa, like the sound of a professional tennis player who had just clinched the first set, then the whole match, and then the whole fucking tournament. Like an approaching thunderstorm it grew in strength, emulating the sound of a gorilla or a rhinoceros or, for all she knew, some Tyrannosaurus rex, having a massive orgasm. "Yes, yes, yes, yes, yes, yes!" It culminated in the crashing of a forty-foot wave hitting the shore or a hundred cymbals being struck simultaneously or an entire football stadium emitting a primal scream.

The doors flew open and there he was. Rod McCain. Big Rod. Rod Almighty. Thick grey-white hair, darkened glasses, loudspeaker ears, and a gold tooth that occasionally caught the light. He had the rocklike physique of a rugby player, with shoulders that were designed to bulldoze their way through the opposition. In media terms this was, indeed, the most powerful player on the planet.

"I did the deal." The voice was a low yet penetrating growl.

"One four five million?" Neville asked eagerly.

"One three eight," screamed McCain in exultation. "Hit me, Neville."

The obedient Australian, the human equivalent of two hundred pounds of condemned veal, hammered a mighty right fist into his boss's solar plexus, a blow that might have had Mike Tyson on his back.

Rod absorbed it with a joyous inhalation of breath and an electric tremble of ecstasy, a pleasure that was only spoiled by the sight of his son.

"Oh, it's you," he remarked coldly.

"Way to go, Dad," cried Vince.

"No," Rod snapped back as he strode past him.

"Can I just introduce someone?" Vince was nothing if not persistent.

"I don't have time," snarled his father. "I'm late for the TV studio."

"But Dad . . ."

"Rod, what do we do about Des Moines?" It was Neville who interrupted, lifting a fax from the boardroom table.

"Close it." Rod barely missed a pace as he strode out of the room.

"It's done." The death of the plant and the loss of a few thousand jobs was pronounced in the sinister tones of a servant who survived through unquestioning obedience to his master.

As Rod emerged into the corridor, Willa expeditiously decided that boldness was the order of the day and introduced herself.

"Mr. McCain. I'm Willa Weston. In fact, we had an—"

"Started today, right?" McCain paused to take her in.

Thank God for Thierry Mugler, Willa thought as she tried to explain: "Your son—"

"You were at Coca-Cola." McCain had a not-accidental reputation for being able to recite minutiae about members of his corporation when most people presumed his head would be filled with the details of his latest deal. He beckoned Willa to follow him down the corridor.

As he made his way, with Neville now pinned to his shoulder, Vince followed in hot pursuit. "Dad, may I introduce—"

"Shut up," McCain barked over his shoulder. He continued to appraise Willa appreciatively. "I've just done a beautiful deal, Willa. Alliance Leisure UK."

"One three . . ." Vince, from behind them, was struggling to remember the bargain his father had struck.

. But Rod continued as if his son weren't even there. "And the sweetest part of it is—I snatched it from under the nose of that bastard Murdoch."

"What are the crown jewels?" Willa was proud of the chance to demonstrate her knowledge of takeover jargon so felicitously.

Rod ticked them off on his fingers: "NorthEast Television and Great British Publishing. Then there's a film distribution company, fourteen multiplexes . . ."

As he paused for a moment Neville continued, reading from a document in his hand. "Three ice rinks, a crematorium . . ."

"Nice little earner"—Rod picked up the momentum again—"and a zoo."

"A zoo?" The words came out automatically; Willa couldn't stop herself from registering her surprise.

McCain may not have heard her as he swept into the company television studio. A prop desk awaited him there, bedecked with hired family photographs and mementoes and college memorabilia, quite different from the arid boardroom.

Vince trailed the others as they went through the door and a member of staff approached him, anxious with some inquiry. "Not now," he said. "We're busy."

"Good morning, Mr. McCain," the crew chorused to Big Rod.

"Morning, boys," McCain responded. Then, in a practised fashion, he isolated a familiar face. "Morning, Ted."

He turned to Willa. "You'll have to excuse me. Tight schedule. Make a lot of money for me with . . . er . . ." His legendary memory deserted him for the moment.

She took his hand. "WOCT."

McCain stopped in mid-shake. "No," he said.

"What?" She was unable to follow him.

"I sold it this morning. Sorry." McCain turned away from her. "Look. I'll talk to you later, okay?"

He moved away towards his television desk. In the interim Vince had entered the studio.

Willa was furious and decided to vent it on the son. "Is that it? I've just left a job I'd been doing for eight years and without batting an eyelid he . . ."

Vince was about to reply but before he could his father returned. "Don't worry, Willa, we'll find something else for you." He switched his attention to Neville. "Check out our liability on the Des Moines pension rights. Should just be a return of employee contributions; don't want to expose us to any topping up."

He knew that Willa was listening but was unaware of just what a state of shock she was in. "Always got to think of the shareholders, Willa," he grinned.

The studio manager approached him anxiously as he eased himself into his seat. "Do you want to rehearse, or—"

"Nah," came the gruff reply. "Let's get it over with."

"Roll tape. Quiet please!" The studio manager was not unaccustomed to such impatience.

Daringly ignoring the injunction, Willa whispered to Neville: "I love zoos."

Neville shook his head, while keeping his gaze fixed on his boss. "Hmm? No. Bit of dead wood there."

Willa persisted. "No. Some animal parks are doing very well. Particularly in Europe."

"Sssh," said Neville at the same time as the studio manager called again for quiet.

"Speed. And in your own time, sir."

McCain fixed the camera with a look of sad sincerity. "My darling Megan," he read from the prepared autocue, "it is with a heavy heart that I send you this message, since pressure of work again prevents my being with you on this our twenty-third anniversary."

His face switched from concern to anger. He pointed at the words on the autocue. "Heavy heart? I said that last year."

"No, Mr. McCain." A copywriter emerged from the dark, waving a blue document. "This was last year's script."

The entire studio held their congregate breath as Big Rod perused it.

"What's your name?" he asked the quivering copywriter.

"Lieberman," came the high-pitched reply.

Willa was far enough away to hope her whisper would not be heard; she wanted to make a mate out of Neville.

"What's happening there?" she asked.

"Where?"

"At the zoo?"

"Nothing," Neville replied emotionlessly. "Rod'll eventually get round to deciding what to do with it. Meantime, as a stopgap, we've got someone standing by from Octopus TV Hong Kong. Name of Lee. Used to be in their police force. Hard-nosed little Chinese bastard."

CHAPTER
3

A tall Englishman in an immaculate linen suit and regimental tie peered inquiringly into the extensive orangutan compound at Marwood Zoo, located just outside Tenterden in Kent in the south of England. The pink bottoms of the frolicking primates bounced around like mobile beacons in the sparkling noonday sun.

It had been a mere three days since Rollo Lee had been given his new assignment by Don Bennetts in Octopus Television in Hong Kong and been told to board the earliest possible flight for London. Rod McCain, he was informed, had just pulled off another brilliant acquisition—a leisure conglomerate in Britain. Most sections of it were running profitably but Marwood Zoo was seriously underperforming. Alliance Leisure had acquired it a year previously, following the death of Sir Marwood, the millionaire philanthropist and conservationist, who had founded it. A committee of local worthies, most of them owning scant knowledge of running zoos, had kept the place going, with a chartered accountant from Alliance Leisure coming down once a month to examine the books. These revealed that while the zoo didn't actually operate at a loss, its profits were barely worth banking.

Take the initiative, Rollo's beer-bellied Australian boss had advised him. There's only one way to cut costs and increase turnover and that's by having a strong, single-minded policy that admits of no exceptions. That way you get the respect of the staff—those you keep on—and, if you move the profits up by the right percentage, the respect of Big Rod as well, or at least he won't come gunning for you.

Rollo had left the office in a state of cold shock. He was forty-nine years old. He hadn't been to a zoo since he was a child. Single-minded policy? What could one do with a zoo except charge people more money to come and look at the animals? Increase the marketing spend, he supposed, but the thought filled him with nausea. He hated marketing and all who worked in it with a vehemence that bordered on the irrational. Let's face it, he admitted to himself as the taxi dropped him off at Kai Tak Airport, I know bugger all about zoos.

After checking in, he had rushed to the airport bookstall in the faint hope of finding some research material on animals. And there lady luck had smiled on him as his eye fell on a thick volume written by one T. G. Parry Jones with a charging rhino on the cover. It wholly absorbed him for the full fourteen hours of the flight; in fact, he read it twice.

"I expect we'll find the keeper over with the gorillas— one of the females is expecting." The information came from a prim lady, dressed like a village schoolmistress with a clipboard cradled in her arm, who was standing beside Rollo. Di Harding had been Sir John's faithful secretary for the last ten years of his life—some said she had been rather more—and had managed to keep the paperwork and accounts in some semblance of order after the zoo had been sold to Alliance.

"Do you have any background in animals?" she asked her new boss politely.

"Well, I've eaten a lot of them, you know," he quipped.

She looked at him as if he had let slip a stream of four-letter words. He sensed that his quirky colonial humour was not going to appeal to Miss Moneypenny, who seemed somewhat deficient in this department.

"Just a joke," Rollo reassured her. "No, I'm afraid my mind is quite uncluttered by any relevant experience. Still, that's the Octopus way." He wished he hadn't said that. Better that the staff remain in the dark.

"Miss Harding . . . ," he began.

"Di," she insisted, and, not letting him continue, explained, "Everyone's a bit nervous."

"Well"—Rollo was anxious to rectify the record—"I know about the entertainment business, of course, from Octopus TV."

"No, I meant Mr. McCain has a reputation for closing things down."

Rollo studiously avoided her anxious eyes and pointed to a gabled building situated a couple of hundred yards to their right. "Now," he said, inspecting the map in his hand, "that's the insect house, isn't it?"

"Not only are these driver ants the most organism-like of all insect varieties, they are famous for their extraordinary ferocity. They will literally eat anything in their path . . ."

It would have been an understatement to say that Adrian Malone, keeper of the Marwood insect house, was renowned for his loquacity. Rarely has a human being on the planet Earth been quite so verbally unchallenged. To Bugsy—a soubriquet which he had once been unwise enough to say he detested and which as a result had become

30

the name by which he was universally known among the other keepers—life was one long soliloquy. And that soliloquy was primarily on the subject of insects. Australian funnelwebs, tarantulas, giant orb weavers, black widows, no-eyed big-eyed wolf spiders—you name them and you can be sure Bugsy had more than named them. The trimly built autodidact, his rimless spectacles and hand-tied bow tie giving him a professorial mien which had no academic qualifications to back it up, could happily hold forth for hours on end on the subject of anything that crawled. His great rival, Sydney Lotterby, keeper of the small mammals, maintained that a Freudian analyst would diagnose Bugsy as suffering from anal arachnophobia.

Rollo listened in amazement; he had never encountered such a type in his life. Bugsy indicated the overgrown ants that were creeping along some logs behind the thick glass of their compartment.

". . . indeed in Africa, nursing mothers take great care never to place their infants anywhere near a driver ant trail, as there are documented cases where these ants have eaten their way right through a baby. Indeed, not stopping at that . . ."

But Rollo did manage to stop him for a moment. "Excellent!" the new zoo director remarked. He discreetly motioned to Di that they should move on to their next port of call. Bugsy didn't appear to notice the gesture but blinked up at them, disappointed that the new director wasn't interested in examining the ants more closely. However, he didn't let a small matter like that halt his diatribe.

". . . in their social organisation there are some surprising parallels with the hierarchical structure found in many termite societies, although of course the driver ants, being more mobile, are correspondingly flexible in their organisation."

31

He glanced up for the director's approbation only to discover that he was now completely alone in the room. This, however, was no reason for him to interrupt himself.

". . . nevertheless the characteristic family behaviour here, as in other hymenoptera of the family formicidae, is indicative of the centralised nature of the colony itself . . ."

He was still probably talking to himself as Rollo Lee and Miss Harding followed the shapely legs of Cub, an American keeper with short, dark hair, down to the big cat enclosure. She had grown up with that nickname as a child, so she sometimes thought she had always been destined to work with lions and tigers and leopards. Unlike Bugsy, Cub was well-equipped with academic qualifications—she had come to London University to qualify as a vet—and unlike Bugsy she said very little. The warmth of her smile tended to say most things for her. She had taken a temporary job at Marwood after she graduated, hoping to get some practical experience before she returned to Philadelphia to administer to the needs of pet cats—they were extraordinarily similar in habits and genetic structure to their wilder big brothers—but she had found the place hard to leave. It was home. The other keepers were an oddball bunch but she had always felt that with her affinity for animals she was something of an oddball herself. So when, three years ago, Sir John had offered her the job as head of department, she postponed her career in domestic surgery indefinitely.

Rollo Lee seemed pleased by her charges, but not very interested in them. She had heard he'd cross-questioned some other department heads quite closely, but all she got was a nod and a peremptory "good day."

Sydney Lotterby, head of small mammals, was without doubt the best operator in Marwood Zoo. He had worked in a fairground before it had become politically incorrect to have monkeys and other performing animals in such places. From his stints on the hoopla and tombola stalls he had an expert knowledge of how to beguile a child into demanding money from its parents to try to win an unwanted stuffed cat or a goldfish in a small sachet of water. Somewhat to his surprise, he discovered that his affection for animals was greater than his affection for fairs, and he found in Marwood a curiously close relationship with the "little brown jobs" that were his charges. With his mop of chestnut hair, scattered beard, pointed front teeth, and darting eye movements he seemed, on occasion, more a member of the animal kingdom than the human one. Nevertheless he inspired committed loyalty in his young staff, especially in Pip, a child-woman with the face of an angel—golden hair and innocent eyes—but a girl who possessed the danger of a scorpion should anyone or thing threaten her animals.

The two of them were feeding raisins to the ring-tailed lemurs when they heard that the new director was on his way to them. It was an idyllic sight as the furry Madagascans playfully ran along human shoulders and arms in order to be fed.

"What sort of temperament do they have?"

Sydney gazed through the cage at the deep, inquiring eyes of the director. Was the man compiling a psychiatric profile of every creature in the zoo? He resisted the urge to tell him that they were a bunch of manic-depressives and decided to play along with the game.

"Very sweet nature, sir," he replied with his pointed-tooth grin, "very sweet."

"Thank you," said Rollo, and without a further word urged his secretary on to their next port of call.

Sydney and Pip exchanged glances but no words.

• • •

The director and Di edged their way down the slippery steps to the sea lion pool, there to be greeted by Reggie Sea Lions. (Many keepers at Marwood tended to refer to themselves and each other by the names of their animals; indeed, some were reputed to have forgotten their real surnames over the years.)

Reggie was a short man, no more than five feet, a fact that might have been less noticeable were it not for the attendance of his assistant, Sky, a willowy Irish girl who towered over him by a further fourteen inches. Several of the staff thought that Reggie secretly relished this juxtaposition—he certainly relished such comely companionship—since in his sixtieth year he had determined to become something of a character, sporting, for example, a military zookeeper hat of a kind not seen since it was commonplace in children's books of the forties.

"We keep the pool very clean." Reggie spoke with the precisely articulated accent of Morningside, an area of Edinburgh that more traditionally turned its sons into actuaries than into zookeepers.

"Mmm." Rollo cast an appraising eye over the area.

"And they're very well-fed. Herrings fresh from the North Sea." Reggie felt more than a little uncomfortable in the presence of this tall colonial and was far from certain what the man wanted to find out.

"What exactly do they do?" Rollo finally asked.

"Do?" Reggie repeated. "Well, they'll leap out of the water and take a herring from your hand. Sky, bring us a bucket—"

But the director raised an arm to restrain him. "Some other time, perhaps," he said with the weakest of smiles.

Reggie felt considerably more uneasy as Rollo left, and even the sea lions picked up on it, the oldest, Sisyphus, clasping Sky in its flippers for comfort.

• • •

Hugh Primates, a solidly built and eternally cheerful Northerner, was waiting by the gorilla enclosure, having encouraged Jambo, his pride and joy, to assume his usual dominant place on top of a small knoll in the middle of their ample compound. With the exception of the pregnant one, all the gorillas had come out of their huts and were basking in the unusually hot summer sun. Perhaps it reminded them of Africa—although none of them had ever been there. They had all been born in the zoological gardens.

Rollo tapped the concrete wall that surrounded the enclosure and indicated the moat on the inside.

"Is that to keep the gorillas in or the public out?" he asked in a half-joking fashion.

"Bit of both, sir." Hugh said, taking him at face value.

"Never the twain shall meet, eh?" The new director seemed to want reassurance on the safety measures. "Is there really any danger?"

Hugh indicated Jambo. "You could play with him three hundred and sixty-four days a year, sir, but on the three hundred and sixty-fifth he might just rip your arm out."

The director permitted himself the slightest hint of a sadistic smile.

Something stirred in Rollo as he gazed at the contented herd of giraffes nuzzling hay from the baskets that were arranged at head height along the front fence of their enclosure. It wasn't just that they were tall and he was tall, it was . . . but he stopped himself from developing the thought. Now was not a time for sentiment; the facts were more important.

"Can I go inside?" he asked the keeper in charge.

"Not today." Gerry Ungulates, the only black head of department, a wiry man with a cheeky grin and impudent eyes, shook his head. "Wrong time . . . for the females."

35

"They'd attack you?" Rollo was amazed.

With mimetic skill Gerry showed what could happen. "The right foreleg comes up like so," he demonstrated, splaying out his own, "and the rear leg comes up like this."

"Oh. Where are the other hoof stock?" Rollo had acquired a fundamental knowledge of the manner in which wild animals were categorised during his fourteen-hour flight.

Gerry indicated his deputy, Fred—a man well beyond the age of retirement but who had nowhere and no one to retire to—feeding the rhinos at the end of the meadow.

"Any angry women in there?" the director joked.

Gerry eyed him solemnly. "If one of those hit a grown man flat out it could toss him forty feet in the air." With his hand he drew an imaginary arc over the copse of chestnut trees that lay behind them.

"A grown man? Forty feet in the air!" Rollo Lee repeated the statistic as if it were some exact scientific measurement.

"Do you want to have a look at the zoo as a whole?" asked Di.

"Why?" Rollo seemed genuinely astonished at the suggestion.

"Well, it will give you a sense of perspective, and there's a simply wonderful view from the top of the water tower at the back of the sea lion pool," she enthused. "On a day like today you can see for miles. It's a bit of a climb. Do you think you can manage it?"

That was challenge enough for the former Hong Kong police officer. He took off his jacket, followed her to the foot of the tower, and went ahead up the 120 iron rungs to the top.

It was, indeed, a wonderful view. Beneath them the translucent green water of the pool, and down the steps from that the big cats—lions, leopards, and tigers. And to the south of them the small mammals—bandicoots and meerkats, maras and capybaras. Beyond the sycamore trees that marked the perimeter lay Kent, the garden of England, and for some the garden of Eden on a clear summer afternoon such as this.

"Did you miss the old country?" Di inquired respectfully.

"No," Rollo answered, wiping his forehead with a starched white linen handkerchief. "Not very much. There wasn't very much to miss. Some people in Hong Kong used to romanticise it the whole bloody time but I never really . . . oh, it doesn't matter."

A large hand descended on the path between the sea lion pool and the insect house and put down a small kiosk and various folded pieces of paper with arrows and information on them.

Another kiosk in her hand, Willa Weston remained in her hunkered position as she pondered her next move. The exact model of Marwood Zoo spread across her office floor like an outsize children's game.

If only she could create a form of mystery tour, she thought, so that the zoo itself contained elements of excitement over and above the animals it housed. Maybe introduce some sort of competition. The art was to get people to spend as much once they were through the gate as they had spent getting in, so the purchase of a book with clues and the promise of a prize, particularly a generous one, might be effective.

"Brought your toys to the office, I see."

She didn't bother to turn her head; the voice was familiar.

"Almost right," she replied.

"How about dinner tonight?" Vince McCain strode into her office, as bold as the bright yellow tie he sported.

Willa rose up, smoothing her leather trousers as she did so, and turned to face him. "Sorry," she said with an apologetic smile, "can't tonight. I've got too much to do." She indicated the sheets of statistics and faxes and zoo brochures that littered her office.

He was genuinely perplexed. "I thought you didn't have a job."

"Not yet," she acknowledged, pushing her hair off her forehead, "but I'm going to ask Rod if I can run that British zoo."

Vince emitted a well-calculated shriek of derision. "What? You want to live in the Third World and operate an animal toilet?"

To some extent she admired his wit, but she knew she had his measure every step of the way. She approached him close enough that he could smell her scent—Le Must de Cartier—and reach out and touch her, which he knew he was forbidden to do.

"Vince," she said, looking deep into his eyes, "what's the big moneymaking idea of the nineties?"

The question caught him on the hop. "Caring?" he suggested. It had certainly been the buzzword in the marketing department.

Willa shook her head. "Caring went out in '95, Vince. It's families. And what do little children love? Animals."

"Computer animals," Vince corrected her, anxious to assert himself.

She took him by the arm and guided his attention towards the model of the zoo spread out across the floor. "Vince, the next thing after virtual reality is going to be reality. This could be the first of a chain of ecological zoos that people can rely on for exactly the same natural experience wherever they are—a kind of Zoos 'R' Us."

Removing her arm, she went across to her desk and lifted a dense printout. "Take a look at the projected figures. With enough zoos up and running, we're looking at a billion dollars here. Octopus can own zoos from Seattle to Sydney, from Tokyo to Tennessee."

"Yeah, from Finland to Helsinki," he joined with enthusiasm, if not accuracy, his face broadening into a beam of comprehension. "I get it. We could buy tigers by the dozen. Membership that enables you to visit one of our zoos whatever country you're in." He lifted a black-and-white panda from the model. "We could import these and colorize them."

She eyed him skeptically.

"When are you going to pitch this to Dad?" he demanded.

"Tomorrow," she said, sitting down at her desk with satisfaction.

"Tomorrow?" he echoed. "What's the rush?"

"I've got to hurry," Willa pointed out. "What if this new guy starts doing a good job, right? I mean, suppose he knows what he's doing . . ."

CHAPTER
4

"'Scuse me, 'scuse me." Adrian "Bugsy" Malone carried a copy of the *Financial Times* under his arm as he threaded his way through the already crowded zoo hall. The paper provided him with well-reported research on international economies and, more than that, indicated to the other keepers that he was, by his own estimate, a cut above them.

But Sydney Lotterby was rarely without some ruse to cut him down to size. He waved a matchbox at the arriving insect keeper.

"Hello, Bugsy. Here—does this belong to you?"

"The name's Adrian and I don't smoke." Malone refused to be drawn further. Or thought he had.

"No, no." Sydney pushed open the box and held it out in his direction. "This ant. One of yours, is it?"

Bugsy glared at him. "I am not responsible for every single insect in this zoo, thank you very much."

"You should get them branded." Sydney was playing to an amused audience. "That way we would know which were yours." He lifted the ant out of the box and fed it to the lemur on his shoulder. "Oh, he loves ants. Got a main course for him?"

Bugsy looked at him pathetically. "At least my brain's bigger than those of my animals. Your sense of humor, Lotterby, ranks as low as—"

But a rising stir in the already tense assembly stemmed even Bugsy's unceasing flow of words. The new director had arrived. Tall, groomed, and authoritative, his Hong Kong–tailored suit in salient contrast to the jungle-warrior green of the keepers' outfits, he sprinted up the steps to the stage, an anxious Miss Harding in his wake. A flip-chart—something quite alien to most of the fifty or so assembled there—was already waiting for them.

"Good evening." Rollo's voice was brusque and no-nonsense. "I apologise for being a little late. Don't get up."

The irony implicit in this last remark was entirely redundant; nobody had shown the slightest inclination to rise to their feet. They were not, after all, at school or in the army or some other formalised institution. In fact, many of them continued to talk among themselves.

"Gentlemen, could I have your attention please," Rollo continued.

"Who?" The interrogative came from Jenni, a solidly built woman who worked with the ungulates.

"And ladies. Thank you." Rollo half-acknowledged his lack of political correctness. "Before I begin—"

"You *have* begun," came a bored and unidentified voice from the back of the hall.

Rollo permitted himself a brief intake of breath. He'd known this was not going to be an easy meeting, but he had not expected to encounter cheek bordering on insurrection.

"Before I begin," he repeated himself, "on the main business of the evening, I should perhaps introduce myself to those whom I've not yet had the pleasure of meeting."

41

He sensed a wave of apathy wafting its way towards him but, undaunted, steeled himself to continue.

"As of 0800 hours yesterday morning I assumed command of this zoo, having been appointed director of Octopus Inc., of which you are now employees"—he chose his words guardedly—"at this moment in time."

Fred, the elderly keeper whom he had seen feeding the rhinos, had his hand in the air.

"Yes, sir?" Rollo's voice betrayed his irritation. This was not question time in the House of Commons; it was a formal meeting to announce the new zoo policy.

"Do you have a name?" the old chap inquired, amiably enough.

"Oh yes, my mother insisted on it," Rollo snapped back sarcastically, fixing his interrogator with an unblinking stare. "Rollo Lee. L-E-E. Though you may find the name 'Director' easier to remember." He looked with satisfaction at the old chap. "Are you similarly blessed, sir?"

"No," said Fred. "I'd like to have been director, but I was passed over."

Laughter began to break out, but Rollo stopped it hastily. "No, your name."

"Fred Hoofstock," grinned the old-timer.

"Well, Mr. Hoofstock"—Rollo's irony was becoming less and less veiled—"I'm sure, in your continuing quest for information, you'll want to know how this zoo now fits into the Octopus Empire."

For the first time, he appeared to have the undivided attention of the hall. Miss Harding flipped a page of the chart to reveal hand-drawn hieroglyphics that showed the pyramid of command from Atlanta to Marwood.

"Now, as you know"—Rollo felt relieved to have obtained their interest—"this zoo was a part of the Alliance Leisure Group, which was taken over by Octopus Inc. last week. So we now report directly to Octopus Inc. in Atlanta, which is, of course, run by Mr. Rod McCain."

Di flipped another page of the chart to reveal a *Time* magazine cover with the brooding, unsmiling features of their proprietor.

"And now"— Rollo indicated a television set beside the flip-chart—"he is going to address you personally."

Di obediently pressed the video button beneath the set. A large Octopus logo filled the screen, then gave way to McCain sitting in the cosy, but artificial, desk from which he had sent his wife his anniversary greetings. "I'm sorry I am unable to be with you today," he began, "but I'm sure you will understand that the pressure of work means that I cannot always be present when some new members are added to the Octopus family."

He rose uneasily from behind his desk in a rehearsed move and edged round to sit on the front of it. "You know, I use the word 'family' advisedly, since that is the unit that functions most efficiently. We may be only distant cousins to some of you, but when you go to work in the plant in the morning I'm certain you'll step up the productivity if you look upon the worker next to you as not just a mate, but as a brother who can give you a hand if you need it. We're creating record profits each succeeding quarter thanks to people like you, and I'd just like to inspire you to keep up the good work and hope that you provide our shareholders with some really healthy dividends. Thank you, and good luck."

Di snapped off the set, not bothering to disguise her amazement.

"Are there any questions?" asked Rollo. "Yes?" He pointed to the young girl with blonde hair and a rabbit in her arms.

"Are there two *l*'s in Rollo?" asked Pip innocently.

"Yes," he snapped back. "Any other questions?"

43

"When was that video made?" It was Bugsy Malone.

"What?" Rollo was slightly flummoxed. "I'm afraid I don't know."

"I'll think you'll find it was 1994. It was on the closing credits in Roman numerals." The insect keeper's tone was superior, to say the least.

"What?" Reggie Sea Lions sounded outraged. "Two years before he bought us?"

Rollo was determined to regain control. "Well, you can't expect him to record a new video every time he buys something. He's a busy man." He looked round the room. "Most people appreciate the personal touch."

This was greeted with ironic laughter.

"Mr. McCain is, as I'm sure you all realise, a remarkable man." Rollo attempted to evoke some enthusiasm from his audience. "Starting with his father's radio stations in New Zealand, he has built up a global empire which is currently worth more than six billion dollars, and growing."

"How much does he want in the end?"

"What?" Rollo glared again at the bespectacled keeper with the *Financial Times* who had posed the question.

"How much bigger does he want to get?" Bugsy seemed quite clear about his request for information.

"Well, there isn't a limit," Rollo tried to explain. "He wants growth."

"You mean, he'll never have enough?" The question, intelligently posed, came from Cub, the American keeper of the big cats.

"Enough?" Rollo couldn't understand this at all. "Enough for what?"

"That's what we're asking you." Bugsy folded his arms and looked smugly around, pleased that he had managed to bring the debate full circle.

44

"At what point would he be satisfied?" Gerry Ungulates felt bold enough to interpolate a supplementary.

Rollo was not prepared to continue this senseless cross-questioning. If they didn't understand what growth was, no wonder they had ended up as zookeepers. He looked around the audience. "Any *sensible* questions?"

"Are you going to close the zoo?" Again it was the angelic-looking assistant from small mammals. A pet rabbit nestled in her arms—she was always nurturing any creature that was sick or below par, and besides, she liked to feel the warmth of a soft animal next to her.

"Er . . ." The question took him to the crux of his speech sooner than he was prepared to go there. He played for time. "I'm glad you asked me that."

"No you're not," spat Sydney from near the front, a lemur climbing over his head like a mobile Davy Crockett hat.

"Yes, I am . . . ," Rollo began, but he was shouted down by cries of "No you're not" from every corner of the room.

"Look!" the director bellowed to quell the insurrection. "This zoo has to make money."

"It does," persisted Bugsy in his high-pitched, know-all voice.

"Yes, yes," Rollo was forced to acknowledge, "but not enough."

"Enough for what?" Gerry Ungulates showed every sign of a man enjoying the fray.

"Don't start that . . . ," Rollo reprimanded him, but then realised he had an exact answer. "Actually, I will tell you. Mr. McCain demands a twenty percent return from every asset in his empire."

He indicated to Di to turn the flip-chart, and there it was in crudely written black and white. 20% RETURN ON CAPITAL EMPLOYED.

"Why twenty percent?" Sydney sounded like a trade union leader, which, in an ex officio way, he was.

Rollo was nearing the end of his tether. Financial logic was not going to work with this cloth-eared bunch. "Because he does, that's why."

"Could we explore that thinking a little?" The high-pitched whine betrayed its provenance.

"No," Rollo screamed at Bugsy. "Twenty percent it is. Otherwise we're all out of a job. So here's the key question: To secure the zoo's survival, how can we bring in more visitors? Now, I've worked in the world of television and I know which programmes attract the largest audience globally—violent ones. Somebody is killed on American television every twenty-four seconds."

The room had fallen silent. Rollo was getting into his stride. "Look at sports. Forget boxing and wrestling and martial arts. Take ice hockey. Do you really think its popularity depends on the subtleties of stick handling? It's the fights. And what about motor racing? In 1994 two drivers were tragically killed at the San Marino Grand Prix. What happened to the attendances there the following year? They rose by twenty percent—our favorite figure. James Hunt, the world motor racing champion in 1976, said, and I quote: 'Spectators come to see someone killed, though they will deny it forever.' Let's take the world of movies. Arnold Schwarzenegger and Sylvester Stallone did not get where they are today by playing in Chekhov and Noël Coward. Violence is the new international language of entertainment. So, in this zoo, we need only animals that are violent. Fierce animals. The others will have to go." Exhausted by his tirade, he indicated to Di that she should turn the chart once more, and the words VIOLENCE-DANGER-RISK-EXCITEMENT surmounted by a snarling tiger confronted the consternation in the hall.

Sydney was on his feet. "What do you mean 'go'?"

Rollo shrugged. "We'll have to find other homes for them."

The uproar intensified. Pip hugged her rabbit closer to her. "But this has always been a conservation zoo," she screamed at the hated bureaucrat on the podium. Small mammals, she knew at once, stood little chance of survival.

"Yes, and I am all for conservation," Rollo came back authoritatively. "And the three things I want to conserve are: the zoo, your jobs, and fierce animals. So over the next few days I will be deciding which of our animals are fierce and which ones will, sadly, have to be relocated."

He strode down from the stage like a man with a mission, Di timidly in his wake as the keepers all rose as one and began to berate him.

It was to no avail. On the platform there remained the chart with three simple, but life-threatening words on it:

FIERCE ANIMAL POLICY

It was a zoo tradition, on Wednesday nights in particular, for most keepers to have a game of darts in the public bar of the Marwood Arms hotel. In Sir John's day they had been very welcome, since he owned the place; indeed, the philanthropic patron had made sure that beer was sold at the cheapest possible price. But after the Alliance Leisure takeover the new management had made strenuous efforts to take the hotel upmarket, trying to attract the sort of customers who like their food flambéed by their table and putting the front-of-house staff—many of whom were Swiss-trained—in dinner jackets, with the receptionists dressed like girls who rent out cars at airports.

Initially they had discouraged the keepers from coming to the bar but, when their hints had been dropped and missed, they acknowledged that a FREE HOUSE, as signs read outside many English pubs, meant that the clientele as well as the beer could come from assorted sources. The management would come to regard the keepers as a sort of sideshow, something folkloric for people in their new Vauxhall Cavaliers and Toyota Coronas to come and look at and be quaintly amused by.

But there was nothing amusing about the angry troop that Sydney led through the gates of the hotel the night of Rollo Lee's speech. A madman appeared to have been put in charge of the zoo, and emotions were running high.

"Diabolical!" Sydney Lotterby, keeper of small mammals, fulminated against the reddening night sky. "Unbelievable!"

Reggie Sea Lions, knowing his aquatic lot looked certain for the chop—if only he had a polar bear, he thought; that would have shown the bastard—trotted to keep up. "It's incredible," he pronounced with anxiety.

"Insane." Gerry Ungulates now realised why Rollo had asked him about the likelihood of being kicked by a giraffe. Thank God he had played it up in his demonstration. And no wonder the director had been so impressed by the velocity of a charging rhino. Gerry had never actually seen a man being hit by a rhino, but he remembered reading in some children's story somewhere about its being able to toss you forty feet in the air. Indeed, it had been a contributing reason as to why he wanted to work with the hoof stock. His animals were certainly in no danger, but he wanted to exhibit his solidarity.

Young Pip, on the other hand, cuddled her baby deer to her for comfort. She had only started at the zoo eighteen months ago as a trainee with the small mammals, and already her career looked doomed. The mixture of fear and rage within her rendered her almost inarticulate as she tried to stumble out her feelings: "It's absolutely . . . absolutely . . ."

"Diabolical." Her boss finished her sentence for her with his favourite adjective.

"Exactly. Yes." That was just what Pip had been trying to say.

Sydney turned his fulminations from the sky to the group of keepers who were now determinedly marching with him across the false Tudor front of the Marwood Arms.

"He knows nothing about zoos. He barges in here, starts firing animals without any . . ." But his eye was caught by Cub, keeper of the big cats, and Hugh Primates in hushed conversation.

"You don't seem very upset," Sydney said accusingly.

Cub put on her sweetest smile. "Oh, we are upset, really." And she really meant it.

"Just because your animals are fierce," Sydney went on, disbelievingly. He turned angrily as Bugsy and his assistants, Ant and Ang-Ling, rode past the group on their bicycles, Bugsy whistled very deliberately as if to indicate he hadn't a care in the world.

"No," Hugh countered, "we think it's . . ."

He and Cub exchanged glances and arrived at the same epithet. "Diabolical!"

The keepers had by now reached the entrance to the hotel, and paused to listen to these final pleas.

"What does he mean by 'fierce'?" Gerry tried to articulate his internal dialogue. "A giraffe can kick a man's head off, but you wouldn't call it fierce."

"Same with sea lions and penguins." Reggie put forward his case with a force that was in inverse proportion to its validity. "People don't think of them as violent, but they can be killers."

He looked around for the comfort of confirmation, but found himself entirely alone; the others had been in greater need of a fortifying pint.

"Why have you all gone quiet?" the timorous sea lion keeper shouted resentfully.

Their possession of bicycles meant that Adrian "Bugsy" Malone and his long-suffering lieutenants, Ant and Ang-Ling, managed to get to the bar before anyone else and were already deep in conversation by the time the other keepers arrived. Well, not so much conversation; Bugsy was delivering an analytical anatomization of the situation and Ant—his real name, and an unfortunate one for an assistant insect keeper—was the main recipient.

"Anyone with half a brain would realise this sub-Nietzschean attempt to turn back the zoological time clock is quite patently doomed to failure . . ."

"Why are you so cheerful, Bugsy?" Sydney demanded as he stormed into the room.

Malone kept a mock-intellectual calm. "First, don't call me Bugsy, please. Secondly, my little chaps are quite adequately fierce in comparison to that collection of cuddly toys you dangle round your neck."

"Fierce?" Sydney took a substantial swig from the pint that the barmaid had already drawn for him.

"Oh yes." Bugsy radiated an air of superiority, but condescended to talk to Sydney in a language he might understand. "They scare the excrement out of most people."

Sydney turned to the others at the bar with a broad guffaw. "That's not fear—that's disgust."

"Name one deadly poisonous mammal," Bugsy came back venomously.

"My lot eat your lot," Sydney scoffed triumphantly, "and you can't kill mine by treading on them."

Bugsy refused to be beaten. "You can't use mine for shaving brushes . . ."

Even before Rollo's pronouncement the two men had hardly been the best of friends; in truth Bugsy was one of life's loners, happy to hold forth to any ear that happened to be in shot. But before this fruitless argument could be carried on into infinity, Gerry stepped in to separate the protagonists. "Come on, chaps. Break it up. We're all a bit jumpy tonight." Cub, too, made an appeal for sanity. "Sydney, we're all on your side," she reassured him, squeezing his arm.

"I'm rather worried, too, if you don't mind." Reggie had at last caught up with an audience and felt excluded by the fact that all the sympathy seemed to be directed towards the mammal keepers.

"We know," the others agreed.

Sydney sank into his favourite chair and idly fondled the ear of the newborn deer that Pip had been feeding from a baby's bottle.

She was in a state of high anxiety. "Do you seriously think he means it?" she asked her boss.

The whole bar went silent in anticipation of his pronouncement. He drained his beer to add to the solemn drama of the moment and then shook his head in despair.

"Oh, he means it all right."

"I'm sure they're upset, Di, but I have a job to do."

Rollo Lee pinned a daily schedule onto the notice board of his new office. He liked order. Institutions and individuals both worked best when they had a sense of priorities and discipline and, above all, clear-cut commands.

"Well, yes, but . . ." Di was just as upset as any of the keepers, and hoped she could occupy the role of an intermediary who might mitigate some of her new boss's excesses.

"Look, I have to be hard-nosed." Rollo was at pains to make her understand that he was a fundamentally reasonable man. "Rod demands toughness. One moment of compassion and you're out."

"You mean that Octopus runs on fear?" Di did not usually mince words.

"No, no, terror more like." In such situations Rollo usually made a nervous retreat into humour. "So I've got this one chance to show that I can do something or I've had it. And, at my age . . ."

His plea for sympathy was interrupted by a temporary secretary's putting her head through the hatch that connected to the zoo director's office.

"Mr. Lee, there's a call from Atlantis."

"Atlantis?" Di knew that the child was about as bright as a very short plank, but for a moment began to doubt her sanity.

"Atlanta," Rollo explained, lifting the receiver from the phone on his desk.

A brusque voice boomed down the line, as loud and clear as if it were in the next room and with the usual swaggering confidence of one of Rod's barons. "Ah, Rolo, Nev here. Rod would like a word with you. Okay?"

"Rod?" If Neville had said "God," Rollo couldn't have been more awestruck. The man himself. He automatically rose to his feet.

"That's right," came Neville's semirefined Australian accent that nonetheless betrayed its rural origins. "Wife and kids settled in yet?"

Rollo's mind was still scrambled by the shock of the situation. "Yes, everything's really terrified here . . . ," he stuttered.

"Hello, Rolo." It was the voice of Rod Almighty. Rollo immediately recognised it from the succession of corporate videos to which he had been constantly exposed in Hong Kong. Enough to programme an entire TV channel in themselves, one sacrilegious fellow employee had noted.

"Got your wife and kids settled in yet?" Rod's inquiry was gruff and far from genuine.

But Rollo was too panicked to take it on board. "Absolutely. Yes, I agree entirely."

"So let me know," McCain continued in a voice that should have been too quiet to be threatening but nevertheless managed to be, "what you're going to do to push earnings up to our favourite twenty percent. Okay?"

Rollo had by now settled his nerves sufficiently to make some sort of sense. "Yes, we're going to have to be very hard-nosed here," he began. "Actually its marvellous to have an opportunity to explain what I have in mind . . ."

"Hello, Rolo." The voice was antipodean but slightly distorted by the satellite.

"Hello again, Mr. McCain." The least Rollo could do was to humour him.

"No, this is Nev," the voice explained. "So your wife and kids are settled in all right."

Rollo had recovered his facilities enough to take this particular bull by the horns. "Look, I don't want to seem awkward, but I'm not married and I don't have any children. What happened to Rod?"

"He's been called away," came the casual reply, and then, more menacingly, "So you'll let us know your plans, Rolo, okay?"

The next thing Rollo heard was the sound of the receiver being put down. He hadn't even had time to point out that his name was Rollo, not Rolo. He was used to the rough, tough Octopus way, but he thought there might have been a little more graciousness in the inner sanctum.

Di eyed him consolingly.

Three thousand four hundred and twenty eight miles away in the Octopus boardroom, Rod had granted four minutes of his preciously allocated time to his little-loved son, Vince, and the new girl, Willa Weston, whose expensive Lawrence Steele outfit in shining azure blue made the very best of her physical assets.

"But think about it, Rod," she was imploring him.

"I don't want to," he countered dismissively. "It's less than two percent of the whole acquisition." Then, picking up a folder from the expansive boardroom table, he added, "I have bigger fish to gut." Willa had not got where she was by being shaken off so easily. "Rod, wait. Hear me out."

"It's a zoo, Willa." She was beginning to annoy him. "They're not moneymakers, okay?"

"Not just one zoo, Rod." She had his ear and she intended to keep bending it. "We're looking at a major franchise potential. Once I turn this place around we can really cut into the leisure sector."

"It could be quite interesting . . . ," Vince put in, attempting to support Willa's cause. This was not to her advantage.

"But Mr. McCain," Willa pleaded, "it won't cost you anything. I think we can do it all with sponsorship."

"That was my idea—I've got several lined up," Vince interpolated unhelpfully.

"It's the gap in your empire," Willa persisted. "Trust me—I can make money for you."

For the first time in their conversation, the great man turned and looked at her. His eyes were cold and ungiving behind his darkened spectacles. But he admired this young woman's tenacity and resolution.

"Do it," he said.

CHAPTER
5

It had been a rare summer in England that year. It was as if God had targeted the sun inaccurately and hit the British Isles instead of Tuscany or the Algarve and bathed the countryside in warmth and wasps for week after succeeding week. (This is always assuming that God is the creator of wasps, something which even the most religious conservationists find hard to justify.) Anyway, it was the sort of weather that made the average Englishman metaphorically knot his handkerchief round his head, pour the family into the car, and sit on clogged motorways for hours on end to admire the way the government scheduled major roadworks for the peak season—presumably to demonstrate to the people how beneficially their taxes were being spent.

Marwood Zoo enjoyed the benefits of this freak summer, and admissions soared with the temperature. Before Rollo Lee had any opportunity to implement his Fierce Animal Policy he found himself with an—albeit seasonally driven—increase in business.

This was of no consolation to the keepers; a pall of gloom hung over the place in the wake of the new director's opening address. After the last visitor had left one humid Thursday evening a week after that speech, a curious sight was to be witnessed in the small mammals area. Sydney Lotterby was in the middle of a compound, poised like a lion-tamer in a circus as he waved a wooden chair to keep a creature at bay.

"Easy, boy, easy." Sydney's voice betrayed his fear, hinting at his belief that at any moment the small brown rodent, about two feet long from its pointed nose to its striped tail, might spring at his throat and tear it out.

There were several watching keepers, who had read the freshly painted sign on the coatimundi enclosure. A map indicated that the animals came from the forests of Central and South America, and beside it was written: "The gruesome hunting habits of the coatimundi can often result in them consuming 100 lbs. of flesh in a single day. A long mobile snout and viciously strong front claws are the tools of the trade for the coati."

Most of the animals in the enclosure were playing quite contentedly on the logs that had been laid out for them, and even the one that had been the focus of Sydney's anxiety seemed less than interested in viewing him as prey.

"Please, sir, stay back." Lotterby threw the admonition over his shoulder as Rollo Lee anxiously approached the spectacle, soon to be surrounded by Gerry, Cub, Pip, Reggie, and Sky, all of whom seemed as anxious as Sydney.

"Fierce? That coatimundi?" Rollo spat out the words derisively. The director looked imposing in the linen tropical suit that had been run up for him by Jackie Tan Tailors in Chung Hom Kok Road, his crisp white shirt, and the familiar regimental tie.

Sydney indicated the creature with a leg of the chair. "It's a wild animal, sir. It's not domesticated."

"Neither is a butterfly," Rollo pointed out, "and I wouldn't call that particularly ferocious."

Sydney stood his ground, backtracking only marginally. "You take a liberty with him and he'll give you a nasty nip."

Rollo sighed in exasperation. "A safety pin could give you a nasty nip, Lotterby. I'll tell you what 'fierce' is." He held out his right arm and smacked his wrist with the fingers of his left. " 'Fierce' is biting your whole hand off."

"Whole hand?" It was Pip, Sydney's assistant, who registered her amazement at this diktat, followed in complaining succession by the other keepers surrounding the director.

"No!" cried Cub.

"Impossible!" Reggie lamented.

But Rollo was in no mood for an argument. "Lotterby, could I have a word with you over here please?" His tone was that of a schoolmaster summoning a pupil to a place of private reprimand.

As the director turned away from the coatimundi enclosure, Hugh, the gorilla keeper, solemnly came up to him and inquired: "Is it all right if it *wrenches* the hand off?"

"Oh yes," replied Rollo, without breaking step.

"Whew!" The look of relief on Hugh's face was palpable.

Sydney, chair still in hand, obediently followed the director as he strode past the various small mammal enclosures.

"Look what a coati did to me, sir," he persisted, indicating a substantial scar on his upper arm.

Rollo threw a contemptuous glance at the wound; the man had probably snared himself on a piece of fencing. He did not bother to read any of the new plaques that now adorned the small mammal department. He had done so before on his way to the coati circus. They had certainly made the "little brown jobs" appear to be animals you kept your distance from:

Pine Marten (Martes martes). Habitat: Forests in America, Europe, and Asia. Vicious carnivore which feeds on porcupines.

Aardvark (Orycteropus afer). Habitat: Southern Africa. Notorious for their fierceness, they kick and slash with their powerful forelegs and razor-sharp claws.

Collared Anteater (Tamandua tetradactyla). Habitat: Savannas of South America. Savage tree dweller that preys on creatures moving beneath. Beware! This animal is very violent.

Accompanied by a still far from contrite Lotterby, Rollo came to a halt by the meerkat enclosure. The long-tailed little mongeese with their black ears and black-ringed eyes scuttled about like children in a sandpit, save for the sentinel member of the family, which remained erect on its back feet to warn the others of any impending danger.

"These are your meerkats, right?" said Rollo, pointing over the low wall of the enclosure.

Lotterby dashed forward and pushed down his arm. "Don't do that, sir, they'd have your hand off in a second."

Ignoring him, Rollo strode over to their plaque. "Meerkat—Suricata suricatta," he read. "These bloodthirsty predators are known to some as 'The Piranhas of the Desert.'" He turned to their keeper. "Is that true, Lotterby?"

Sydney nodded his head emphatically. "Yes sir, they can strip a human carcass in three minutes."

Rollo looked closely at the woolly-haired, pointy-teethed man in front of him to ascertain whether the chap was a complete idiot or whether he thought that Rollo was a complete idiot.

Sydney Lotterby was unable to stop a bead of perspiration from appearing on his brow, but retained his composure.

Not for long. Rollo reached into the deep side pocket of his Jackie Tan tropical suit and pulled out his trump card: David Macdonald's *Encyclopedia of Mammals*—over four hundred world species in colour with information on classification, habitat, and much more.

Like Dracula confronted with a clove of garlic; Sydney took a step back. Rollo flicked through to entry number 297: a picture of a sentry meerkat in a sandy desert. He showed the page to Lotterby. "It says here that meerkats are easy to tame and are often kept as pets."

"Well, you haven't been attacked by one." Lotterby was not prepared to give in just yet.

"Nobody's been attacked by one," Rollo snapped, moving on to the neighbouring enclosure, "or if they have they didn't notice."

"They've got diabolical temperaments, sir." Even the enunciation of the small mammal keeper's favourite epithet seemed to have lost its bite.

Rollo had reached a new sign. "Patagonian Maras—Dolichotis Patagonum," he read. "These deceptively docile-looking creatures hunt in packs. Maras have been known to devastate entire Argentinian villages.

"Shocking to watch," Lotterby interpolated, more in desperation than in hope.

Rollo smacked his book against his palm. "It says here they eat grass."

"That's for hors d'oeuvres, sir." Sydney was prepared to take this argument to the wall. "When their blood's up—"

But Rollo cut him off with a roar of rage. "Be quiet. You are deliberately and fraudulently trying to deceive me into thinking that some of your animals are fierce . . ."

"Only the rogue ones, sir." Lotterby knew he had reached the last-chance saloon. His plea was ignored.

". . . when," continued Rollo, "they are, in fact, lovable, cuddly, and surplus to requirements."

Sydney was, for once, lost for words. He took a deep breath. "You want every animal here a psycho?"

The new director of Marwood Zoo could see with satisfaction that he had at last got through to his most implacable opponent. "Exactly. I want a lethal weapon in every cage."

He was rather proud of the phrase. They had run the *Lethal Weapon* films on Octopus TV in Hong Kong and, although he had strongly disapproved of Mel Gibson's policing methods at the time, he knew the words would go round the zoo like wildfire.

"So what do we do with the other animals?" demanded an outraged Lotterby.

"Simple," Rollo called over his shoulder as he pocketed the encyclopedia and headed back for his office. "Get rid of them."

The keepers had managed to derive a degree of pleasure from the glorious summer by taking their meals out-of-doors on the terrace of the staff canteen. Accordingly, the next morning, they assembled with their traditional cups of tea and bacon sandwiches expecting a breakfast postmortem over the failure of Sydney's scheme. The only person to be displeased by the weather was Adrian "Bugsy" Malone, head of insects and boring people to death. Rain was usually the only reason that any number of visitors entered his domain, less to see the spiders than to find shelter. Not that this had any effect on his unquenchable need to share his knowledge with whomever was unlucky enough to be within earshot, be it human or animal.

Most keepers savoured this precious time before their day was interrupted by the arrival of visitors. It wasn't that they disliked members of the public; it was just that, as Sydney had once pointed out, the zoo could have operated so much more efficiently without them.

On this particular Friday morning, however, Sydney was nowhere to be seen; nor was his assistant Pip, or Reggie Sea Lions, or Sky, or Gerry Ungulates, or Ant. Nobody particularly noticed their absence save for the fact that by now Bugsy and Sydney would usually be engaged in some arcane argument about the merits of the tropical ogre-eyed spider over the Siberian raccoon, the sort of discourse to which the other keepers had grown so accustomed that they treated it as a form of background music. It was better than listening to the news of the real world on the radio and letting accounts of human evil and folly enter an environment where man and nature coexisted in a form far more logical than at the average office.

Bugsy seized on the absence of his sempiternal rival to regurgitate some newly acquired knowledge from a history book he had been reading. Most of the other keepers were able to ignore this unwanted information, but Fred and Ang-Ling had the misfortune to be sitting at his table and the politeness to feign interest.

"The Thirty Years' War, of course, as most people know, was concluded with the Treaty of Westphalia in 1648, which gave France southern Alsace and certain Baltic provinces to Sweden."

Ang-Ling essayed a sympathetic smile, whereas Fred, a melancholy man at the best of times, looked mournfully at the tea leaf floating on the top of his tin mug.

"Another thing about the Thirty Years' War," Bugsy went on, oblivious to the widespread disinterest of all around, "is that it saw the introduction onto the battlefields of Europe of what we now know as the modern grenade. Scholars were amazed that in postmedieval . . ."

But then, without warning, the other keepers became just as amazed. Something quite remarkable was emitting from Adrian "Bugsy" Malone: silence. They terminated their individual conversations and turned in mute astonishment to see what could possibly have truncated his never-ending stream of garrulity.

Bugsy was gazing out at the grassy slope that led from the aviary down, past the canteen, to the director's lodge. A small procession was emerging over the brow of the hill, led by Sydney Lotterby, clutching a coati to his breast as if paradoxically seeking warmth on this sultry morning. He was followed by Pip, who was rarely without an animal in her arms but whose expression today mirrored the look of the ring-tailed lemur she was carrying. (When naturalists had discovered the species in Madagascar at the end of the eighteenth century, they had called it lemur after the Latin for "spirit of the dead" because of the animal's deep-set, mournful eyes.)

No less cheerful was Gerry, next in line with a mara in a comfort blanket, followed by Cub, who had a tiny wallaby still in the canvas pouch that simulated a home for it in the absence of its dead mother. Reggie, ever the small stationmaster in his old-fashioned zoo hat, was struggling with a baby ostrich that would have clearly rather been somewhere else, and Sky and Ant brought up the rear with some cages in which the occupants—if there were any—could not be seen.

Most of the keepers, but especially Bugsy, watched in openmouthed amazement as this mournful troupe filed by.

Turning their heads neither to the left nor the right, they walked past the canteen terrace in sombre silence and down the grassy hill past the picture window of the director's quarters.

Rollo Lee had his back to them, so didn't see them pass by. He was having a working breakfast with Di. It was a habit he had picked up at Octopus—an unseemly habit, he had always thought, since the only companions a gentleman should have at breakfast were his mail and newspaper. But in view of the avalanche of overnight faxes he'd received from Atlanta, today it seemed a fairly necessary one.

"Another fax from Octopus." Di handed an extended sheet to him, adding disapprovingly, "The cost!"

Rollo drained his orange juice—it tasted like the stuff they served on planes; had the British forgotten how to squeeze fresh oranges in his absence?—and studied the sheet with a shiver of disgust.

"Marketing! Have you ever met any marketing people?" he asked Di. Without waiting for a response, he went on. "The worst. They'd sell advertising space on their wife's coffin. The founding father of modern marketing was Jospeh Goebbels . . ."

His peroration was interrupted by a knock at the dining room door.

"Yes, come in," he shouted in some annoyance.

"My late husband was in marketing," Di whispered nervously.

"Of course, some of them . . . ," Rollo began, but any attempt to cover his tracks was completely overwhelmed by what he now saw before him. Sydney and his four animal-carrying companions portentously crossed the room and lined up at the table, with Sky and Ant in attendance behind them.

Rollo was totally taken aback. "Yes?" was all he could say.

"Here are the animals, sir." Sydney's statement was as matter-of-fact as if they were something Rollo had requested.

The director eyed him with suspicion, mindful of Sydney's masterly hyperbole when it came to the subject of man-eating meerkats. "What animals?" he inquired suspiciously.

Sydney, shifting uneasily from foot to foot, indicated his colleagues and their charges. "The first batch of animals that are definitely not fierce, sir."

"Ah, good." Rollo attempted to resume his equipoise. He indicated the creature now on Sydney's shoulder. "The coatimundi, I see. Excellent."

"They're going to have to go, sir." Pip cuddled her lemur to her like a child.

"Yes," Rollo agreed. "Good. Well done."

His seemingly calm acceptance of the fact caused a disconcerted ripple to pass through the assembled staff.

Gerry broke the silence. "We've tried to place them with other zoos, sir," he explained, "but there were no takers."

Rollo was genuinely surprised by this. When he had formulated the Fierce Animal Policy, he had naturally assumed that any zoo would welcome a free animal. If someone were to ship him a giant panda, he mused, he would accept it with open arms—well, not open arms, since the 350-pound carnivore had a penchant for more than bamboo, as many Chinese had found to their cost.

"What?" he demanded. "Do you mean to tell me that of all the zoos in this country, you can't find a single one that would—"

"Zoos are taking fewer and fewer species, sir." Sydney pointed out.

"They're all trying to get *rid* of animals." It was Reggie who underlined the point, from behind his ostrich.

"You can't just add these to other animal groups, you see. They'd kill them. Wrong scent." Cub spoke with soft American authority.

Rollo knew she had a first-class degree in veterinary sciences, and he respected her knowledge. He was beginning to feel more than a little uncomfortable. "What about people taking them as pets?" he suggested.

"Pets!" Sydney raised his furry eyebrows with a snigger.

"They need expert attention." It was Di, by his side, who could contain herself no longer.

"Anyway, we're not allowed to. Quarantine regulations." Reggie was always happy to add to any argument.

"Well, can we release them back in the wild then?" Rollo had recently learnt that this was the ultimate aim of a conservation zoo.

A cacophony of negatives assailed his ears. "No safe habitat for this one, sir" . . . "Takes months to prepare them for rerelease" . . . "They don't know how to feed themselves" . . . "This one's been hand-reared" . . . "Sorry, sir, sorry . . ."

He raised his hand to terminate the tide of reasons. Now was the time for straight dealing. "All right, all right. So what do you propose?"

It was Cub who had clearly been deputed to handle this one. She fixed him in the eyes with her own, dark and determined. "There's only one solution, Mr. Lee, and it's the one Lord McAlpine, the boss at London Zoo, proposed a few years ago when the government wouldn't give them any more funds. You probably read about it in the papers."

Rollo hadn't. He had been abroad. "What was that?" he inquired.

"Shoot them," Cub said softly.

A clang broke the silence in the room as the director dropped his teaspoon onto his saucer. Pip began to sob and Reggie followed suit. The others managed to restrain any emotions they were feeling.

Rollo scanned their faces with close scrutiny. "Are you seriously telling me there is no other way of getting rid of these animals?"

They shook their heads with uniformity. "No, sir" . . . " 'Fraid not, sir" . . . "Sorry, sir" . . . "Tragic."

"Not"—Sydney spelled it out slowly—"not unless you were to change the Fierce Animal Policy, sir."

"No," Rollo snapped.

The small mammal keeper tried again. "You're quite sure about that, sir, in the circumstances."

"Perfectly sure, thank you Lotterby, yes."

"They're very dear animals, sir." Reggie was beginning to break up.

"That's not in dispute," Rollo acknowledged.

"But you would like them killed in line with your policy?" Gerry seemed more incredulous than sad.

Rollo was not prepared to be swayed by this emotional blackmail. His days on the Hong Kong force and later with Octopus had at least taught him the stamp of strong management. "If you've really explored all the other options, yes."

He picked up his spoon and resumed eating his by now stone-cold hard-boiled egg to indicate that the meeting was at an end, pretending to make sense of the marketing jargon that was the prime content of the fax from Atlanta. But he very soon became aware that nobody was leaving the room; instead, there came the sound of objects being placed on the table.

He looked up. "What are you doing?"

It was self-evident. The keepers were putting their animals into their cages.

"Well, it's just that we'd rather not shoot them ourselves, sir." Cub was choking back a tear as she hung her pouched wallaby in its box.

"We're very fond of them." Reggie had long ago abandoned any self-control as he closed the cage door on the ostrich.

Pip could barely bring herself to part with her lemur. "We're keepers, and now we're not keeping them," she exploded bitterly.

Rollo assumed his most matter-of-fact air. "Oh, I see. So *I'm* shooting them, am I?"

"If it's not too much trouble, sir." It was hard to tell whether Sydney's response was deferential or ironical.

"Right," said Rollo, turning to Di. "Have you got my diary there?"

Pip could see he meant business, and reluctantly slid her lemur into its cage. "You will make it quick, sir, won't you?" she pleaded.

Rollo looked at her innocently. "You mean I'm not allowed to torture them a bit first? Just for fun?"

Sydney had to restrain his assistant from physically launching an attack on the director. "Good God, you wouldn't do that," she screamed.

"I wasn't being serious, you stupid girl," he said patronisingly.

"Hardly a time for jokes," sniffed Reggie as he bent down to bid farewell to his ostrich. "Good-bye, Cindy."

Sydney took up the refrain as his coatimundi stuck its pointed nose through the bars. "Good-bye, Suzie. I tried."

Cub bit her lip. "Be brave, Mitzi," she counselled the bewildered wallaby, and then went to the door.

"Bye, Petal." Gerry tried to put his cheek next to that of the mara. "Godspeed."

"Bye-bye, Rollo" was all Pip could manage through her tears as she turned away from the lemur.

Whatever the circumstances, the director was not prepared to stomach cheek like this, especially from so junior a member of staff. "I'd prefer it if you called me Director," he said sternly.

Pip howled bitterly from the door, "I was talking to the lemur."

Lee was puzzled. "The lemur is called Rollo?"

Sydney came forward and put his arm around Pip. "It's all right, sir," he explained. "She named him after you when you first arrived, as a mark of respect."

Rollo turned determinedly to Di so that none of the leaving keepers could read the expression on his face.

"Could you pass the marmalade, please?" he said.

Less than an hour after the last visitor had left, and when all the animals had been fed and watered and locked up for the night by the various keepers, the zoo was alive to the sound of laughter. It came from the selfsame canteen terrace which had been the location for Bugsy's lecture on the Thirty Years' War less than ten hours previously.

Now the insect keeper remained in relative silence, occasionally picking his teeth with a match, as those about him rollicked and rolled with mirth.

Sydney was on his feet, holding forth. "I'd completely got him by the short and curlies."

Reggie, choking down his tea with minor convulsions, turned to the keepers who had not been there. "You should have seen his face when he realised he was supposed to shoot them." The very thought of it made his minor convulsions major.

"What was it you called your coati?" Gerry asked Sydney.

"Hoover?" Sydney grinned his toothy grin, savouring the success of the scheme. "I called him 'Suzie.'"

Reggie squeezed Pip's knee theatrically. "You were wonderful, darling."

"Wasn't she just," Gerry chimed in. "Did you see her? 'Bye-bye, Rollo.' " He dabbed his eyes with a tissue in mock admiration.

A nasal note of dissent cut through the renewed mirth.

"Without wishing to detract from your award-winning performances"—Bugsy, like Queen Victoria before him, was clearly not amused—"may I be so bold as to inquire what you are hoping to achieve by this prank?"

"It's not a prank, Bugsy." Cub was angered by the implication. "We were trying to confront him with the reality."

"Exactly" . . . "That's it" . . . "You've got no imagination, Bugsy." The other keepers rallied to Cub's support.

But Adrian Malone was quite used to a situation where he was the only soldier in step. "If you paint him into a corner . . . ," he began, but Sydney could tolerate him no longer.

"Shut up," he yelled belligerently. "He's not a cold-blooded murderer. And we've given him the five sweetest, cuddliest, most lovable—"

Now it was Sydney's turn to shut up. The sound that stilled his was not that of a human voice, but a noise that cut through the evening air like a sliver of ice. It was the sound of a shot from a gun.

There was no mistaking it. Or, if there was, there was no mistaking the next sound. Several keepers rose to their feet. As they did so a third shot rang out, causing everyone else— with the exception of Bugsy—to join them. It was by now possible to ascertain where the sounds were coming from—

the other side of the copse, possibly in the glade that led down to the flamingo lake.

The keepers stood, many with their eyes closed in prayer. But they were not prayers that were answered. A fourth shot rang out, just as loud and fatal as the first.

Pip could contain herself no longer. "It was your idea," she hissed at her boss through clenched teeth.

Indeed it had been. Sydney's hands were clenched in knots so tight that he feared he might never unclench them again, as he waited for the inevitable fifth shot. He did not have to wait long.

Eventually they approached the clearing, with stealth and under cover, fearful that the madman who was now running the zoo might turn his weapon on one of them. At least he had made a decent job of it. Five freshly dug graves lay under the shade of an elderly sycamore tree, each with an animal cage as a form of headstone. Rollo was patting down the last one as the first keepers neared the edge of the glade. He had taken off his jacket for the executions and, as a mark of respect, wore a black band on his right arm.

Sydney watched in fear and loathing as the former Hong Kong police officer blew on the end of his service revolver, put it back in its holster, threw his spade onto a wheelbarrow, and went off downhill in the direction of his office.

The keepers emerged stunned from their observation points among the trees into the open glade. Pip ran tearfully towards the lemur's cage and knelt in front of the grave in silent prayer. The other four followed suit, with the rest of the zoo staff keeping a respectful distance, some wiping their eyes, many too shocked and stunned to evince any emotion.

"I told you so. Nobody listened."

There was no need for anyone to look to see who had spoken.

Pip leapt to her feet in fury. "Shut up," she screamed, and advanced for the second time that day with the intention of attacking a man.

Again Sydney held her back. "Bugsy, he'll start on yours next," he warned, with bitter menace in his voice.

The rabbit was nearly six feet tall. It had been tethered to a stake, its paws tied behind its back. On its head it wore a racing driver's helmet, covered in marketing logos for all manner of products from gasoline to Italian knitwear to lager and chocolate bars. The Mexican firing squad, belts of bullets making cross-diagonals on their chests, were pointing their rifles, cocked and ready for the order to fire, at the trembling animal. Behind them Generalissimo Rollo, in heavily epauletted uniform and shining boots with spurs, finished his small cigar and ground it sadistically into the dirt.

"Take aim. Fire!" he ordered.

The five rifles cracked off simultaneously and the rabbit exploded into a ball of fur, white down dropping onto the village square like snow. The bell in the church clock-tower began to toll. Louder and louder and louder . . .

Rollo sat ramrod straight up in bed. Where was he? What was it? He drowsily came to his senses: he had been asleep and the telephone by his bed was ringing loudly.

He leaned over to switch on the bedside light, knocking off his chest an opened book on mammals that he must have been reading when he nodded off. Gingerly lifting the receiver, he inquired: "Yes?"

"Rolo?"

The voice was male and American and pronounced his name incorrectly.

"Yes?" he inquired again.

"It's Vince McCain and Willa Weston. Are we interrupting dinner?"

His brain began to wake up: it was that dreadful marketing couple from Octopus in Atlanta who had been bombarding him with insane faxes.

"Dinner?" Rollo peered at his bedside clock. "It's two o'clock in the morning."

"Oh, were you asleep?" Vince asked innocently.

By now Rollo was fully awake and in full flow. He propped himself up against the pillows. "Yes, I frequently am at two A.M., I'm afraid. Filthy habit. Must have picked it up in the Far East."

"Look, if this is a sleep-interruptive call," Vince apologised, "we can retelephone you later."

Rollo looked at the receiver in disdain; didn't they speak English in America any longer?"

"Oh no, it's not sleep-interruptive," he assured the imbecile. "Let's chat now. I can always catch up on some rest. At Christmas, probably."

"Okay," said Vince breezily. "Let's talk marketing."

"Oh good." Rollo wondered if they understood irony in America anymore, either.

"The figure for marketing you sent us . . . ," Vince went on, but his sentence was interrupted by strange sounds from the English end of the transatlantic line.

"Careful! Get off! Please!"

Vince and Willa were sitting side by side on a sofa in the latter's well-appointed bachelor pad. Bright prints of Cezannes and Manets and Monets adorned the walls and prominently displayed on the bookshelves were a series of self-help books running from *How to Stop Your Mind from Killing Your Body* to the collected thoughts of Mark McCormack.

Willa had offered to have Vince over for supper after work to reward him for what she supposed was his part in clinching McCain's green light for her plans to run Marwood Zoo. He had accepted with alacrity, ever hopeful that she might provide a richer reward than just dinner. Slightly to his surprise, on entering her apartment, she had suggested they call the zoo in England. She had been babbling about it all through the journey home—not that Vince had been paying attention—pointing out that here was a unique opportunity for her to make her mark in Octopus Inc. As they listened to the speakerphone on the low table in front of them, her contention that the place was currently being run by a half-wit seemed to bear fruit.

"Hang on! Suzie! Get your leg off!"

Willa leant towards the phone. "Willa Weston here. Are you all right?"

"Fine," came the harassed and far from convincing English voice at the other end. "Suzie, no, I can't fool around with you now. Move over, will you. I'm sorry, I'm going to have to put you on hold. Just for one moment." Rollo pressed the button on the phone.

"Another filthy habit he picked up in the Far East," Vince suggested knowingly.

The lemur had been the first animal to fall on Rollo, a direct hit on his head. This had woken the others up. The wallaby and the ostrich had started to play a game of tag round and round the room, crossing the bed at irregular intervals. The mara had decided to lick his toes and the coatimundi, seeking warmth, was trying to get under the sheets.

Worse than any of this, the lemur now leapt across the bedside table, treading on the hold button of the phone to release the sounds of the room to Atlanta.

"Suzie, take your tongue out of my ear! Mitzi, get off, will you? Just go over there, both of you, and play with each other."

Vince looked at Willa in amazement. "He's got two girls there."

"Don't pull, please. I'm talking to those marketing moonies. Cindy, don't bite!"

Willa, more than a little amused, held up three fingers. "Three girls?" Vince mouthed.

"Look what you've done. That is disgusting." The sound of Rollo's agony—which they presumed was his ecstasy—came to an abrupt stop. Unknown to the Atlantans, the lemur had wrenched the receiver off the phone, snapping the wire. Rollo, meanwhile, was staring at his soiled hand; he had tried to brush the ostrich off the bed and its hind quarters had proved less than hygienic.

Vince was incredulous, and not a little envious. He got up from the sofa and stomped across to the bookcase behind them. "He must have eaten an entire rhino horn. How does he get three girls?"

Willa coolly adopted a sangfroid attitude. "He's just taken charge of the place. They're jockeying for position."

"Simultaneously?" Vince had had a few office lays, but never to this extent.

"Why not?" She smiled. "Henry Kissinger. Power is the greatest aphrodisiac." She made an invisible set of inverted commas with her fingers.

She arose from the sofa, her back almost entirely naked in the tight-fitting black Hervé Leger dress, indicating to him that he should remain there, and went across to a half-open door. "Give me a couple of minutes."

From inside the room she shouted: "He's from Hong Kong. It's probably the tradition there—after you've been to the opium den."

Vince was aroused—in both senses of the word—by this aberrant behaviour. "He's in England now," he yelled back. "Bastard. I expect there's lots of young female keepers—damn him."

He slipped off his purple Japanese designer scarf and silk Armani jacket and folded both, placing them neatly on the sofa beside him. As he began to undo his trousers he yelled: "I think it's disgusting how some people abuse positions of trust for personal sexual gratification. It's offensive to women."

In the kitchen Willa was removing not her clothes but a take-away Chinese meal that she had given a boost of heat to in the microwave. She had carefully told Vince that she would "give" him dinner, not "make" it, since cooking was not amongst her skills. Why bother? she had reasoned as she'd watched her mother spend a lifetime in the kitchen. We live in an instant world today, her thinking went: faxes, E-mail, the Concorde. Nobody with any nous hangs around waiting for dishes to come to some simultaneous state of preparation. Leave that to the guys in the big white toques. Why did God give us the microwave if he didn't intend us to use it?

"At least they knew about each other," she called.

"What?" said Vince, struggling with a shirt button.

"The girls. If they're all in the same bed they know about each other. It's not as if he's cheating on any of them."

Vince stopped undressing to ponder this logic. It was true, but such a remark, he figured, could only come from a real swinger. He felt a little intimidated.

"Tell me about the sponsorships," she said, as if the question of sex had now been resolved.

He was perplexed. "What sponsorships?"

"The ones you told Rod you'd fixed up."

"Oh, yeah. No, I made that up," he replied casually, at last getting the final button on his shirt undone. He couldn't get that English geek out of his mind. "Bastard! I hope he has a seizure."

As he stood up to drop his trousers, Willa emerged from the kitchen door carrying a tray laden with takeaway Chinese food, most of it still in neat white boxes.

She was incredulous. "What are you doing?"

A confident smile radiated from his handsome features. "Undressing."

She seemed astonished.

"For sex," he explained. "I thought you were in the bedroom."

She indicated the kitchen. "I was getting dinner."

"Okay," he said with a grin, "you want to eat first."

"Vince," she said. There was more than a note of reprimand in her voice.

"Yeah." He tried to sound as casual as he could.

He was standing in front of the sofa in a pair of pink boxer shorts, his trousers down by his ankles.

"I'm undressing," he explained as he opened his shirt. "For sex. Fourth date."

She put the tray down on the already set table, sidled towards him with a knowing smile on her face, and dropped deftly down on one knee at his feet.

He closed his eyes, "Oh yeah—yeah, yeah, yeah," he yelled in anticipation.

But the only sensation he received was that of his trousers being pulled up and buttoned at the top.

She brought her face up level with his, and he leant forward eagerly to kiss her. As his tongue wriggled out, an admonishing forefinger was placed across his lips.

"I invited you here tonight to thank you for helping me with Rod. Not to jump in the sack with you."

76

He backed off, perplexed by this temporary setback. "Time-out," he requested, forming a T with his hands. "Not to jump in the sack with me. What is the problem? Willa, you're someone who'd really appreciate me."

"Look," she began. She didn't want to humiliate him. "You're a very attractive man . . ."

Vince looked at her as if she was deranged. "That's the problem? Because normally it's 'I have a headache' or 'My boyfriend's coming back tonight and he has a gun' or 'There's been a death in the family' or 'I can't find my diaphragm' or 'I don't do it with people from the office' or 'I've just had root canal work' or 'It's the wrong phase of the lunar cycle' or 'I'm too depressed about the environment' or . . ."

As he paced the room to deliver this tirade, Willa attempted to attract his attention to get a word in. Eventually she succeeded.

"Vince, we haven't known each other long enough."

"I knew I'd missed one!" he howled in abusive triumph.

Willa calmed him down and managed to persuade him to pick up his chopsticks and eat some dim sum.

She took a sip of wine and attempted to move the conversation onto a more rational level. "Look. I really like you. Who knows what might have happened . . ."

". . . if you weren't going to England tomorrow," he completed the sentence for her.

She nodded with enthusiasm, delighted that she seemed to have got away with it.

"Exactly."

Vince nodded too. "Look, I understand."

She put down her chopsticks in surprise. "You do?"

"Mmmm." His mouth was full of noodles, but his agreement was evident.

This was strange. She ran it past him one more time, spelling out the words with care. "You don't mind?" she asked.

"Really," he assured her.

Thank God, she thought. I'm off the hook. I may never have to fend off this half-wit again. "Thanks," she said. And she meant it.

He got up from the table and ran back to the sofa. She watched him suspiciously. Ferreting around in the pocket of his jacket, he pulled out a document and waved it in front of her.

Her heart fell. She knew what it was. A ticket.

" 'Cos I'm going with you," he announced in triumph.

"What?" was all she could say.

He strode back to his chair and sat down, delivering the ticket like a writ on the table between them and enthusiastically picking up his chopsticks. "Surprise! Yes, I asked Rod. He thinks it will be good for me to get away from Atlanta. You'll manage the zoo; I'll market it. We'll be a great team."

"Great." Willa summoned up a weak smile, but felt sick to the pit of her stomach.

CHAPTER
6

"I never thought I'd get rid of him so easily," Rod McCain confided to Neville as they crossed the television studio floor. "And it'll get his mother off my back."

"You'd better send a good bookkeeper with him," Neville warned. "Pity to lose Willa, though."

"Nah, we'll find out if she can cut the mustard," countered McCain. "If she suggests turning the place into a golf course, she's cut it."

Neville laughed. "Yeah. And then you can give her something real big to close down."

The studio's floor manager deferentially guided Rod to his seat. Opposite him were a black moderator, an earnest female with long dark hair, and a laid-back type with thick glasses wearing an Armani suit.

"You must be the intellectuals," said Rod. "What do you want to know?"

"Hard-nosed."

Rollo traced his finger down the battered dictionary he had discovered in the desk drawer of his new office. "Hard liquor," "hardmouthed," "hard-nosed." He discovered the expression meant "hard-bitten," so he had to trace his finger back up again to that word. "Steeled in battle," he noted with a scintilla of a smile. There was a quote from T. E. Lawrence—"hard-bitten tribesmen, their faces flecked with the blood of the fighting."

Well, that was what Big Rod wanted. It was the style of management that had made Octopus Inc. the $6 billion conglomerate that it was today. Rollo had been more than a little confused during the induction course when he'd joined Octopus TV in Hong Kong: the station manager had harangued them about the need to cut costs, whereas the company appeared to be awash with cash. "Slim and fit" was the frequently repeated maxim, but all it meant was that when they took over their main rival station they fired all the staff (despite assurances to the contrary).

In fact it had fallen to Rollo, as a personnel officer, to call in the less senior employees and explain the policy. Ironically, by being the mere messenger of a command that presumably originated in company HQ in Atlanta, it had earned him the epithet "hard-nosed," although he had no alternative course of action other than to resign himself. He had been glad enough to find another job in the Crown Colony when his Hong Kong police days had ended, and he was not about to sacrifice it.

Maybe the world of business had changed during the three decades he had spent in the ordered environment of the police force. Maybe all companies now motivated their workforces by fear—it certainly seemed to have replaced loyalty in the case of Octopus. *Fear Is the Key.* Rollo remembered the title of the book by his favourite author, Alistair MacLean, and the words had echoed in his brain as he had studied T. G. Parry Jones's book *Fierce* on the Cathay Pacific flight.

One passage in particular had caught his imagination. In 1852 Horatio Girling, the first keeper of serpents at London Zoo, had got very drunk one lunchtime and was bitten by a cobra. In two hours he was dead. The next day the zoo saw queues like it had never seen before as thousands arrived to look at the lethal reptile, which, oblivious to its newfound fame, lay curled up asleep in its glass tank. Rollo knew he would have to do something to make his mark on Marwood Zoo or he was out, and the notion of a Fierce Animal Policy seemed the perfect solution to cutting costs, with fewer animals to feed and hopefully an upturn in revenue.

He glanced again at the dictionary. "Hard liquor." He found his gaze lingering on the closed top drawer of the metal filing cabinet. Inside was one of the half litres of Smirnoff he had bought duty-free on the flight from Hong Kong. No, he instructed himself, not yet, not until the sun was over the yardarm. On the other hand, he reasoned, glancing at his watch, by now it would be well over the yardarm in Honkers. He could do with a stiffie. The events of the past days had taken their toll—although he had kept up a bold front in the face of the concerted opposition of the keepers. But no. Why go for Dutch courage, his father always used to counsel, when you could dip into the reservoir of your own.

Firm government. That was the policy that always worked. The people didn't always like it at first, but once they came to respect it the result was invariably positive. Look at Castro; look at Thatcher; look at Deng Xiaoping. The thought of the Chinese leader made him homesick for the Crown Colony. In less than a year's time mainland China would resume control of Hong Kong. He still intended to be there, standing by Government House, a reminder of the British way.

The inhabitants hated the prospect of their new masters—just as the keepers hated him. Rollo had known that his Fierce Animal Policy would meet with some resistance, but he had never envisaged he would be in the isolated position in which he now found himself.

Christ, he had forgotten the programme!

He had even placed a portable television set on his desk to watch it. There was still time to catch the last ten minutes, but as he flicked through the channels in a state of panic, he wondered if he would even see that much, since he couldn't remember which channel the fax from Atlanta had said Rod was on. Not one that Octopus owned; Rollo could remember that much. He would just have to tell pushy Ms. Weston that he had been too busy with an emergency in the ungulate enclosure to watch, a sound excuse, since he was fairly certain she had no idea what an ungulate was. He liked the idea of it—an ungulate emergency—and began to think of titles for movies: *Ungulates on the March, Revenge of the Ungulates, Ungulates Unbound.*

But there he was—Channel 46—the familiar features of Rod McCain: a controlled white mane of hair, fastidiously trimmed moustache, half-moon spectacles to add gravitas, and a look that could switch from charmingly sincere to icily severe at will. Apart from his photograph, which was splashed over the world's press on an almost daily basis, Rollo had only seen him in the flesh once, when he had swept through Hong Kong. "Almighty Rod," they called him at the station, and there had been something superhuman in the solid bulk and fearsome presence of the man. He seemed in full flow now, confronted with three intense journalists—a Harvard highbrow, a groomed woman in her middle years, and a smooth black chairman—who made up the panel of *In the Spotlight.*

"The trouble with you people," Rod was saying accusingly, "is that you seem to think I am able to control prime ministers or presidents or whatever—"

The female interlocutor raised her pencil to remake her point. "No, what I was suggesting was—"

But Rod was not a man who enjoyed being interrupted. "Let me finish. I have no control over anybody except my own employees—and not always them."

He chortled at his own joke, and the chairman took the opportunity to slip in a supplementary point. "But, Mr. McCain, it is a documented fact that before you make any major acquisition in any country you do tend to hold meetings with the prime minister or at least—"

It was Rod's turn to interrupt again. "Who's documented it? You?"

The black journalist seemed prepared for this. "Didn't you have talks with President Chirac before Octopus took a majority shareholding in Chanel Encore in France?"

"What's the crime?" McCain looked incredulous. "Am I meant to alienate politicians? What you've got to understand is that a large part of Octopus is in the communication and leisure business. We have a reputation for giving the people what they want in many countries throughout the world. So doesn't it make sense to enter into a full and free dialogue with their elected leaders? That's what democracy is about."

Rollo found himself rather impressed. He had never particularly associated democracy with the Octopus organization, but he found Rod most persuasive.

The lady opposite his boss in the television studio was less persuaded. "So you would agree that your editors tend to support governments, especially just before elections, when you might need permission—"

Rod had swatted away this particular mosquito many times before. "What my editors do or do not do is for them to decide. I do not control the editorial content of my newspapers."

"But you do appoint your editors," the interviewer reminded him.

He smiled sarcastically. "Do you expect me to get someone else to?"

The woman was nothing if not persistent. "Surely the presence of several former politicians on the Octopus board is an indication—"

McCain's hackles were beginning to rise. "I don't know what you're trying to imply. My shareholders are best served by having a board with top-level international experience."

"You talk about a board," the woman challenged him, "but isn't it just you alone who flies around the world running your various companies?"

McCain put the tips of his fingers together and leant forward, as if explaining something to a child. "Listen, it's not a question of hands-on management. You appoint managers to manage. If I have a skill, it's putting the right guy in the right country at the right time."

Is he talking about me? Rollo wondered. But the black American interviewer who was chairing the panel seemed sceptical. "And removing people at the right time as well. Am I right?"

Rod shifted in his seat. "Look, all companies make changes. They evolve. Men outgrow jobs and jobs outgrow men." He glanced at the female interviewer on the right of the panel with a seductive smile. "And women."

She wasn't to be seduced so easily. "But it is said, Mr. McCain, that as soon as anyone working for Octopus, in whatever country, begins to make an individual public reputation, they tend to be replaced."

" 'It is said'? 'It is said'? Who says it?" McCain intended to put the woman in her place. "When journalists work for me they attribute their quotes to sources."

The silent member of the panel, a man in an Armani suit with close-cropped hair and the sort of glasses that darken in the sunlight, stifled a laugh.

The woman was not to be done down. "Let's say that I say it."

McCain smiled. "Then I would have to say that you are wrong. There are several people in Octopus who have worked with me all the way, right from the early days in New Zealand."

"But that makes my point," she insisted. "They are invisible men, wise enough to keep a low profile, whereas the moment—"

"I'm going to have to cut you off, Elizabeth." This time it was the moderator who interrupted her. "We're nearly out of time, Mr. McCain, and we've heard very little about the private side of your public face. Would you describe yourself as a family man?"

"Very much so." McCain seemed relieved at the shift. "Megan and I spend as much time together as possible. There's nothing we like more than a quiet evening in front of the television. And working with me in company headquarters is Victor, the son of my first marriage . . ."

"Vincent?" The man in the dark glasses actually spoke.

"Sorry. We often call him Victor. Family pet name." McCain was nothing if not adept at covering up his errors.

But the exchange was not lost on Rollo, who was, at this moment, frozen to his chair in a state of shock. His worst

85

nightmare had just come true. A large black spider that had presumably escaped from the insect house was steadfastly making its way across the desk towards him, its black abdomen covered in bright red hairs and its spindly legs spelling out death with every step.

Trying not to let the creature notice he was making any movement, lest it increase its pace, Rollo looked anxiously around for a means of defence. The dictionary was too small, but on the shelf beside it lay his prized copy of *Fierce*. His right hand snaked out and he gingerly lifted the book by its spine. Just as he raised the volume above the desk, the spider came to a halt, as if sensing the impending battle.

"Scared?"

The beaming face of Adrian "Bugsy" Malone popped round the half-open office door. Rollo was too terrified to deny the accusation; besides, it was entirely accurate. Usually the sight of Bugsy was itself enough to cause strong men to hide. His seemingly uncontrollable stream of verbiage—however well-informed—was a penance to his listening victim. At this moment, however, the loquacious insect keeper was just the man Rollo wanted to see.

"I've always had a bit of a thing about spiders," gulped the zoo director.

"Irrational, but not uncommon," Bugsy intoned as if he were talking to himself—something, Rollo surmised, he often did if there was no human ear to punish.

Bugsy advanced airily towards the desk and protectively lifted up the spider. After checking to see that it was unharmed, he popped it in the pocket of his jacket. Rollo could feel rivulets of chilled sweat trickle down his neck.

"The point I'm making"—the glint in Bugsy's eye indicated his delight at finding a captive audience—"is that Terry here wouldn't hurt a fly."

He thought for a millisecond and corrected himself. "Well, he would hurt a fly, actually, being an Euathlus Smithi—to the layman, a Mexican red-kneed Tarantula—and thus particularly partial to flies. No, the point I'm making is that Terry has a bite relatively harmless to human beings, and yet you reacted to him as if he were fierce, which he isn't. So my understanding of your so-called Fierce Animal Policy—"

"It isn't so-called." Rollo had recovered his equilibrium sufficiently to attempt to gag this terrible man.

Bugsy hardly appeared to have heard him. "—is that if creatures are *thought* to be fierce, then that is sufficient—"

But this time his unceasing babble was interrupted by a more dramatic disturbance. The door to the director's office flew wide open and three keepers—Hugh, Cub, and Ant—dashed in, followed by a breathless and apologetic Di, the director's secretary, who began to unlock the gun rack.

"Sorry, Mr. Lee," Hugh, the gorilla keeper, explained. "Animal's escaped. We've got to corner it."

As each of the keepers removed a rifle from the case, Rollo rose from his chair. "What about the tranquilizer darts?" he inquired.

"Derek's got those," Cub, the big cat keeper, reassured him.

"I'll take one, too." Rollo, already unsettled by the tarantula incident and now greatly alarmed, strode towards the open case.

Ant, from insects, attempted to restrain him. "Don't worry, sir, we can handle it."

Hugh pulled him away. "Let's go. It's all under control, sir."

The keepers swept out of the room as swiftly as they had entered. Di dutifully relocked the gun case, but not before

Rollo had removed a rifle and checked to see that it was loaded.

He ran out into the corridor in pursuit of the keepers. Behind him a plaintive Bugsy was continuing his suit. "You see, it's all a question of perception. The public think pandas are pets; however, they'd maul you as soon as . . ."

But his words were lost in the hue and cry that greeted the two men as they stepped into the bright daylight. Visitors—men, women, and children—were being pushed back from a cage on a trolley over by the capybara enclosure.

"What's going on?" a mother with two small daughters anxiously asked Rollo.

He tried to sound as casual as possible. "Just recapturing an animal. Keep back, please. Nothing to worry about. It's not fierce."

"Why have you got a gun then?" one of the daughters asked, eyeing Rollo suspiciously.

"Just a precaution," he hastily explained. "Don't worry. Everything's under control."

Which, indeed, it appeared to be. Rollo made his way towards the recaptured animal. The keepers were still covering it with their guns and Derek with his blowpipe. At the same time they were attempting to convince the approaching crowd that the danger was at an end. "It's all right. We've caught it. Relax."

Rollo decided to assert himself. He walked through the agog members of the public with a reassuring smile. "All over now. Thank you for your cooperation, ladies and gentlemen."

Sydney Lotterby, the keeper of small mammals, seemed to be attempting to wheel the aminal away before Rollo could get a good look at it.

The zoo director restrained him. He looked through the

bars of the small cage. A docile animal with a protuberant snout was cowering inside.

"Is that an anteater?" he inquired of Lotterby.

"Spot on," came the cocky Cockney response. "Careful, sir, it's still angry."

"Angry?" Rollo was incredulous.

"They've got wicked tempers, sir," Lotterby warned him.

Rollo smelled a rat. Lotterby had already attempted to delude him by putting up notices asserting that all his mammals were fierce, and this seemed an extension of the same ploy.

"Devastate small towns, do they, Lotterby?" The director's suspicion was not hard to detect.

Sydney looked surprised and hurt in equal measure. "No, sir. Not these. But look at the claws. Diabolical. You can never be too careful with an anteater, sir."

"Nevertheless, and correct me if I'm wrong"—the note of irony in Rollo's voice rang more stridently than before—"it is an anteater, not a man-eater."

Two keepers went by carrying a stretcher with a heavily blanketed Pip, looking like a casualty from the First World War, but Rollo failed to notice them, so intent was he on getting a truthful response from Lotterby.

"You have overreacted," he snapped at the head of small mammals.

Lotterby was down but not out. He indicated a woman and her infant by the steps leading up to the sea lion pond. "What if it had jumped on that pram over there? What would you be saying to the mother now?"

"I would be saying," Rollo replied, " 'Madam, you are the victim of an eight-billion-to-one chance—a jumping anteater, an evolutionary mutant previously unknown to naturalists.' "

"They can climb like monkeys, sir," Lotterby persisted.

"You did not need three guns to recapture this." Rollo gestured with his own. "A sharp stick would have sufficed."

"A sharp stick, sir?" Sydney countered. "Believe you me, these jaws would splinter—"

"Will you shut up!" Rollo screamed at him. "Get this fluffy pet back to its enclosure and stop insulting my intelligence. Now!"

Sydney dolefully led away the trolley party with the recaptured anteater as the stretcher with the wounded Pip, which had gone past Rollo unnoticed, came round again.

"You all right, Pip?" Sean, one of the stretcher bearers, called down to her with more volume than appeared necessary.

The cute blonde keeper grimaced. "Yes. I'm fine . . . I'll be okay."

Rollo at last noticed them, took this exchange on board, and hurried after them. "What's wrong? Is she hurt?"

"A little difficulty with a bandicoot," Tim, the gangly keeper at the other end of the stretcher, reassured him.

The girl was apparently in agony. Rollo, wondering whether he should call an ambulance, lifted the blanket that was covering Pip to examine the extent of her injuries. He took a step back in horror. Her right leg was bandaged from thigh to toe and blood was seeping from a succession of wounds.

"My God!" he exclaimed.

The assistant small mammal keeper was nothing if not stoic in her response. "Just a flesh wound, sir." Her blue eyes gazed up at him as she attempted a brave smile. "Few stitches and I'll be back at work in a week."

"Are you sure?" The director wondered if gangrene was likely to set in.

"Don't worry." Little Pip seemed to be trying to comfort him. "It's part of the job with bandicoots."

Before he'd had time to issue any orders, the stretcher

90

swept away. "Just be careful of those bandicoots, sir," Sean shouted over his shoulder.

"Right . . . bandicoots," Rollo mumbled to himself, trying to remember where their enclosure lay. He could see Di fast approaching, having given instructions to the stretcher bearers on her way.

"Pity about Pip's leg," she said with a casualness almost bordering on cheerfulness. "Still, it's good for the zoo, isn't it?"

Rollo's mind went blank. Good for the zoo?

Di read his expression and tried to explain. "I mean the fierceness."

"Oh, yes." Rollo collected his thoughts. "Yes, indeed. Our policy precisely. I'd like to take a look at the bandicoots, Di, can you remind me . . ."

"Just beyond the meerkats, sir." Jenni, the stocky keeper from the camel house, had overheard his request. "I'm going that way if you'd like to follow me."

Rollo thanked her and proceeded to do so. As they set off, he noticed that her left arm was heavily bandaged up to the elbow.

"What happened to you?" he asked.

"Just a bite," came the nonchalant reply. "You come to expect them in our business."

"Come to expect them," Rollo repeated ruminatively. He was about to delve more deeply into the cause of her accident when he was nearly knocked to the ground by a trio of boys who went charging past him. These were not keepers but members of the public. His surprise was mitigated by a certain satisfaction that these young men in their late teens or early twenties were precisely the age group that zoos found hardest to attract. And they were not alone. Innumerable men of varying ages, from eighteen to eighty, were now streaming up the hill beyond the souvenir shop.

91

Rollo excused himself from Jenni and Di and hurried after them, his gun still in his hand. He changed his step as he recognised the svelte back of the Chinese student keeper by the shop.

He tapped her on the shoulder. "What's happening?"

Ang-Ling swung round to reveal a black patch over her left eye. "Sea lions, sir," she informed him, indicating the men scurrying up the steps.

Rollo was completely taken aback. "Sea lions? Are they attacking someone?"

He found himself somewhat out of breath by the time he reached the pool. It irritated him that he was no longer in the peak physical condition he had maintained during his years in the Hong Kong police, but his time as an Octopus executive had proved considerably more sedentary. A crowd of more than a hundred people—most of them men—completely occupied the tiered steps by the pool. Rollo pushed his way through them to what he presumed was the site of the accident.

"Excuse me," he said politely as he made his way forward. "No cause for concern. It's all under control."

Several visitors tried to impede his progress. "Get back!" a long-haired youth yelled at him. "Oi," joined in his beer-bellied mate, who was lighting up a cigarette, "we was here first."

Rollo prudently moved to the side of the steps, where, thanks to his height, he was able to get a clear sight of what was happening. It was not quite what he expected.

Sky, the six-foot-two assistant to Reggie Sea Lions, was standing on the rocks at the far end of the pool. In front of her was a tubfull of herrings. Gracefully she took one from the top and threw it to a waiting sea lion, who caught it in his mouth, swallowed it, and then rewarded her with a grateful bark and a flurry of applause from his flippers.

Feeding time always attracted some extra visitors, but rarely numbers of this order. The fact that Sky, her blonde hair flowing down her back and her body tanned like that of a girl in a holiday brochure, was clad only in the smallest of bikinis which barely covered her ample, springy chest and only about three of the forty or so inches of shapely leg, might well have influenced the size of the audience.

"Nice crowd today, Director." Reggie Sea Lions, a genial Scot whose own upward development was no more than five feet, had insinuated himself beside Rollo. "We're doing very good business."

Rollo was forced to agree, while keeping an ear open for the comments coming from the men near him.

"Stunning creatures, sea lions," said an old-age pensioner in a blazer and military tie. "Wonderful plumage," his companion agreed—somewhat to Rollo's mystification. "God at his best," went on the first.

Sky bent down, the ring in her immaculate stomach glinting in the strong afternoon sun, and threw another herring.

"How long has this been going on?" Rollo inquired of the short keeper beside him.

Reggie paused for thought. "Well, we only started it on Monday," he began, then quickly added, "but we've been thinking about it since Friday."

"It seems to have caught on," Rollo was forced to acknowledge.

Reggie beckoned the director to lower his head so that he could share a confidence with him. "Between you and me," he whispered, "I think the girl helps."

At this moment Sky executed a perfect arched dive and swam the length of the pool, a sea lion on either side of her, to tumultuous applause from her nature-loving fans.

"You do?" said Rollo, a faint trace of irony in his voice.

Reggie had another confidence to impart as he threw a herring to the girl, who expertly caught it in her mouth. "And she has a Ph.D."

The crowd applauded. "Wonderful thing, nature," the old-age pensioner confided to his mate.

As the crowds were dispersing from the sea lion show, a woman in a red dress, who had been attempting to take a photograph of her husband and mother beside a large bronze sea lion statue while she was standing on a stone bench, accidentally slipped, badly grazing the inside of her leg and twisting her ankle. Some keepers ran up to help her. But Rollo was oblivious to this, as he was more concerned in escaping from the small sea lion keeper, who was pleading the case for his watery charges.

"Of course, she couldn't do that if they were fierce." The short man trotted along, trying to keep up with the giant strides of the zoo director, who was nearly a foot and a half taller than him. "I mean, I'm a hundred percent in favour of the Fierce Animal Policy, but obviously with some animals—like mine—the attendances speak for themselves. I mean, the purpose of the policy is to increase attendances, isn't it, and where the attendances are very high for non-fierce animals there obviously has to be an exception to the general rule."

But Rollo's attention had been directed elsewhere. He had just caught sight of a young female keeper emerging from the hut which served as the zoo workshop with a bloodied and bandaged arm. She turned and waved it, showing no signs of discomfort, to someone whom he was unable to discern in the doorway, then slipped it into a sling and strolled off whistling in the opposite direction.

Rollo turned to the still-babbling Reggie. "Stay," he commanded, as an owner might address a dog.

Tucking his rifle under his arm, he strode into the hut.

Ant, the assistant insect house keeper, was naked to the waist, and was lying on a trestle table while two other keepers applied liberal quantities of theatrical blood to his stomach. Chuckling as they did so, they failed to notice the director in the doorway.

"Bit more," said one of the painters. "Not too much," warned the other. "Got to keep it real."

"You're right," concurred the first. "I don't think we should do anyone else today, otherwise he might get suspicious."

"Yes," a laughing Ant agreed from his prone position, "we don't want to make him too fierce."

The loud sound of a gun being cocked caused them all to look round in surprise. Rollo Lee was standing in the doorway looking like John Wayne in a John Ford western.

"I have a suggestion," he said, raising the rifle to his shoulder. "Let's make those wounds as realistic as possible."

"No! No! Help!" The keepers flung themselves to the floor as three shots rang out. With an expertise acquired in the Hong Kong police, Rollo picked off the three mugs sitting on a ledge behind them. Not that he was going to tell the keepers he had been aiming for them.

"Dear me," he exclaimed casually, glancing at the smoking rifle, "there must be something wrong with the sights."

The keepers gibbered in relief.

"You three," said Rollo, "see me in my office at nine o'clock tomorrow morning."

He turned and strode out of the hut as a terrified Reggie ran in past him, galvanised into action by the sound of the shots.

Reggie covered his mouth in horror. "My God," he wailed as he saw the blood dripping from Ant's stomach.

Secretly proud of himself, Rollo marched down the hill back towards his office. In the distance he could discern a gathering crowd of visitors and keepers, just near the spot where Pip's stretcher had been. That too—he cursed himself for having been so easily fooled—had been a total fake, he now realised.

But this time it wasn't Pip. In fact it was she who came towards him now, running up to him from behind the hut, and screamed tearfully: "Have you been shooting more animals?"

"No," Rollo reassured her. "Just culling a few keepers." And, then, noticing that this "seriously wounded" girl hadn't so much as a limp, he added as an afterthought: "Leg better, is it? Miracle recovery?"

The young keeper opened her mouth to offer an explanation, but no words came out, since she could think of none.

Rollo marched through a carefully tended flower bed to where the latest prank was being acted out. He intended to put a stop to this "injured by the animals" charade once and for all. His policy was not biddable; the staff had better believe it.

He had gotten close to the crowd when Reggie emerged from the workshop hut, screaming at the top of his voice: "He just shot a keeper—watch out!"

"No I didn't!" Rollo bellowed back.

"He's in there dying." Reggie's terror was palpable. "Look out. He's gone mad."

Many of the zoo visitors turned away from the scene of the latest accident to see Rollo levelling his rifle at Reggie, who was trying to hide behind a tree, with Pip running away as fast as her uninjured legs would take her and the two keepers from the hut popping their heads back inside the door as quickly as they had popped them out.

"Be quiet!" Rollo shouted at Reggie. "Stop ranting or I'll—"

He suddenly became aware that he was being watched by members of the public, so he turned back to the crowd and, lowering his gun to his side, approached the new victim on a stretcher with as much decorum as he could muster.

"Right," he muttered to himself. "Right."

Sydney tried to forestall him. "Ah, Director, I'm afraid there's been an accident . . ."

"Of course there has," snapped Rollo. "And I can assure you it's the last one, Lotterby."

Cub attempted to remonstrate with him. "This lady fell off some steps, Mr. Lee. She was taking a photo . . ."

"No, surely she was savaged by a koala bear," the director corrected her, "or gored by a chipmunk or ripped to shreds by a canary."

He pointed to the keepers bearing the stretcher. "I've had enough of this. Put that down, now."

As they did so the woman in the red dress who was lying on it protested: "I fell."

"She did, Mr. Lee. Scout's honour."

But Sydney's intervention did little to help the woman's cause. "I warned you, Lotterby." Rollo's patience was by now threadbare.

"What are you doing?" demanded the victim's husband, a balding, red-faced man with a semimilitary moustache.

Rollo looked down at the man's wife. "Come off it, friend," he said patronisingly. "Just get up and stop shamming, will you."

The husband was incredulous. "She needs treatment."

"No she doesn't," came the imperious reply.

"She does." The man pointed to his wife's body, now prone on the stretcher on the ground. "She's hurt her leg."

"It's fake," Rollo explained to him.

"What?"

"It's fake blood." Rollo kneeled by the body and with his finger, took a smear from the woman's ankle. "Taste it."

"Mr. Lee . . . ," Cub said in a last-ditch attempt to intervene.

"Fake," Rollo pronounced to the husband. "Try it."

The man assumed he must be in the presence of a lunatic. He turned pleadingly to the keepers. "Who is this?"

Sydney smiled willfully. "He's the director of the zoo."

Such had been the commotion caused by the incident that nobody had noticed during this exchange that a black London taxi—an unusual sight in Marwood—had drawn up by the zoo offices and two smartly dressed people had emerged with their baggage. They were Vince McCain and Willa Weston from Octopus Inc., the new bosses of the zoo.

Rollo shook his head at the woman in red. "You've been rumbled, old girl."

"What?" the injured woman managed to reply, still in a state of shock.

"The game's up," Rollo insisted.

Her husband was about to hit him. "What's going on?"

"Don't you know?" Rollo patiently explained, "This is theatrical blood. It's a charade. It's been going on all day. She's not hurt."

"She *is* hurt," insisted the husband.

Rollo shook his head. "No. She's just one of the keepers' wives. Taste the blood."

"She's *my* wife," the enraged man replied.

Rollo was in the process of licking the spoor from his finger. "She's your wife?" he repeated, registered a scintilla of doubt.

"She did fall down, Mr. Lee." Cub still saw some hope of extricating him from the situation.

Rollo was now in deeper doubt. In panic he lifted the woman's ankle to his lips to taste the blood once again.

A handbag caught the side of his head. "He's drinking her blood," the woman's mother screamed. "Will you stop that!"

Rollo fell back, dropping the leg. The woman on the stretcher howled in agony.

"Sorry," Rollo apologised as he regained his equilibrium. Then he turned to the husband. "Are you sure she's your wife?"

"Of course I'm sure," the man exploded, threatening him with raised fists. "Get away from her."

Rollo attempted to calm things down. "Wait, wait. Let's be sensible."

"Sensible," screamed the husband. "Count Dracula's telling me to be sensible."

Willa Weston, who had been observing all this in amazement, stepped forward from the crowd. "What's happening here?" she demanded in a deep voice from the American South.

"He's sucking her blood," the mother pointed out.

"He's what?" Willa thought she had seen this when she'd got out of the taxi, but still she could hardly believe it.

"Look at his lips," said the mother.

Rollo brushed the back of his hand across them. A deep red smear appeared on it.

"He's the director of the zoo," the husband mouthed unbelievingly.

"You're Rolo Lee?" Willa demanded.

"Christopher Lee, more like," the mother interjected.

"Yes," Rollo admitted.

Willa indicated the woman. "She needs attention. She's injured."

Rollo was angered by this unwarranted intervention by some pushy American visitor. "I know she injured," he answered patronisingly.

"But you just told everyone she wasn't," the husband unhelpfully reminded him.

"Before you bit her," added the mother.

"Look . . . ," Rollo began, but Willa was now taking control. She crouched down by the body. "Are you in pain, Mrs. . . . ?"

"Mrs. Pike. No," the woman acknowledged, "but it's very tender—"

"I can manage this, thank you," Rollo interrupted.

"Not on the evidence so far," Willa said, and turned back to the woman. "We'll get you straight to hospital, Mrs. Pike."

"No you won't," Rollo bellowed at her. *"I'm* in charge here."

"No you're not," the American riposted through tightened teeth.

"Yes I am. Yes I am." Rollo raised himself to his full six foot five in mounting fury. "Now why don't you bugger off? You Americans think you run everything. I mean, who the hell do you think you are?"

"Willa Weston," replied the woman.

"Vince McCain," said the Armani-clad man standing beside her.

A hush fell over the assembly of crowd and keepers, and no one was more silent than Rollo Lee. All eyes were on him. After a while he spread his arms. "Welcome to Marwood Zoo . . . Can I offer you a coffee . . . or something?"

"Cappuccino," said Vince with a smile.

Before either of the Americans had time to respond, the diminutive figure of Reggie Sea Lions came running from behind the souvenir shop, with two policemen in hot pursuit.

"That's him," Reggie said, breathlessly indicating Rollo.

The taller policeman took Lee by the arm. "You're under arrest," he said.

The police sergeant explained to the astonished crowd: "He shot one of the keepers."

"He also shot five animals." Little Pip was bitterly determined that all of Rollo's crimes should be aired.

Vince McCain and Willa Weston were incredulous. What had Lee been up to? Had he been running a zoo or a madhouse?

"No, he missed." It was Ant, a lone voice coming partially to the director's defence.

Reggie strode across to the keeper who had been prostrate in the hut. "Missed?" he queried. "What about this?"

He pulled up Ant's shirt to reveal the appalling injuries to the man's stomach. People screamed; the stretcher bearers dropped the woman in red onto the ground in amazement; the police sergeant stepped across to remove Rollo's rifle, but as he did so a swinging handbag from the woman's mother caught Lee on the side of the head and the zoo director crumpled in an undistinguished heap in front of his new American masters.

Willa lowered her sunglasses to make quite sure that what she was witnessing was for real.

CHAPTER
7

Marwood Zoo Hall had never seen anything like it before.

Not in the Edwardian days when it was convivial with cigar smoke and laughter at the conclusion of sumptuous banquets; not when it served as a temporary hospital ward for recuperating officers during the Second World War; and certainly not when Sir John used it for visiting naturalists and explorers to give lectures to the keepers and interested members of the local public.

A vast screen had been erected in the centre of the stage and an audiovisual onslaught had hit the keepers with dazzling images of happy families, contented customers, cute animals, smiling staff at fast-food restaurants, whirring turnstiles with cash accumulating at the gate in rapidly increasing piles, and, above all, merchandising, merchandising, merchandising—hats, T-shirts, jackets, cuddly toys, soft drinks, sweets, key rings with first names on them, pencils, jigsaws, cups, plates, glasses, and even wine.

All this, and more, came across to the rampant accompaniment of a hip music track that might have been more appropriate for Rollerblading on Venice Boardwalk in California than for introducing a new zoo policy. It was a "little something" that Vince had asked the marketing department to run up for him and Willa before they left for England, and even as she cued the succeeding images on her laptop, Willa acknowledged to herself that it was, perhaps, somewhat excessive for the occasion.

But the keepers seemed to respond to this introductory lecture with glowingly positive rapture—not so much because they welcomed any form of change; they didn't. But they were overjoyed by the fact that Rollo Lee was no longer in charge. The mass murderer sat alone at the back of the hall, shunned by the others like a child molester in a prison.

Willa Weston, in her metallic high heels and her luminously shining silver Via Spiga silk suit, which ended enticingly far enough above the knee to distract most male attention from the display behind her, wore a state-of-the-art headset and microphone to address the troops.

"To summarise"—she looked with satisfaction at the appreciative eyes—"we want you to join the Octopus family. But families work because they have a lot in common. So let's see what we have in common."

Vince McCain took centre stage, dressed all in all black save for a bloodshot tie. He raised a portable microphone to his lips as if he were Tony Bennett in concert. "You all want job security. Miss Weston and I want you to have that security."

"You love your animals," Willa took up the rehearsed refrain. "We respect that and know this zoo cannot succeed without that love."

Vince looked at her admiringly. "I love the sound of that." He glanced at a note in his palm. "Now, I'm told conservation is the heart of your work here. No problem. Sounds great to me. It's what we all want. But for us to carry on this work the numbers have to be right, and they depend on customer pull-through. The stats are all visitor-volume-sensitive. Sadly, zoos face growing competition. In the last decade there's been a fivefold increase in alternative-family-orientated-ticketed-leisure opportunities."

At the back of the hall Rollo thought he was going to be sick. Marketing! Its practitioners came from a planet all of their own. Reggie Sea Lions looked at Sky in the hope that the younger generation might be able to follow what Vince was saying, but all he got was a shrug of incomprehension. In fact, the body language of many communicated bewilderment.

Sensing this, Vince hunkered down at the very front of the stage to make himself clear. "So we must acknowledge our core business and orient our marketing to position ourselves not just as an adventure-outlet-recreational-leisure-environment venue, but also as a multiple-facility-merchandising-opportunity situation."

Images of everything from ice cream to Indian tepees scudded across the screen in time to the music to illustrate this concept.

"May I ask . . ."—the zoo's own master of verbosity was on his feet with a question—"may I ask whether the epithet 'theme park' effectively defines what you're trying to—"

"Not yet," Vince snapped back brusquely. "Willa."

"Thank you, Vince." She gave the audience her best number two smile, and even several female keepers felt themselves seduced. "Our aim must be to give each visitor a warm, buzzy experience. And I believe passionately that we can do that only if communications between all of us are re-

104

ally open. So that we can ask you how you feel about what's happening here at the zoo and, in turn, each and every one of you can feel free to ask us anything you like . . ."

"Well, if I may ask something . . ."

Again the voice came from near the back of the hall. Willa could see him. It was the same irritant, in his bow tie and rimless spectacles and his hair parted in the centre, waving a copy of the *Financial Times* to obtain her attention.

"Please, let me finish," she pleaded. "Ask us anything at all about, for example, zoo policy . . ."

"Yes, that's what I'm trying to do." Bugsy was on his feet.

She sensed that the rest of the audience did not have much sympathy for the man and made the decision to ignore him. "We will be organising a series of seminars for this purpose."

"Are you planning a theme park?" Bugsy's nasal whine rose to maximum decibels.

Vince now stepped forward and glared at the insect keeper in barely suppressed rage. "Not now. Haven't you ever been to one of these things before? Shut up."

"That's ironic, Mr. Communication . . . ," Bugsy muttered, but another maniacal scream of "Shut Up!" from Vince shocked him into resuming his place.

Sydney, who was sitting two rows farther forward, turned round to him. "Better a theme park than a shooting range," he shouted.

The assembly concurred, many eyes fixing on Rollo at the back, who made a point of assiduously straightening his tie.

"So, to summarise." Vince indicated a large white rhino on the screen. "Conversation remains the aim of this zoo."

"Conversation?" Bugsy chuckled to himself, and many of the others were equally mystified.

A chart with a massive dollar sign and a graph snaking upwards replaced the rhino. Willa pointed to it. "Two. The zoo is in no danger, provided we increase income."

"And three." Vince knew this was the coup de grace and threw his fist in the air. "The Fierce Creatures Policy, the brainchild of Mr. Rolo Lee, is no longer in force."

The keepers rose as one man, stamping and cheering. Willa and Vince could hardly believe their luck. They clenched hands and raised them together, like a newly elected politician and his wife.

Following the lead of Sydney, most of the keepers turned to sneer in triumph at the deposed director.

His chair, however, was empty.

But not his room—not the cramped attic room to which he had been forced to move the evening the Americans arrived. It was full to overflowing.

Vince and Willa had given him no opportunity to explain why, at the very moment they turned up, he happened to be licking blood from the ankle of a lady visitor to the zoo. Rollo realised that it was understandable that they might regard this as an act of complete insanity. However, there was a wholly logical explanation, which he had rehearsed over and over in his head and which he fully intended to deliver the moment the opportunity arose.

Actually, in some ways it had been a stroke of luck, he realised, that they had gone off for some candlelit dinner at the Marwood Arms after ordering him to vacate his rooms. That way he had been able to smuggle the five animals up the stairs to his new quarters undetected by any human eye.

But for how long? He had assiduously completed the report they had demanded on the "customer flow-through," as the detestable Vince had put it. In fact there had been a slight upturn, Rollo noted with a modicum of pride, although he knew it was due more to the clement summer weather than any policy of his, fierce or otherwise.

"Will you two calm down!" The ostrich and the baby wallaby had ignored the two glasses of water he had given them and were romping round his bed like children in a playground, leaving the sheets a crumpled mess. He sometimes wondered if they were trying to mate, shuddering at the thought of what the progeny might look like.

Although he knew it was bad form to have favourites, the lemur and he had become bosom chums. After all, they did have the same name. Those eyes, so mournful and reflective. As he fed the little creature from a bowl of grapes, he wondered if the animal was sympathising with his dilemma. At least it provided a sympathetic ear.

"The big question is: What am I going to do with you lot?" Rollo sat at his desk looking at the mara warming itself by the window in the afternoon sun. It was the best behaved of all; sometimes he thought it was stuffed, unlike the coatimundi, which was always sticking its interfering snout into everything.

"Because I'm almost certainly on the scrap heap, you see," he explained to the snuffling little animal.

He fed Rollo another grape. "Pity. I like it here. But you can't stay in this broom closet which they've put me in. So either I come clean—which is embarrassing—or I start putting you back in your cages one by one, hoping that nobody will notice . . . Oh, look what you've done!"

What the coati had done was to tip the contents of the bowl of milk and muesli it had been sniffing right into his lap. Rollo rose to his feet and looked down at the mushy mess that spread across his fly and upper trouser legs.

"Honestly! That's the second time," he warned as he started to remove his trousers. "Don't they teach you any

107

table manners in Argentina? You do that again and I will shoot you."

The lower half of his shirt was covered in the stuff, too. He would need an entire new outfit before he was summoned for his meeting with the Americans. He was just in the process of pulling the shirt over his head when a formal knock came at the door. Damn it! The summons was earlier than he had expected.

"Hang on!" He supposed it must be Di. "Shan't be a moment."

Whoever it was, they mustn't see the animals. What was he to do? Rollo grabbed hold of the ostrich and whisked it into the bathroom.

There was another knock, more peremptory this time. "Coming," he called, trying to sound as relaxed as a man with his shirt half-pulled over his head and his trousers round his ankles while he was trying to catch a wallaby could sound.

His panic might have been even more feverish had he known it wasn't Di outside the door.

"I still say we should fire him." Vince stood impatiently tapping his toe.

"Okay. Fine," Willa challenged. "You call your father."

Their conversation was halted by the curious combination of noises emanating from the room: low whispers, the opening and closing of doors, a clink of glasses.

Vince couldn't believe it. He had seen the guy now: he looked like a schoolmaster, not a sexual athlete. "He's at it again," he whispered to Willa in amazement.

She was about to agree when the door was flung open and before them stood the perspiring and dishevelled figure of Rollo Lee, clad in a short lemon dressing gown with ferns on it—a joke leaving present from the Hong Kong police to which he had become rather attached.

He was more than a little surprised to see them. "Oh, hello" was all he could stiffly say.

"May we come in?" Willa, uninvited, took a pace into the room,. "You *are* working, aren't you? It is three o'clock in the afternoon."

Rollo watched Vince peer round the door, his censorious eyes travelling from the grapes to the two glasses to the rumpled sheets on the bed to Rollo, seemingly naked beneath his short lemon dressing gown.

"It is a bit of a mess—I just spilt something," the tall Englishman acknowledged, adding, in an attempt to change the subject, "Ah yes, you want the report."

He delicately extracted the document from under the coati's feeding bowl and handed it to Willa.

She didn't bother to examine it. "Look, Rolo." She, too, seemed to have a prepared speech, and he braced himself to hear the worst. "We've been reviewing your situation, and we've decided to move you to an administrative position."

"Oh." He could hardly suppress his relief and surprise; they weren't going to fire him.

"Away from the public," Vince added pointedly.

"You saw the local paper?" Willa inquired.

"Er . . ." Rollo was disconcerted. Who hadn't seen the local paper?

Vince had thoughtfully brought a copy with him. He held it up for Rollo to see and with some relish pointed to the headline. "The 'Vampire Gunman Runs Amok' story," he said.

"Oh that . . ." Rollo attempted to laugh it off. "Bloody newspapers . . . hah!"

There was a moral conundrum here. Of course, he wanted to clear his name, to explain what had really happened. But it was his word against that of forty keepers if they felt bloody-minded enough to deny their subterfuge, and since they believed he had executed five of their charges, it seemed more than probable that this would be the case. On the other hand, if he managed to convince Vince and Willa of the valid reasons for his seemingly irrational actions, that would dump the keepers in it. Then again, from what Rollo had seen at the Americans' ghastly slide show, they were about to be dumped in pretty deep anyway, whether they realised it or not.

Besides, he reasoned, he had managed to keep his job. So he kept his counsel as well. Also, to his relief, the couple seemed about to leave.

"So will you report to me at nine tomorrow, please," Willa reminded him severely, "and we'll discuss your new position."

"And your new office." Was there a hint of malice in Vince's pointed remark?

Just as he was about to breathe a sigh of relief at their impending departure, a loud clatter came from the bathroom, probably the sound of his tin of shaving foam being knocked into the washbasin. Damn that coati, he thought.

"Absolutely," he shouted in a lame and ineffective attempt to cover the noise. "Look, one thing before you go. About those five animals I'm supposed to have shot . . ."

Vince turned on his heel and pointed at him. "Smart career move, bub."

Rollo was astounded. "What?"

"Killing them." Vince started once more to go "saved your ass from extinction, pal."

Willa could see that Rollo was in a state of total and acute amazement. She benignly offered an explanation. "When we told Rod, he said: 'I like his style. Keep him. He's got balls.'"

"Oh, I see." And, in that split second, Rollo did see. It was just the sort of fear-inducing gestapo-type management de-

110

cision that would appeal to Rod McCain. Balls, eh? Why ruin his incorrectly gained reputation, he mused; he might as well make the most of it.

"Yes, I see," he said to Willa in as matter-of-fact a tone as he could muster. "Well, it wasn't an easy decision obviously, but, you know, toughness is the name of the game, and you've got to be hard-nosed if you want to deliver no-nonsense management."

At that moment his credibility was delivered a perilous blow as the sound of clattering in the bathroom interrupted his flow. To Rollo it sounded like an agitated mara looking for a way out; to Willa it sounded like a woman in high heels.

Again Rollo tried desperately to distract her. "I mean, toughness is what it's all about, really, at the end of the day. That and hard nasality, as I mentioned just now, are the bottom line, as Rod so frequently says." The sounds in the bathroom were getting louder, and Rollo raised his voice accordingly, reaching a dry-throated, high-pitched cry. "A remarkable man—six billion dollars; how extraordinary . . ."

But he was no match for the unmistakable sound of a lavatory being flushed. Had the three of them been able to see through the bathroom wall they would have witnessed a slightly surprised lemur hanging from a chain.

Rollo kicked the radiator by the bathroom door. "Damn radiator. Couldn't sleep a wink last night."

Willa stifled a giggle. This guy was too much. "I'm not surprised," she said, smiling.

Vince marched up to him accusingly. "Listen, Rolo, I don't like you. You're weird and unattractive. You'd just better reposition your attitude to your relationships vis-à-vis certain members of the female staff or you're going to be out of here."

"Certain members of the female staff," Rollo repeated. He genuinely had no idea what Vince was on about.

But Willa did. "Oh, come on," she said with a shrug as she and Vince closed the door.

Rollo tightened the cord of his dressing gown. At least he had a job; that was okay. And he had five animals who were now making one hell of a racket whom he had to thank for helping him keep his job.

What in heaven's name was he going to do with them? But these allegations about relationships with certain members of the female staff—the idea was so outrageous it was laughable. Vince and Willa must be as mad as hatters. But there again, he reflected, so were most people in marketing.

Where does a giant gorilla sit down? Anywhere it wants to. The old joke rang resolutely true as Jambo settled his 352 pounds in his accustomed position on the crest of a grassy knoll to be the sole recipient of the final warming rays of the sun that found their way through the surrounding trees. Other male gorillas and females with their babies grouped in separate shaded parts of the compound, prudent enough not to occupy their leader's favoured spot or to disturb his meditation.

Jambo—his name was the Swahili word for "hello"— seemed somehow to know that he was the pride of Marwood; he was certainly its oldest resident, having been born in the zoological gardens some thirty years previously. Animal activists who'd thought of liberating Jambo and his family and returning them to their native habitat were faced with the problem that it would have meant an almost certain death sentence.

When the German army officer Captain Oscar von Beringe discovered mountain gorillas in 1902 (endowing the race with the Latin tag "Gorilla gorilla beringei"), there were thousands of them. Today their numbers can barely be measured in hundreds. In beleaguered Rwanda the needs of the locals come first, and they hunt the animals not only for food but to make money by selling the gorillas' hands and heads to tourists as trophies. Until the day that education changes that, England will remain a safer habitat than Africa for this endangered species.

Willa had spotted the magnificent silverback on her second day at the zoo, and when Vince had suggested an evening meeting away from the eavesdropping ears of the office staff, she marked a spot on the zoo map down by the gorilla compound.

As in Atlanta, clad in her black, skintight Ralph Lauren exercise pants and an equally clinging blue top with the United States logo embossed on it, she went for a jog at least once a day—that pencil-slim waist and those perfect legs could only be maintained at a price—and, as in Atlanta, she used the opportunity to record her thoughts in her feather-weight headset with its microphone and recorder.

"We should work towards having a computer-operated information system with outlet screens near every major enclosure. Members of the public can be informed of the feeding times of various animals—these should, where possible, be staggered—and, for educational purposes, we can provide much more ecological information about natural habitats. The zoo's image can in that way be enhanced as a place of education, and we can offer competitive rates for school parties and thus sustain a customer flow during the less popular winter months."

But this was not a winter month. It had been a glorious summer evening, the russet mantle of the setting sun cloaking the place—peaceful now that the visitors were long gone and the keepers had finished their work—in an enchanted

113

hue. Willa knew she had made the right decision. Compared with the toxic fumes of urban Atlanta, this was heaven.

Vince, too, had been working out. With one of his ubiquitous silk scarves knotted Apache fashion round his brow, fashion-accessory sleeveless woollen jacket, and designer track suit, he was practising ballet moves, using the low outer wall of the gorilla compound as a barre. In fact he was quite proficient, having trained as a child, and was fully aware that the suppleness of his body movements might prove more alluring to Willa than they had been to his father, who'd once come to his ballet class and dismissed the students as a "bunch of pooftahs."

"Sexy? That bloodsucking stick insect? Did you check out his cologne? Eau de monkey fart." Vince was obviously still in a state of irritation about what they had heard in Rollo's room. "What a hemorrhoid. He's a geek, a loser. And the way he moves. He looks like he's borrowed his body for the weekend and hasn't figured out how it operates yet."

As if to demonstrate the contrast, Vince pirouetted and spun three hundred and sixty degrees with practised dexterity. Willa, amused by this brewing macho battle, put the running weights that she had been carrying on the wall and placed a finger against her neck to check her pulse.

"Well, he's got *something,*" She avoided Vince's eyes and stared into the compound, as she knew she was being provocative. "He's just been demoted and the girls are still all over him."

"I bet they're real dogs." Vince turned away from her. "Mangy, nearsighted Weight Watcher rejects."

Willa leaned over the low wall of the compound. "He's so male," she purred admiringly.

"Him? Are you suffering from early Alzheimer's?" Vince sputtered, spinning round in astonishment and anger.

"No, not our vampire friend." Willa indicated Jambo, still impassively soaking up the sun. "The gorilla. Wonderful."

"Oh, yeah." Vince's concurrence sounded less than convincing.

Willa put her elbows on the wall and, cupping her chin in her hands, stared dreamily at the animal. "He reminds me of my father."

"Was your father ugly?" Vince was unable to stop himself from saying.

She couldn't calculate whether this was a joke or for real. It didn't matter. She had, for the moment, been transported back to an earlier, carefree life.

"No," she replied absentmindedly. "It's just that he used to take me to the zoo. He was a pilot with Delta, and he was away a lot. But when he did get home he'd always say, 'What shall we do today?' and I'd say, 'The zoo' and we'd go and make straight for Willy B. He's the gorilla at Atlanta and he's been there for about thirty-three years and he looked magnificent. We'd spend hours there. That's when I felt close to him."

Vince gave her a quizzical glance. "To the gorilla?"

"No. To my father." Her thoughts were years away. "Life just seemed so simple then."

"Simple?" He was still not quite on her wavelength, in fact was very far from it, but he was certainly not going to indicate this. "Yeah, yeah."

She retreated into the silence of her memories, which had the effect of making Vince feel excluded. He needed to be the centre of attention—at least of her attention.

"Is that all he does?" he remarked out of the blue.

"What?" Willa said, coming back into the present day.

Vince indicated Jambo. "I mean, this zoo's after the entertainment dollar, right? So is that the show?"

115

The gorilla remained stately and impassive. "I mean, if this is the evening performance, I'm glad I missed the matinee." Vince climbed up and sat on the wall, satisfied with his joke and anxious to embellish it. "What does he do for an encore? Fall asleep?"

Willa looked at him inquiringly. "You don't really like animals very much, do you?"

"It's not that I don't like them"—Vince was anxious not to alienate her—"it's just that I don't see the point of them. When I was about five my mother gave me a dog. I didn't 'get' it. I mean, I didn't have any sticks that needed to be fetched. So I sold him."

Willa shook her head. "That's so sad."

"He got over it," Vince replied brightly.

"No," she explained. "For you."

"Ah, yes." Vince had always found the best policy was to agree, at least to begin with. Then he added: "In what way?"

"That you couldn't love the puppy."

"Oh no. No. No." The time had come to assert himself with her and to adopt a different course of action. He held out his hands as if pushing something away and walked backwards towards some bushes.

"What?" She wasn't on his wavelength at all.

Vince pointed at her. "I've been in this situation before. This is the kind of conversation that two people have if one of them is female."

He had by now reached the bushes and, with the élan of a conjuror, pulled out a small drinks trolley which he had earlier hidden behind them. On it was a blood-red rose in a tall slim vase, two long-stemmed glasses, and a bottle of Dom Pérignon.

"Surprise!" His mood changed abruptly as he wheeled the trolley towards her. "Champagne! To celebrate our partnership."

Willa was indeed taken by surprise and touched by the gesture. "Our partnership," she echoed.

Vince began to open the bottle of champagne. "Just one thing I couldn't help noticing," he mentioned casually. "We still seem to have separate bedrooms."

Thankfully for Willa, the popping of the cork obviated the need for her to make an immediate response. She just smiled appreciatively as he poured the champagne and giggled flirtatiously as he ran his glass along her collarbone, still moist from the jog, and collected drops of her sweat in his drink.

"To us," he pronounced, wriggling his snakelike tongue suggestively into the glass and then downing the entire contents.

"To us," she said, sipping hers and still smiling.

As she feared, he returned to the subject. "We've taken over the zoo and we're here in England . . ."

She moved closer to him. "I think we should wait."

This time Vince suppressed his instinct to agree. "Why?" he demanded.

She affectionately tapped his chest. "Because what we have is special."

"No, it isn't." He hadn't been able to stop the words from coming out.

"Yes it is." She put a finger against his lips. "Can't you feel how different it is?"

"Yes. Yes I can. Different. Yeah. Absolutely," he agreed, but then added: "In what way?"

"You know," whispered Willa as she kissed him on the lips. His tongue slithered into her mouth like an eel and she drew away, pushing it back with her finger. "It's too soon."

She put her champagne down on the wall, retrieved her weights, and set off jogging down the path.

Vince stood anchored to the spot, absolutely stunned.

"How too soon?" he bellowed after her.

But all he got was a cheery wave as his eyes followed her trim, unobtainable shape disappearing in the direction of the rhino enclosure.

Vince was vibrant with anger. His usual psychotic behaviour when he found himself in such a state was to vent it in a physical attack on an inanimate object or, in extremis, an unlucky person.

He stared accusingly at Jambo. "This is all your fault," he yelled. But a sense of self-preservation stopped him from climbing the wall and attacking the beast. He then glanced at the drinks trolley and the rose in its elegant vase.

"Too soon," he repeated, and with the entrechat of a trained ballet dancer, rose four feet in the air and brought his full weight down on the fragile wooden structure, crunching it apart. In his fury to complete the demolition, he trashed the remains, performing a kind of Indian war dance as he smashed the harmless object into smithereens, incanting angrily, "Too soon, too soon, too soon."

Jambo watched him with seeming interest; in his thirty-three years at the zoo he had never seen behaviour like this before, save occasionally in a rogue gorilla.

Unnoticed by either of them, there was another witness to this display. Rollo Lee, purposely clad in his dark blue suit to be less conspicuous in the twilight, had been moving quickly but cautiously along the narrow zoo track that at one point fringed on the border of the gorilla compound. In front of him he pushed a small wire basket on wheels, the kind that elderly ladies favour on shopping trips. He stopped and stared in mute amazement at Vince's violent attack on the wooden trolley; it confirmed his fears about the mental stability of the zoo's new boss.

Rollo had no desire to be spotted, however, by Vince or anyone else. He was on a top-secret mission and had determined that no one must—

"You!" The word rang out like a rifle shot.

Rollo froze and turned around with as much dignity as he could muster. "Oh, hello. Sorry to intrude. Lovely evening."

"What are you doing with that?" Vince was levelling a piece of broken wood at the contents of Rollo's metal cage.

Rollo looked down and Rollo looked back up at him. They had been caught.

"Oh, the lemur?" The Englishman feigned surprise to find that he was in possession of one.

"Yes." There was definite menace in Vince's tone.

"Just putting it back. In its enclosure." Rollo could think of no other immediate explanation save the true one.

"Putting it back?" Vince was not going to let this one slip away.

"You know, I was just taking it for a walk." Rollo was becoming more inventive. "Bit of exercise at this time of night."

"Exercise!" Vince exploded. "It can hardly move in there."

"Oh, no," Rollo explained patronisingly, "the exercise is for me."

Being treated as an idiot did little to calm Vince's temper. "Why do you need the lemur then?"

"Why do I need the lemur?" Rollo repeated. "Good point. Like a dog, I suppose. Well, perhaps next time I won't bother. Thanks for the advice. Have a nice evening."

He started on his way again, but Vince was not to be fobbed off with this claptrap. "You were stealing it, weren't you?"

"Stealing it?"

"Yeah, you can make a lot of money out of selling animals, especially the right ones."

"I wouldn't dream of stealing any animal." Rollo was mortally offended.

It suddenly came clear to Vince in an instant. "No, of course, you were taking it out for a little target practise."

The remark rankled Rollo, but he was not prepared to be humiliated by this half-wit. "I took it out because it was lonely."

"Lonely?" Vince emitted a manic laugh.

"Yes." Rollo assumed a superior mien. "Lemurs happen to suffer from loneliness. That's what the word 'lemur' means in Madagascan, incidentally. If they're not given personal attention they can go into irreversible decline, leading to rickets and secondary carcinomas."

"Bullshit!" screamed Vince. "You're lying."

"You don't even know how many legs it's got," Rollo retorted.

"I see, you're just a guy who spends his evenings wheeling round a trolley with a soft toy in it. That is, when you're not sticking your fangs into a paying customer or porking your way through the female staff teaching them disgusting group sex perversions you picked up in some Oriental knocking shop. I'm onto you, Casanova. You're sick."

Rollo listened to these rantings with mounting amazement. "Is there a history of insanity in your family?" He tried to modulate his sarcasm; the man was, after all, his boss. "Or is smashing up trolleys the latest American craze?"

Vince pointed at him threateningly. "The latest American craze is firing weirdos like you."

Rollo looked down at the lemur, which had remained placidly undisturbed by this adult exchange. "Come on, Rollo," he said, continuing his journey up the path, "better get you home before some loony attacks your trolley."

"Come on, Rollo." Vince needed no further evidence that this erect Englishman was out of his tree. "He talks to himself and he calls *me* a loony. Weirdo."

As Vince turned away he could see that Jambo was still watching him intently.

"Hello," he called to the gorilla. The animal still didn't move. "Hello." Vince grabbed the champagne bottle from the wall and hurled it at him with a shout of "Have a drink on me."

Still the mountain gorilla maintained its poise and, unlike either of the two humans it had just witnessed, its dignity.

Vince thrust a middle finger towards it. He had read somewhere that these animals were meant to understand hand signals.

"Sorry. I'll leave you to your meditation," he called as he stomped off. "Get a job. Get a life."

CHAPTER
8

"I wonder if you could help us?" The chap in spectacles and a flat hat was definitely from the north of England, Yorkshire possibly, Northumberland more likely. "My wife and I—"

Before he could complete his inquiry Hugh Primates breezily stretched out a hand. "Hi. My name's Hugh."

The visitor shook his hand, despite being somewhat taken aback by the gesture. "Er . . . hello, Hugh. We . . . er . . ."

The man's smartly dressed wife, definitely from a class above him in the English social order, took over. "We'd like to ask you what animals we should look at," she inquired in a prim voice.

Now it was Hugh's turn to be thrown. "You deal with this," he whispered to Gerry Ungulates, who was standing beside him.

"Hi. I'm Gerry," he said, beaming. He also proffered a hand, which both the man and his wife shook, looking somewhat discomforted. "What animals do you like?"

"Well, what animals do you have?" The Northerner seemed anxious to reassert himself in front of his wife.

"We've got lots," Hugh replied enthusiastically.

Gerry eagerly mirrored this. "Today's specials are . . . er . . ."

"We like lions." The wife seemed anxious to help her husband out.

"Well . . . we recommend the lions then," Hugh suggested obligingly.

"Good idea." The husband was happy, the keepers were happy, everybody was happy.

"Just one other thing," the wife added. "Could you possibly tell us where they are?"

Gerry knew he could handle this one. "Straight on to the bandicoots, take a left, hang a right at the kinkajous, and they're just past the pumas."

The couple nodded their thanks and set off as directed, barely noticing the diminutive figure of Reggie Sea Lions beside the path.

"Hi!" He grinned from ear to ear. "My name's Reggie."

"Good-bye, Reggie," said the wife politely.

Reggie looked extremely miffed.

"Just a moment," Gerry called after the couple.

They stopped and turned. "It's been our pleasure to facilitate your enjoyment of this leisure-ticketed-environment-pull-through venue today," the hefty keeper smiled.

"What are you talking about?" Willa Weston rose from the bench upon which she had been watching this attitude exercise. "Environment-pull-through? It doesn't make sense."

"I know that," Gerry agreed. "I was just trying to sound more like Vince."

Reggie added, "You know, more consumer-friendly."

Willa looked down at him. "No. No. You're very formal."

"Thank you." Reggie smiled.

"No . . . no." Willa had been misunderstood. "I want you to be warmer and more friendly."

"Warmer?" Reggie repeated the adjective apprehensively.

"More friendly?" Sydney almost choked on the word as he entered the fray.

"But last week you showed us—" Reggie began.

"Last week I was trying to eradicate out-and-out rudeness," Willa explained firmly. "This week I'd like to move on to something more positive—helping people. What we have to work on here is developing a more positive attitude towards our visitors. We want to give them a warm, buzzy experience. That way every visit leads to a return visit. And we start by getting close to our customers. Yes?"

She looked around at the anxious faces. They were the familiar ones, but the uniforms were not. Out had gone the casual khaki that had been the trademark of Marwood Zoo. Instead the keepers were now clad in an array of subphosphorescent safari outfits with a vulgar logo reading THE OCTOPUS LEISURE EXPERIENCE backed by a pink octopus attached to each one. The colours of the new uniforms were various—Sydney, Hugh, and Gerry were in strawberry; Reggie in lemon, with his old-fashioned cap covered in the same; Pip in cobalt blue; Cub in acute violet—but they were united in their vulgarity. In truth, Willa found them abhorrent to her eye, but she knew, having withheld her body from him for quite a few weeks now, that she had to allow Vince some indulgences.

But she was not prepared to indulge the attitude of these semi-Bolshevik keepers. People favoured restaurants not just for the food but also because the staff created the right atmosphere. It was her intention to make them understand that the same marketing principle applied throughout the leisure sector.

124

She indicated to them that they should come and sit on the benches of the small amphitheatre where Fred used to do his bird displays before the day, some years ago, the hawk had flown off and failed to return. The rumour was that the farmer next door shot it, but no body was ever found.

"Okay, fine." Willa clapped her hands together. "I think we need to talk about our feelings here."

"Feelings?" Reggie was, by nature, an anxious man, and after the ordeal of the Fierce Animal Policy was worried about any sort of change—especially now that he was togged out in this lemon outfit.

"Yes." Willa was unbending.

"Do we have to?" The disapproving voice came from Di, who had played the part of the woman visitor in the attitude exercise. Bugsy had been her husband, and he remained determinedly in his flat hat and raincoat, so uneager was he to reveal the bright blue uniform underneath.

Besides, he had knobbly knees—hitherto unseen by the other keepers. Willa looked Di straight in the eye. "Why not?"

"Well, it's embarrassing," the older woman replied.

"They're private," Hugh tried to explain to her.

The others nodded their assent. "It's just not very British to sit about discussing one's feelings; there are plenty of American sects you could join if you were interested in doing that," Sydney pointed out.

Willa opened her arms. "I'm not asking you who's screwing who." She had used this line in her seminars before, and she smiled inwardly as she observed one or two uncomfortable glances among the group.

"I just want to know your *professional* feelings, okay?" she explained. "So, how do you feel about our customers?"

"They're pests." Bugsy pronounced this as if it were an undisputed fact.

"Pests?" Willa was completely taken aback.

"Yes, annoying the animals . . ." Pip never missed an opportunity for some mischief-making.

"Feeding ice cream to the fish," Sky added.

"Dropping litter," said Gerry.

"Asking questions," added a shrugging Hugh.

Delighted with the backup from a group that was usually unsympathetic to his statements, Bugsy continued: "All they ever want to know is where the lavatories are. And, of course, whether—"

But Willa could stand this no longer. She was almost speechless with horror. "Don't you understand? One—they pay your salaries. Two—they're people. People. Don't you like people?"

"Not much," said Reggie.

"No." Hugh was more emphatic.

"That's why we became zookeepers, really." Bugsy slightly surprised himself—and the others—with the remark, but having uttered it, he knew that there was more than a grain of truth in it.

"We don't even like each *other* very much." Since they were being candid, Reggie felt free to go all the way.

"If you don't like people"—Willa was close to exploding—"why did you come into a people business? Why didn't you become lighthouse keepers or novelists or snipers or something?"

This time nobody came up with a reply. They all knew the answer: they weren't in a people business; they were in an animal business. But she could never be made to understand that.

"Okay." She felt she had made, if not won, her point. "Let's go back to last week."

"Do we have to?" whispered Reggie.

126

Willa ignored him. " 'Have a nice day,' right? Have you been practising?"

The group rose to their feet reluctantly and formed a ragged line.

"Cub." Willa approached her countrywoman. "You're American. Remind us."

Cub shrugged; it was a phrase that came like second nature to her. "Have a nice day."

A loud raspberry of disapproval emanated from an untraceable source.

"Excellent." Willa was heartened. "Okay, now all together."

"Have a nice day." The congregate tones of the keepers were deliberately funereal.

"Again," Willa demanded.

"Have a nice day." It didn't sound much more enthusiastic. Bugsy, for one, had deliberately adopted the tone of the wartime BBC newsreader who allegedly used to begin his bulletin with the words: "Here is Alvar Liddell with news of fresh disasters."

"Smile," screamed Willa. They smiled and said it again, but it had little effect.

She was reduced to pleading with them. "Say it as if you mean it."

Reggie held up his hand for attention. "Can we say it as *though* we mean it?"

"What?" Willa was confused. "I don't follow you."

Reggie was precise, but polite. "What I mean it: Is it all right if we don't really mean it?"

She could hardly believe her ears. "Why wouldn't you want your customers to have a nice day? Oh, I forgot—you hate them, don't you?"

"No, we don't *hate* them . . ." Reggie wanted to make the keepers' position quite clear.

"You'd just like them to die in car crashes on the way home so that they don't come and annoy you again." Willa was in the full flush of sarcasm and had no ears for this obdurate attitude. "Hey, we could put up a notice at the exit saying: HOPE YOU HAD A LOUSY VISIT, NOW GET LOST."

She had to be told, and Reggie found himself the spokesman. "Miss Weston, people come here to see the animals, not to form relationships with us."

There was clearly a gulf between them that would take several more seminars to bridge. But Willa didn't want this one to finish with the keepers thinking they had gained the upper hand. Besides, she sensed she was near the end of her tether. "Look, I'm not asking you to become their best friends or invite them for Sunday lunch or send them presents at Christmas. I just want you to smile at them and say: 'Have a nice fucking day.'"

"Have a nice fucking day," the keepers immediately chorused with new enthusiasm.

Even Willa could scarce forbear to grin at this. They would come round to her way of thinking—eventually. Almost everybody did. But, she wasn't going to let them get away with it that easily. "Fine, fine, very funny. Now each one of you is going to say, 'Have a nice day,' and anyone who says it unconvincingly will be on the Customer Complaints Desk for a month. Believe me, I mean it."

She pointed at Hugh to start, and the thought of having to deal with lost umbrellas, missing children, and the accusation that the tigers were always asleep was too much for him to contemplate. "Have a nice day," he cried in a way that would have brought a smile to the face of Ronald McDonald.

The others, struck by the same fear, followed suit, right down the line—Bugsy, Di, Gerry, Ant, Reggie, Sky, Cub, and Sydney. It was only when Willa got to Pip that she encountered a resistant silence.

"Come on, kid," she urged, "have you forgotten the lines?"

But Pip was literally dumbstruck. She lifted a dainty finger and pointed in a shaky fashion towards the nearest small mammal enclosure.

"Rollo!" was all she said.

Rollo was seated behind his new desk working on staff holiday charts. Relieved as he had been to hold on to a job of any sort at the zoo, he knew the words "personnel" and "downsizing" were frequently contiguous in Octopus Inc. and that he soon might be having to implement a policy of getting rid of people as opposed to unfierce creatures. However, so far, not so bad, he thought. Willa seemed to have been much more interested in training the keepers than in sacking them and the madman had been too obsessed with the image and marketing of the zoo to even notice the keepers—or the animals, come to that.

A bun landed on his desk, followed by an unseen giggle. With a hidden sigh of exasperation he picked it up and threw it into his wastebasket on top of the pile of other buns already accumulated there. Rollo had been given a disused cage as his temporary office, the old-fashioned kind with thick iron bars on three sides. It had been an unremittingly hot summer so he had appreciated the ventilation, but not the mockery of the keepers, who still saw him as a mass animal murderer. Hence the buns and sniggers. Nevertheless he tried to retain as much dignity as possible: his desk was neat, his files were well-ordered, he had pinned his organisational charts to the rear wall, and each day he wore a clean white shirt and neat tie and his best office suit, an image that was marred only by Vince's insistence that his jacket carry a large and hideous OCTOPUS LEISURE EXPERIENCE badge on the back.

He felt very isolated. Vince regarded him as some kind of lunatic—talk about the pot calling the kettle black, Rollo thought—and Willa connived with her partner in the wholly unjustified belief that he was engaged in nightly orgies. And none of the other staff would talk to him. So, in one of life's ironic reversals, he found himself quite pleased to hear himself being addressed by a voice that, in his days as director, he had grown to dread.

"We've got to do something about it, you know. I mean, I couldn't make head or tail of him, and I regard myself as a reasonably intelligent member of the human race."

Adrian "Bugsy" Malone, Rollo observed, looked a rather peculiar member of the human race in his light blue bushranger's hat with its luminescent orange undertrim and safari suit to match, and with advertisements for Guinness and Pilkington Glass attached to it. Above all—or, to be precise, below all—his knobbly knees were just visible below his elongated shorts.

"So I said to him: 'A zoo has an educational purpose, Mr. McCain' "—the outfit clearly had no diminishing effect on Bugsy's incessant stream of verbage—"and he said: 'It's a waste of time talking to the public about animals when you could be selling them things.' "

Rollo rose from his desk. "I know what you're saying; however—"

But Bugsy hadn't finished. "I can only assume he's going to turn the whole zoo into a supermarket where he can sell videos about animals in other zoos."

"Yes, I can see exactly where—" Rollo made another abortive attempt to get in his point, but in vain.

"Actually the zoo shop looks like a supermarket *now,*" the insect keeper continued, "with people buying Korean-made stuffed souvenirs of animals they haven't had time to see because they've been too busy shopping. I'm surprised he hasn't started selling our animals yet."

Another bun landed at Rollo's feet. He picked it up and chucked it in the bin. He was an obsessively tidy man. "Look, the point is—"

"Special summer sales, antelopes fifty percent off"— Bugsy was in full swing and quite oblivious to the insult of the flung bun—"ocelots two hundred pounds each or six for a thousand; rhino horn—just the thing for a Friday night."

"Would you please let me speak?" Rollo pleaded.

"One free porcupine with every purchase of two over-priced T-shirts."

"Please!" Had it not been for the presence of some visitors passing by the cage, Rollo might have employed physical force.

Bugsy pointed to his new outfit. "I mean, it's bad enough having to wear this rubbish."

And, looking down at it in disgust and remorse, he actually interrupted himself for a moment.

"Thank you," said Rollo. "I just—"

"If you ask me—" Bugsy was off again.

"I don't," Rollo screamed, visitors or no visitors. "I can't get a word in edgeways, let alone ask you anything—"

But, once again, he was interrupted—not this time by the chattering insect keeper, but by the door beside his wall chart flying open and Pip and Cub rushing into the cage.

All Rollo could see were blue and violet streaks dashing towards him and then leaping onto his body, clinging to him with hugs and covering his face with kisses.

"You didn't kill them." Pip threw her arms round his neck, lifting her slight body completely off the ground.

131

"We've checked," Cub told him between kisses. "They're all alive. You never shot them."

Sydney and Gerry had followed the two girls into the cage, somewhat surprised to find Bugsy already there but more than anything else relieved that the five mammals were safe.

"He never shot them," Sydney informed Bugsy with glee.

"Just figured that out, have you?" came the knowing reply.

Rollo was just beginning to think that life was taking a turn for the better and was enjoying, for the first time in ages, the sweet warmth of the female embrace when a voice boomed out behind him. "What the hell do you think you are doing?"

It was an American voice, and a greatly unwanted one. Vince McCain, in his unchecked drive to commercialise the zoo, had instituted a series of visits from potential sponsors and today, unfortunately, was the first of these. Thus three sharply suited men with briefcases and, worse still, three elegantly groomed female executives, one in advanced middle age, followed in the wake of the Armani-clad marketeer. They had just passed the capybara enclosure, where a large photograph of Gabriela Sabatini, the Argentine tennis player, had been erected on Vince's orders in the belief that an international personality might draw some interest to the four-legged inhabitants of her land.

He had secretly been looking forward to the moment of humiliation when he showed them Rollo at work in his cage and had rounded the corner with his back to it, delivering his idea of an ecologically correct joke: "This used to be the old lion house, but obviously it's no longer suitable for animals so we're using it for middle management."

Thus it came as a doubly distressing disappointment that his personnel director should be discovered with two female keepers draped around him, not least because it confirmed to Vince visually what had hitherto only been surmised by aural evidence. "Will you, for God's sake, put a lid on it till the sun goes down," he snapped. "You're supposed to be working, not prancing round your cage like a flamingo with a boner."

He swivelled round to the sponsors, but could not bring himself to catch the eye of Willa, who was following at the back of the group. "Ladies and gentlemen, I'm sorry. We're having a little problem getting the right balance with his medication."

When he turned back to Rollo, Pip and Cub had released their embrace but stood loyally on either side of the acquitted killer.

"This is a family zoo, not the Playboy mansion," Vince hissed at him in an audible whisper. "You pervert. This is your last warning, Lee."

He moved away, beckoning the amazed sponsors to accompany him. "Follow me, ladies and gentlemen. Sorry about that. He'll be all right. This way."

The oldest female executive found it hard to take her eyes off this extraordinary spectacle. "I suppose that's why they have to keep him in a cage," she remarked to Willa, who said nothing but lowered her sunglasses in Rollo's direction and made sure he registered her deliberately inscrutable expression.

"I'm sorry, Mr. Lee." Cub dared to put a consoling arm back on his shoulder. Sydney and Gerry had joined them to show their solidarity.

Rollo gripped the bars of his cage, his knuckles white with anger. "I'll break his bloody neck," he muttered.

The potential sponsors, still in a state of bewilderment at what they had just witnessed, found Vince's continuing harangue on the art of marketing a little incomprehensible in parts. Maybe, they figured, this was how everyone spoke in America nowadays. "What we're talking about is a whole new concept in sponsorship that completely eliminates the nonevent-impact deficit," he assured them.

He stopped in front of a low brick wall which bordered a well-manicured lawn on three sides, with a set of curtains twelve feet high at the back of the enclosure. "For instance, what have we here?" Vince asked rhetorically. "A Galápagos tortoise. Look at it."

The small shell, no more than twelve inches across, lay motionless in the centre of the lawn. No head or legs were currently visible. Vince leapt the wall into the enclosure and indicated the animal. "Who gives a shit?" he said disparagingly. "My grandmother's grave is a bigger attraction. But wait!"

He moved with balletic grace to the back of the lawn and pulled a tasselled rope by the side of the curtains. They parted to reveal a life-size picture of Bruce Springsteen in full performance, from bandanna to banjo. The song "Born in the U.S.A." blared out from speakers on either side of the portrait and, like a manic karaoke addict, Vince went into a full Springsteen routine, if anything more frenzied in its body-lowering and limber gymnastics than the real thing.

"This is not some nonentity tortoise now," he bellowed at the sponsors, high on his own adrenaline. "This is Bruce Springsteen's tortoise. Immediately it's an event. If the Boss has sponsored this tedious little runt, it's positively a celebrity itself, right?"

The sponsors seemed unsure.

"Does he come and visit it?" It was the attractive blonde woman in the expensively cut black suit whom Vince had especially been trying to impress.

"Whenever his schedule allows," he responded unhesitatingly.

A serious-looking man who had been making copious notes looked up from his leather-bound pad. "So he actually has agreed to sponsor it?"

Vince pulled out a mobile phone from the inside pocket of his jacket and brandished it like a piece of evidence. "I'm expecting his call at any minute. Look at the potential. We can market little Bruce Springsteen tortoises for the kiddies. Do you know that *Jurassic Park* made half its income from little plastic dinosaurs? And they're even deader than this heap of shit."

Resisting the urge to kick the tortoise with his well-polished toe, he jumped back over the wall and, like a tour guide, urged them on to the next attraction.

The sign read "Brazilian Tapir (Tapirus terrestris). It possesses a sparse mane, a long proboscis formed by the upper lip and nose, and a tail that is virtually inconspicuous. This solitary species lives in forests—a habitat that is being fast destroyed—and is extremely timid, fleeing at the first sign of danger, but is capable of defending itself by biting. Its main enemy is the jaguar."

Vince allowed his guests time to digest this description and the accompanying drawing of the less than decorative animal. "I must admit, I've dated better-looking women in my time," he joked, then indicated the sign derisively. "And who needs all that Latin shit—what are they trying to do, frighten customers away because they're not educated? Now, what we propose is to educate them and sell at the same time. Listen to this."

He pressed a small information box at the front of the still-empty cage. "Brazilian tapirs are solitary three-toed ungulates which inhabit the lowland forests of sunny Brazil, reachable now in less than fourteen hours and for less than seven hundred pounds on British Airways nonstop flights direct to Rio de Janeiro, the city of samba with a rhythm all of its own . . ."

As music began to play, Gerry Ungulates, dressed in the uniform of an airline steward, backed into the cage, bending down to offer a tray of canapés to the tapir that unsteadily followed him. It wore a full body stocking with the words "British Airways" on it. The blue screen at the back of the enclosure was suddenly filled with footage of a jumbo jet taking off, as the commentary breezily continued: "Where looking good in your beachwear has become an art form. Yes, from the legendary sands of Copacabana to the towering majesty of the Corcovado, you can have the holiday of a lifetime."

Vince punched the button again to terminate the display and looked at the sponsors for their approval. Most seemed surprised but impressed; Willa, less so.

"Is it endangered?" the attractive woman asked him as they left the building.

"If it isn't it ought to be," Vince replied flirtatiously. "Nothing that ugly deserves to have sex."

An extremely long queue of people, maybe the longest in the history of Marwood Zoo, snaked its way from the tapir house, past the other ungulates, two-toed and three-, in between the lemurs and the meerkats and all the way to the side of a bizarre structure which looked as if a ruined temple in Egypt's Valley of the Kings had been attacked by New York subway spray-paint vandals.

The queue was deliberately slow-moving—Vince had made sure of that to obtain the maximum number of people (and not a few paid stooges, identifiable by their lack of interest in the animals)—to impress the sponsors. Prancing backwards with the fleet-footedness of which he was justly proud, he assured his potential sponsors: "In the immortal words of Ralph Waldo Emerson—'You ain't seen nothin' yet.' "

And, indeed they hadn't. Out of the false masonry of the structure protruded a giant tiger's head, at least twenty feet in height, painted an abnormal colour of orange with eyes flashing like a lighthouse and a stalactite row of jagged dentures from which were suspended large, pendulous globules of what looked like congealed blood. Behind the mouth of the effigy lay artificial jungle, denser and more menacing than the real thing. On one side where the visitors paid to enter there was a prominent first aid box, and on the other side were two student keepers dressed as nurses, as if in anticipation of some accident.

Vince jumped adroitly onto the Day-Glo pink tongue—modelled more, it appeared, on Mick Jagger than on any Indian or Siberian quadruped—that sprawled out of this monstrosity and held his hands aloft like a visionary preacher. "Here's yet another commercial-slash-sponsorial opportunity, and a part of our zoo policy of facilitating the processing of the joys of nature."

The sponsors looked up as he indicated the words above him, CANON PRESENTS TIGER TERROR. At the entry, where people were finally being allowed in, there was written the challenge: "Dare to experience a fully authenticated Tiger Attack," with the ominous rider: "No people with Heart Conditions or Pregnant Women may be admitted to this exhibit."

The crowd shuffled past a notice board on which were pinned pictures of suitably terrified human victims with their heads perilously close to what, indeed, looked like an authentic tiger.

Vince smiled as he watched them absorb all this: it was his pièce de résistance. "This is a simulated attack by a Bengal man-eater," he announced with pride, "a real white-knuckle-brown-underpants job."

"How's it done?" The Asian sponsor was indisputably impressed.

Seeing the spell had been woven, Vince tried to sound as casual as possible. "It's a high-tech animatronic tiger operated by two guys with incredible sound effects. It's Belgian."

On cue, a fearful, bloodcurdling, ear-shattering seismic roar, louder than a Concorde landing, more terrifying than anything heard on Krakatoa, East of Java, emanated from the psychedelic mouth of this weird creation, causing everyone within earshot to reel back in terror. The only person unshaken by the experience was Vince, who stood on the luminous tongue with the smug smile of a ringmaster.

"What happens?" The attractive sponsor had recovered her senses sufficiently to be intrigued.

Vince smiled knowingly. "For two heart-stopping minutes you get stalked by a serial-killer tiger—it costs only four pounds—and for another three you receive a commemorative photograph of the moment it kills you. Great for Christmas cards."

A small boy, aged no more than nine, was dragged out of the mouth by an overweight father in a Hawaiian shirt, perspiration dripping down an alabaster face.

"Can we do it again, Dad?" pleaded the child, stubbornly trying to resist his parent's pull.

"Wouldn't you like a big ice cream instead?" wheezed the father. "Sweets? Popcorn? Anything?"

Vince pointed to the departing parent with pride. "Now, that man has had an experience. Do you think we could get a real tiger to do this? Hell no. They sleep for more than twenty hours a day. Look, tigers have had great PR over the years. But if they're not attacking you, they're boring. No, this is the way zoos have got to go: automatic, digital, experiential, and interactive."

A peaked yellow hat withdrew behind the gaudy notice board with pictures of past victims. Reggie Sea Lions wasn't quite sure of the meaning of any of Vince's last four adjectives, but he knew what they spelt: the end of Marwood as he and the other keepers knew it.

CHAPTER
9

In a peculiarly British way, every Wednesday evening the keepers met up in the public bar of the Marwood Arms, ostensibly for a game of darts. In fact it was a time—although no one would acknowledge this—when they could call a truce on their petty rivalries and discuss any problems, professional or private. Heaven forfend that anyone should look upon this as a form of group therapy: that was far too direct and American a way of dealing with such matters. No, this was a casual darts competition, and if someone happened to mention that their animals or their marriage needed help or that they were deeply in debt or in love, then maybe somebody else could give some advice. Casually.

It was Hugh Primates's turn to throw his darts when Reggie Sea Lions burst through the door as fast as his little legs would carry him.

"Vince McCain is going to get rid of all our animals and replace them with anima . . . anima . . ." He stumbled on the word.

"Animals?" Gerry suggested mischievously.

"Animatronic ones." Bugsy, sitting snugly at his favourite table—he made a point of being there but never joining in the game, which he saw as a complete waste of time—came to the sea lion keeper's rescue. "It's undoubtedly his long-term strategy."

"Shut up, Bugsy," Sydney snarled, as he did on nearly every occasion the two men met—their rivalry was a little more than petty. He turned to Reggie. "Relax. You're always going on about some disaster that's just about to happen."

"Well, it is." Reggie choked on the double gin and tonic that Sky had thoughtfully ordered for him. "It's worse than the Fierce Animal Policy—much worse. Even *you're* in danger, Cub. Someone's told him that tigers sleep twenty hours a day, so he wants those automatic ones that will pretend to attack people."

The news did not come as a total surprise to the American keeper. "He did tell me he wanted notices saying what time the animals have sex," she said solemnly.

"You see," Reggie rounded again on Sydney. "And he told those investors or whatever they are that he was going to have rows of synchronised swimmers dressed as penguins performing Bugsy Berkeley routines in my sea lion pool."

"*Busby* Berkeley," the insect keeper corrected him.

"He told me he wants ostrich races for people to bet on," Fred Hoofstock added with resignation.

Hugh released a dart that just managed to hit the edge of the board; the burly keeper had the shape of many of television's beer-swilling darts stars but not, regrettably, the ability. "I've got the chimps booked in for their first skydiving lesson next Thursday," he mentioned nonchalantly.

"No. Not possible." Several of the keepers at the table rose from their seats.

"No . . . it was a joke," the big man apologised. "Sorry."

141

"It's not funny." Reggie was on to his second gin and tonic by now. "It's not going to be a proper zoo anymore."

A pall of silence hung over the room. Hugh couldn't bring himself to throw his third dart. Many of those there were beginning to fear that Reggie's habitual anxiety was this time rooted in reality. Inevitably it was Bugsy who cut into the gloom.

"Who was it, I wonder," he smirked, "who first mentioned the phrase 'theme park'?"

Cub, bright-eyed in full makeup and curvaceously appealing in her off-duty slacks, nevertheless assumed the role of den mother. "Look, let's not get excited."

"Why not?" Ant, Bugsy's right-hand man and eternal audience, only removed his pipe from his mouth when he had something essential to impart. "I saw a lot of money changing hands with those sponsors."

"See, see, see." Reggie was almost gleeful over this verification of his fears.

"Speaking personally, I don't trust him further than I could throw a wet mattress up a spiral staircase," Bugsy added unnecessarily.

Nobody at darts night now doubted that Vince was intent on destroying the zoo as they knew it in his zealous pursuit of profit.

"The trouble is, there's no way of knowing how far he's going to go." Gerry had visions of his beloved rhinos being turned into another circus act.

"*He'd* know." Bugsy indicated the television set behind the bar, which was showing the *News at Ten*. Most of the keepers had little interest in the world beyond Marwood so the sound was rarely on, but Bugsy always kept a vigilant eye on the main events, which he knew he could read in detail in his *Financial Times* the following day.

142

"What's he saying?" Cub searched for the remote control on the bar.

"Turn it up," Gerry urged.

On the other side of the Thames from the Palace of Westminster—a location favoured by TV news directors—stood the solid and unmistakable figure of Rod McCain, familiar to all at the zoo since Rollo had played the video and displayed the *Time* magazine cover with his face on it at his introductory lecture. He was obviously on one of his spot-check visits to Britain. And he only condescended to appear in television interviews when there was some message he needed to get across. Habit had taught Rod that before any meeting with a prime minister to discuss acquisitions and inevitable redundancies it was useful to paint a worst-case scenario in public from which he could offer concessions in private. Whatever the story might have been, they had missed it. The sombre New Zealander had said what he had intended to say and was now swatting off an upstart reporter with corporatespeak.

"We're a multinational company. Globally we have a record—a proud record—of job creation. But country by country we may need to downsize operations that are simply not cost-effective."

The intrepid ITN reporter, clearly not a man who was looking for future work in any Octopus-owned station, had the ambitious nerve to try and translate the magnate's circumlocutions into plain English.

"So, in effect, what you're really saying," he began, "is that there's a strong likelihood of redundancies in your British—"

But Big Rod was too old and experienced a hand to let himself be caught by this newsboy.

"I'm not saying anything about our position in the UK until we evaluate the figures and see what makes financial sense. Thank you."

It didn't require any great intuition on the part of the reporter or any viewer to realise that the interview was thereby terminated.

"Rod McCain in London today," the jowly studio newscaster intoned, underlining the fact that it was, indeed, the man from Atlanta. "Another Conservative MP," he went on to the next item, "has been forced to resign because of sexual intrigue . . ."

But the news held no intrigue for those watching in the Marwood Arms, and Cub snapped off the set. They had heard enough to inflame their fears.

"We've got to find out what's happening." Reggie felt a curiously perverse satisfaction in at last being taken seriously, albeit as a harbinger of doom.

"*We're* becoming endangered." Bugsy voiced the unpalatable probability that nobody wanted to face.

"What do you think's going on?" Cub addressed her query to a lofty man in fawn trousers, an army-green short-sleeved zoo shirt of the kind the keepers had worn before the absurd Octopus outfits were forced upon them, and a traditional Marwood Zoo cap which had been ceremonially placed on his head many pints earlier.

Rollo Lee, newly hailed by the keepers as a non-animal murderer and one of them, was about to throw a dart. "Do you think they'd tell *me*?" he asked Cub, seeking sympathy.

"Okay, no." She realised, not least from his new office, that Rollo was not in favour with her fellow Americans. "But maybe you could find out something."

Rollo let fly a dart. Bull's-eye. He was rather proud: at least some of his time in the officers' mess hadn't been wasted. "Okay, I'll try," he conceded.

144

Pip, a little lamb in her frail arms, approached him with a gleam in her wide, innocent eyes. "Why don't you just break his neck?"

"What?" Rollo was so startled by this suggestion that his final dart hit the wall.

"Like you said," Pip reminded him.

"Oh, right," he replied, remembering his anger in the cage. "I'll put it in my diary."

"Careful. If someone killed Vince you'd be facing twenty . . ."—Bugsy had the annoying habit, and he had many annoying habits, of chortling at his own jokes before they were even complete—"or twenty-five hours of community service. At least."

Nobody else was ever quite as amused by Bugsy as Bugsy. On the contrary, there was a mild uproar and shouts of protest as Gerry's dart thudded into the centre circle.

He lowered the zoo blowpipe from his lips—Gerry always carried it in case an animal had to be sedated in an emergency—and indicated the board. "It's a dart," he protested.

Rollo, wearing his cap with pride, was in a state of rare exhilaration and fair intoxication as he made his way back from the Marwood Arms. Although he certainly practised the colonial habit of a stiffie at sundown to loosen up after the cares of the day, he seldom permitted himself to get very drunk, since his life was predicated on being in control of himself and his emotions. But this had been a night quite unlike any other in his forty-eight years. He had been welcomed into a family, albeit a divided and bickering one, that, in its fashion, was as eccentric as any that Charles Addams could have imagined. They were disparate people drawn together by a simple common cause: a love of animals and a desire to protect and preserve them. But they didn't go about it in a saintly way; on the contrary, their bluff, gruff exteriors masked much of their emotion. He recalled the moment in *The Wind in the Willows,* which he had read as a child, when Toad chides Ratty for always going on about his beloved river. "I don't think about my river, Toad," Rollo recalled Rat as replying, "but I think about it—I think about it all the time."

Rollo knew he would be happy to spend the rest of his days among these people—much better than the prospect of being the secretary of some Australian golf club or a bursar at a school. How worthwhile to go knocking at heaven's door with an earthly reputation for having saved the Arabian oryx or the Père David deer from extinction and returned it to the wild.

The prospect of his empty attic room with no animals for company actually made him maudlin. He had grown to love those "little brown jobs." And love was something that had played little part in Rollo's life in recent years. But now that bastard Vince was going to wreck the place and turn it into some fucking funfair. Rollo exculpated Willa from being part of this madness. He had noted the expression on her face when she'd watched Vince humiliate him in his cage in front of the sponsors, and somehow she had communicated sympathy—maybe even something more than sympathy. No, he was fooling himself. All those innuendos about his utterly nonexistent sex life. What sex life? he thought as he unsteadily tried to put his key in the outer door of the main zoo building.

The next morning dawn, ripe and red, rippled across a pale blue sky, a harbinger of the heat to come, as the keepers left their lodgings to set about seeing to their animals.

"Well, now we know what we're up against," Reggie sighed resignedly, his bright canary-yellow outfit at odds with the darkness of his thoughts.

The half dozen or so others gathered by the sea lion pool nodded in mute agreement.

They all knew that now was the time for action. But what?

"Look out. Enemy on the starboard bow." Ant, the assistant keeper, seldom spoke—he seldom had a chance to with Bugsy as a boss—but when he did it was in epigrammatic naval terms. He had once been a sailor.

All eyes switched to the kitchen entrance of the main house as a radiant Willa emerged to embark on her daily jog. She began a series of elaborate warm-up exercises against the side of an Octopus Leisure Jeep parked outside. She looked up at them and gave a cheery wave.

"Can we trust her to tell us what Vince is up to?" Gerry whispered.

"Trust no one," said Sydney.

Willa glanced at him through her legs—the woman certainly had a supple body—and grinned again.

Sydney waved. "Have a nice day," he smiled, and the others, inspired by his initiative, took up the refrain.

"Thank you," Willa replied, surprised and rather pleased that her lesson had made an impact at last. With a weight in either hand, she began her jog down the hill towards the old wishing well.

Over the years children had habitually thrown pennies down it; the fun was in waiting to hear how long it was before their coins actually splashed in the water several hundred feet below, as well as the anticipation of their wishes coming true. But Vince had ordered a bold new sign that read: WISHING WELL: £1 MINIMUM. EXTRA SPECIAL WISH: £5. And he had a sheet lowered on ropes each morning to a depth of ten feet which was hauled up with the day's take when the zoo closed in the evening. No longer could anyone test the depth for a penny.

Willa disapproved of this piece of petty embezzlement, especially since the victims were primarily children and their dreams. But then, she disapproved of most of Vince's marketing initiatives: they were crude and, for the most part, dishonest. Once she got the books in good enough shape to confront his father, she would have him on the next plane to Atlanta.

She ran on, past the giant Doritos packets, the Perrier poster and sales stand, and the vast raspberry-coloured octopus that now sat on top of the stately elm tree in the middle of the lawn. "The garden looks beautiful," she dictated into her headset, "but the trash needs to be picked up twice a day due to the increase in junk wrappings."

"Have a nice day," another group of keepers chorused as she trotted between the giant blowups of Tina Turner and Steve Martin on either side of the okapi enclosure. "Okapi johnstoni," Vince had read sneeringly when he saw the original notices. "They look like fucking failed giraffes. Nobody's interested in them. But Steve and Tina . . ."

Sponsorship, yes, Willa thought; that made sense. But when the sponsor dwarfed the animals, the zoo's very reason d'être fell into question. She was certain her own customer relations policy was having a much more beneficial effect.

"Have a nice day." The two girls by the bears were smilingly eager to greet her.

She had now reached the most relished stretch of her jog, the one that made it all worthwhile. She deliberately slowed down as she trotted past the gorilla enclosure. Where was Jambo? His favoured position was empty. Plenty of his family were about, but none of them dared occupy it. A bit Big Rod, she mused.

Several keepers were taking their early morning tea in the outdoor cafeteria just beyond the gorilla house. She gave them a friendly wave and they responded with similar good cheer. Hugh Primates kept some bottled water in the small refrigerator of his inner sanctum, and he was more than happy to let her have some on her jogs. It was her habit to make a pit stop there, after exactly—she glanced at her pedometer—one mile three hundred and eighty-eight yards.

"Hugh?" she called as she pushed open the door.

There was no response. He was a solitary soul who welcomed her company for a few minutes. He liked to hear her stories about Willy B and Atlanta and said he would go and visit him one day if ever he could afford the fare. And he let her feed oranges to the gorillas through the bars which they would delicately peel. Fruit was their favourite food; they were, he told her, largely herbivorous save for the occasional nourishing insect, which gave them some protein.

Willa bent over the refrigerator and removed a bottle of icy water. Nectar, she thought as she took a swig, was better than champagne if you need it enough. But it was then that she became aware of the fact that she was not alone. Something stopped her from swinging round.

"Hugh?" she said again, more softly this time. But there was no response. Just the creak of a door hinge and the sound of something coming towards her. Her instinct told her to turn very slowly.

It was Jambo.

His cage door was wide open and he was moving steadfastly towards her. Willa, at first, froze, and then tried to edge her way to the door with her back to the wall. But 352 pounds of gorilla blocked her passage.

She wanted to scream for help but, in her short time at the zoo, she had learnt that any unexpected noise frightened most animals. So she just stood her ground and watched the vast anthropoid approach.

Was he going to kill her? Why? She had done him no wrong. She adored him. She stood there, poised between life and death, realising for the first time in her thirty-two years what real power was. She was at the mercy of this creature. But the experience wasn't only terrifying: she had rarely felt more alive.

Here it came. Jambo reached out his arm, not much longer than a human's but with a wrist three times the size of a heavyweight boxer's, and with great delicacy took her headset by the small microphone and lifted it off her head.

Good—he wanted a plaything. She realised now that the perspiration caused by her jog had been joined by a new source of sweat: her glands were pumping liquid fear.

Jambo seemed to sense it, too. Discarding the headset, he did something quite extraordinary. He reached down and took hold of her hand, which was nervously pressed to her thigh. His great leathery palm and fingers were soft and un-threatening. She allowed him to lift her hand, which he pressed against his broad, flat nose, sniffing it.

Hope he likes Chanel, she joked to herself in order to keep her spirits up. But she knew, of course, as Hugh had told her, that that was how gorillas identified other creatures, by their scent.

Jambo knew now that it was her. She could tell by the way he wrinkled his brow, twitching the crest of short hair on his forehead. He knew she meant him no harm. And he meant her no harm.

He released her hand, satisfied with this discovery. Something told her that it was her turn to respond. So, reaching out both hands, she took his palm and pressed it against her nose. And at that very moment something went off within her: an explosion of joy and exultation and love and happiness and, above all, understanding. She knew that she would never in her life again experience the ecstasy of this enshrined moment. She also knew that from this moment on her life would never be the same.

"You all right?" Hugh came out of the gorilla cage in his singlet and shorts. He had obviously been mucking out.

"Yeah," she assured him. "Fine."

Hugh put a hand on Jambo's back. "Better go now, big lad. Sorry about that. He sometimes slips his bolt when my back's turned."

"That's all right," she assured him, and then looked with deep affection at the departing Jambo. "Good-bye," she said.

When she emerged into the daylight, the dazzled expression on her face was due to more than just the strong morning sun. The keepers were still there, finishing their tea.

"Are you all right, Miss Weston?" Gerry Ungulates looked genuinely concerned. The others turned round to see what might be wrong.

"You look a little dazed," Cub observed in a friendly fashion.

"No, I'm fine." Willa was having difficulty finding the appropriate words. She gestured behind her to the door and waved her hand inarticulately. "I . . . just . . . right now . . . with the gorilla."

"Oh! You made contact." Gerry was almost casual about it.

"Yes." Willa took a grateful step towards him; he had encapsulated what she had been trying to say.

The keepers smiled and glanced knowingly at each other, making approving murmurs.

"It was . . ." Willa felt obliged to explain, but again the words just wouldn't come.

"We know," Cub said, nodding sympathetically.

Willa, still disconcerted by what had happened, scrutinized the assembled faces. "Oh. You all know."

"Yeah, that's why we became zookeepers," Sydney explained. "I mean, it's hardly the money, is it?"

The others laughed good-naturedly.

Willa was still not sure. "But you never talk about it."

"No, no, we don't." It was Reggie's precise Scottish accent. "There's no point, really."

"You either understand or you don't," Pip explained.

Gerry looked warmly towards her. "We always thought you might."

Willa had never felt so many streams of emotion course through her body at once. At the same time an illumination was taking place in her mind that began to cast light on so many matters that she had deliberately kept in the dark. Nothing was clear, not yet, but one thing she knew—there was a rare offer of comradeship in the air.

She also knew she had lost all restraint and was going to break down into floods of tears. Too bad. They're going to see the boss is vulnerable, Willa thought. But since when is vulnerability a crime, she told herself.

"Thank you" was all she said as she turned and hurried away, her cheeks glistening in the morning sunlight.

The zoo was exceptionally crowded that afternoon due to the fact that it was Whitmonday, an English bank holiday. Bank holidays—ordained by the Banks Act of 1871 to cut down on the number of holidays taken by banks rather than increase them—now applied to everyone and his car, so the whole of England turned into an enormous traffic jam and fathers frequently turned to zoos to answer the perennial question from the family: "What are we going to do today?"

Sydney and Pip, still not keen to wish the visitors a nice day, had wandered across to join Cub by the big cats enclosure and watch the public watch the lions, who remained perversely asleep in the long grass.

"She seems to have got what the zoo's about," Sydney suggested to the American lion keeper.

Cub nodded. "And she's strong; she can control Vince."

"It's going to be all right." Reggie Sea Lions, an edgy smile on his face, came across to them, with Rollo in his wake.

"Good." Rollo agreed in an abstract manner which indicated that maybe he didn't agree. "Good."

Cub shot a penetrating glance at him; she knew something was wrong. "What's the matter?" she asked.

The worried look on Rollo's face made Pip feel uneasy, too. Surely he should be celebrating Willa's seeming conversion, she thought. "Why aren't you excited?" she inquired tentatively.

Reggie sensed a possible conspiracy. "I thought you were on our side," he said accusingly.

"I am," Rollo insisted. "I am."

"He doesn't care." Sydney had never quite welcomed the former zoo director back into the fold, not after the cruel way he had called his bluff on the lemurs and capybaras.

Rollo rounded on him. "I do!" he exploded. "I love this place . . ."

"Well, what's the problem then?" demanded Pip.

Now Rollo *did* become conspiratorial. He noticed that several members of the public, unable to find sufficient entertainment in the dormant lions, were paying more attention to the keepers—especially after his outburst.

He beckoned the others to him and dropped his voice. "It's the figures," he whispered.

"The what?" Pip was sure she had misheard him.

"The figures," he repeated. "I've taken a look at the books. We're nowhere near making twenty percent."

Sydney guffawed and indicated the well-populated pathways. "With these crowds?"

"I know." Rollo was talking between his teeth. "I just don't understand it. But look . . . it means . . . what it means is McCain could close us down."

Sydney was outraged. "He'd never dare."

"He'd never get away with it." Pip was attempting to convince herself as much as anybody else.

"Think of the protests," said Reggie. "We'd organise them ourselves."

"Yeah, and it wouldn't be just us protesting, but all the friends of the zoo and local animal lovers," Cub added.

But Rollo was unswayed. "It takes time to organise that stuff. That's why he strikes like a cobra. You can't protest when you're dead."

A chilled hush hung over the small group. They had all heard that this was the McCain way: act first and answer questions afterwards.

"Will you ask Willa what she thinks?" It was Cub who broke the silence.

Rollo affected a derisory guffaw. "She'd never tell me something like that."

Cub looked him knowingly in the eyes. "Rollo, she likes you."

Rollo found himself easing his collar with his finger; it was hot that afternoon.

"Look, I spoke to Bruce Springsteen direct."

The visitors had long vacated the zoo this bank holiday, and two lean figures were engaged in an animated conversation on the far side of the tiger enclosure.

"Direct?" repeated Willa. She wanted to check that he knew the meaning of the word.

Her companion made a "trust me" gesture with his hands. "He said: 'Vince—you have my blessing.' "

Willa waved a lengthy piece of paper in front of him. "Then why have I got this pissed-off fax from his agent?"

Vince spun on his heel with a dismissive laugh. "It's a negotiating ploy. Just offer him fifty percent of the total tortoise revenue."

She slapped the fax with the back of her hand. "There *isn't* any tortoise revenue."

"Exactly." Vince levelled his forefinger at her like a congressman who had just won an argument. "The point is—"

"The point is—" Willa interrupted him in her iciest voice, "the point is *I* am running this zoo and I need to know what you're doing. I don't want to stumble across any more of your crackpot ideas."

"Like what?" Vince's arms shot out like a man falsely accused.

"Like that." Willa's own arm pointed undeviatingly at a prowling Siberian tiger who had come to life now that the sun had gone down and the visitors had left. Its four-hundred-pound body was enveloped in a red and white body stocking with the word MARLBORO printed on it.

Vince looked at her in amazement. "There's not one major advertising award I won't win with this."

Willa turned to leave. "It is not acceptable."

As she departed down the beaten track towards the small mammal enclosures, she didn't even deign to turn her head to utter her final condemnation. "Try to work out why."

She was tight with anger that he could humiliate an animal in this fashion, especially one that had the nobility of a tiger. Her annoyance was compounded by the fact that she knew that never, not in a hundred years, would she be able to explain to Vince what he had done wrong. Sensitivity was simply not in his makeup.

To her surprise, she was not the only person who'd been drawn to the small mammal area that evening. A tall figure was feeding snacks to a ring-tailed lemur through the wire of its cage. Rollo Lee.

Willa's mood changed abruptly. She smoothed down her skirt, at the same time pulling it up slightly above her knees, and adjusted her jacket so that the moon was allowed to cast its light on at least part of her bosoms. And then she walked purposefully towards him.

"Good evening," she said.

He was clearly startled. "What?"

And then he saw her, like an apparition in the twilight, so beautiful and so untouchable. "Oh, hello" were the only words he could find.

She came closer to him. "What are you doing here?" she asked.

He gave a nervous laugh. "Just seeing a little friend."

"Plenty of them at the zoo, I gather," she replied pointedly.

The innuendo sailed over his lofty head. "Absolutely," he eagerly agreed.

He looked into her eyes. They shone like crystal, as if possessed of their own radiance. "Look, can I ask you something?"

A smile curled round her lips as she rested a shoulder against the cage. "Sure."

"About last month's balance sheet," Rollo blurted out, "have you and your fiancé by any chance had time to examine—"

"My fiancé!" Willa straightened up in shock. "Vince and I aren't together. I'm quite unattached."

"Oh good." The apology came tripping off Rollo's tongue before he even had time to formulate it.

"Good?" She repeated the word as if she wanted him to elaborate on it.

There were moments in Rollo's life when he stumbled over sentences as if they were self-set trip wires. This was one of them. "I'm pleased you're not with, er . . ."—he could see the trap at the end of the tunnel, and just managed to avoid it—". . . anyone in particular," he finished.

Willa seemed tickled by his embarrassment. "It's a warm evening, isn't it?" she observed apropos of nothing.

"Yes, warm." Rollo would have agreed it was warm if the temperature had been minus-50-degrees centigrade, so relieved was he to be let off the hook.

Willa slipped her jacket off to reveal a skimpy grey top with thin straps and shoulders that were lean and brown and altogether enticing. Rollo's eyes were fixed on the equally tanned bosoms that, while remaining on the side of propriety, were very evident now.

"They're gorgeous, aren't they," she said. "They just make you want to handle them."

Rollo realised she must be reading his thoughts. Who was she? Some female Uri Geller? "Yes. Yes, I know what you mean," he readily agreed.

She came closer to him and to the ring-tailed lemur he had been feeding. There was an enrapturing smell about her, so fresh and feminine.

"Yes, I like him breast—best—of all the small mammaries—mammals!" he stammered, looking helplessly at her, knowing his corrections had merely compounded the twin Freudian slips.

"He's called Rollo, actually," he gulped.

Looking at him disingenuously, she whispered in a low, alluring voice: "Tell me more about Rollo."

He paused for thought. She was playing games with him. And he rather liked it.

"Well, he's from Madagascar, about four years old, eats mainly fruit and vegetables but"—he purposefully took a peanut from his hand and fed it to the creature—"he just loves his nuts."

"Does he?" She had to restrain herself from bursting into laughter. "And is he very sexually active?"

Rollo took her question at face value. "Well, he's on his own at the moment, obviously."

"Is he?" Willa raised an eyebrow with practised expertise.

"Yes," Rollo continued airily. "However, if he had a partner . . ."

"Just one?" she inquired.

"What?" He didn't quite follow.

"That wouldn't bore him? I mean you had two in your cage the other day," she pointed out.

"Oh, very good, very good." Rollo got the joke and decided to put her newfound warmth to a more serious purpose. "Incidentally, about the profit-and-loss account . . ."

She wasn't sure she could believe her ears. "Rollo, do you really want to discuss the zoo?"

This unnerved him. "Well, yes, er, I do."

"Then let's do it over dinner."

"Dinner?" The stark invitation hit him straight between the eyes. No woman had ever asked him to dinner before, especially a creature of this radiance.

"Why not?" she said with a shrug. "Tomorrow?"

"Yes . . . yes, that's fine," he stammered. "I don't think I've got anything on this year."

"Tomorrow then," she confirmed casually, as if they had made an appointment to discuss work rotas.

Deliberately she removed the packet of peanuts from his hand and took one out and fed it to the lemur. "Rollo," she said, "I think you're cute."

And then, almost before he realised it, she was gone, her jacket over her shoulder as she strode off with style down the beaten track.

He stared after her. "Fucking hell," he said under his breath.

She stopped. Had she heard him? He could have killed himself. He hastily looked for a peanut to feed the lemur, then realised she still had them.

"Damn!" Willa turned and came back to him. "I'm having dinner with Rod McCain tomorrow."

"You're going to London."

"No, he's passing by here. In fact, I think he's going to spend the night in the Marwood Arms. Can you do the evening after?"

"Sure." Rollo hoped his eagerness wasn't too apparent. "Will you be able to find out what he's thinking about the zoo?"

She came up to him. That scent again. "Rollo. You've been an Octopus employee long enough to know he doesn't tell anyone what he's thinking. Except Neville."

"Neville," Rollo repeated.

CHAPTER
10

"You do know the history of the phrase 'sub rosa,' don't you? In medieval times, towards the end of the fourteenth century, when a group of men gathered in a room and agreed that the contents of their meeting would be strictly secret, the practice was to hang a rose above the table. In succeeding centuries carpenters would actually carve roses on to ceilings to denote that that particular room was to be used for precisely that purpose. Nowadays, with the dire lack of education among the young—and the rest of the population, come to that—very few, if any, people realise this fact, and most look upon such a carved rose as mere ornamentation. So there is more than a little irony"—Bugsy began to choke on his own high-pitched chuckle—"in the fact that I am attaching a bugging device to the sacred symbol of secrecy, indeed . . ."

"Where shall I put this?" Rollo could feel his arms lengthening as he stood in the bedroom doorway with an outsize tape recorder in his hands.

"Oh, on one of the beds in our room."

Bugsy seemed unconcerned about its position. He was more concerned about extolling the virtues of the device he was screwing into the ceiling. "This phase-coherent microphone has a remarkable response in its unique ability to minimise interior acoustics . . ."

"Haven't you got anything smaller?" Rollo remarked as he lowered onto the bed the ponderous machine with its two oversize reels, each threaded with old-fashioned quarter-inch tape.

"The Revox A77 was always known as being heavier than comparable models," Bugsy explained, "due to its three-motor design and ten-and-a-half-inch reel capacity . . ."

Rollo was no longer listening. Somebody was outside, knocking on the door of the room he had booked. He glanced at his watch. Christ, surely they hadn't arrived this early!

". . . it also features a signal to noise specification that has never been effectively superseded," Bugsy continued merrily, wholly oblivious to his companion's distress, "since its arrival on the scene in 1957. The BBC Home Service, now distressingly renamed Radio Four—such ingenuity!— which used to set the benchmark for this standard of recording, would no more dream of bending its knee to that miniaturised Japanese rubbish than . . ."

The knock came again. Rollo, because of his Hong Kong police days, was no stranger to dicey situations; sometimes the only course of action was to bite the bullet. You never knew . . . He took a deep breath, nervously took hold of the handle, and opened the door with a bold flourish.

"Would you like your bed turned down, Mr. Lee?" It was the maid, a lanky teenager in laddered tights with a trolley stacked high with towels and breakfast menus and little bottles of shampoo and bath lotion.

161

"No, no. Thanks. Everything's fine." Rollo hoped his relief wasn't too palpable.

"A chocky mint for bedtime?" Was there a hint of flirtation in the young girl's manner?

"No, no," Rollo insisted. "I'm just fine. Fine. Thank you. Good night."

He closed the door with emphatic finality. Thank God, he thought. Until that moment he hadn't realised just how tense he was. It had been quite a few years since those days in the police, and then he had usually been in the habit of detecting crime rather than committing it. But, as his brother used to hold forth at the family dinner table after he had acquired one term's knowledge of jurisprudence, sometimes a greater moral imperative justifies a smaller misdemeanour. Otherwise, he would pronounce with recently acquired wisdom, you end up with Vichy governments implementing Hitler's law, and we all knew what that led to: a society which was in itself criminal.

They had to find out what Vince's plans for the zoo were, and more important, Rod McCain's response to them and his own master plan. It had been relatively easy to discover—Sydney was having a wholly carnal relationship with one of the receptionists, a married woman, as it happened—for which night Vince had reserved the Churchill Suite at the Marwood Arms: Saturday 22nd June. The hotel's largest room came with an adjoining bedroom to the left and, if necessary, another to the right. The latter could also be let separately and, as luck would have it, Vince hadn't bothered to book it and neither had anyone else. Thus Rollo Lee had nonchalantly taken it for the very same night.

He ran through the connecting door, which could only be opened from the bedroom side, into the main suite. He also ran into a wall of words.

". . . what I've done is to combine this with a phase-coherent cardioid microphone specially designed to use in a situation such as this when an overall acoustic response is required . . ."

"Please." Rollo was finding it difficult to restrain his exasperation. "How much longer will—"

". . . meanwhile this FM transmitter provides a high-quality . . ."

"Please!" Rollo implored. "Please!"

". . . wire-free connection." Bugsy did not take well to interruptions.

"Will you shut up!" Rollo screamed. His accomplice was so taken aback by this outburst that Rollo felt somehow constrained to add an apology. "Sorry! Sorry. I'm anxious . . ."

Bugsy, dressed in a well-worn tweed suit and his habitual bow tie, pulled a fob watch out of his waistcoat pocket and casually flipped open the lid. "We've got plenty of time."

"We have not got plenty of time," Rollo countered through gritted teeth.

Adrian Malone pointed to the dial. "McCain isn't due for half an hour."

The man must be mad, thought Rollo. Or a fool. Doesn't he countenance the possibility that people occasionally arrive ahead of time? Especially those being driven in high-powered cars through empty English byways on a summer evening.

"Do you know the risk we're all taking here?" Rollo tried to infiltrate some sense into the boffin's brain. "If he finds out, we're all dead meat."

Bugsy pointed at Rollo's bedroom. "But we'll all be safely in there."

Somehow he had to imprint the immense danger of the enterprise on this insensate insect keeper. "You do realise this is a criminal act, don't you?"

163

"Oh, yes," Bugsy replied. "Section 5 of the Wireless Telegraphy Act of 1949, revised in . . ."

"How soon?" Rollo was reduced to pleading. "How soon?"

"Just one more microphone to check," Bugsy assured him.

"Good. Right." Rollo looked at his watch. Time to double-check the girls. He stealthily but rapidly made for the corridor.

". . . another interesting thing about the combination of the A77 with a standard hypercardioid microphone is that it solves . . ."

Then, miraculously, Bugsy actually stopped talking. However, this time he interrupted himself. His eye caught a dead wasp on top of the carefully arranged bowl of fruit on the occasional table beside him. He picked it up and dropped it into the large side pocket of the tweed jacket he was wearing.

"Lucky you, Terry," he mumbled fondly into the pocket, and then continued: "The whole problem of achieving full auditory quality with maximum ambient reach . . ."

Rollo rushed down the hotel staircase, only slowing his pace when he encountered a couple of elderly ladies coming up towards him after an early supper. "Lovely evening," he said, smiling graciously. And they nodded back politely.

In a controlled fast walk he passed reception—without, he thought, attracting any undue attention from the woman on duty—and made for the public bar. It had been coyly renamed the Lion's Den by Alliance Leisure, to justify both the somewhat bizarre presence of the zookeepers and the fairly tasteless animal sculptures and pictures that adorned the walls. There was some sort of rugby crowd at the bar, but seated by the window with a clear view of the rear entrance to the hotel was Pip. In a tight-fitting black cocktail dress, and with her short blonde hair fashionably styled to one side, her white matte makeup, and her delicate rouge lips, she looked more like a Milan fashion model than the apprentice keeper she really was—save for the presence of a sickly lamb on her lap which she was feeding milk from a baby's bottle.

"See all right?" Rollo inquired quietly, adjusting his cravat anxiously, aware that one or two of the rugger buggers were watching to see if he was chatting her up.

"Everything," she reassured him, sensing his unease.

"About half an hour," he reminded her.

"Okay," she said with a nod. "Don't worry about me. Everything okay up there?"

"Apart from the conversation, yes." Rollo's retort brought a perfect smile to her sweet face.

Rollo returned with despatch to the lobby. Where was Cub? She was supposed to be here. He casually stepped out of the main door of the hotel onto the gravel drive. Perhaps she was hiding, behind a bush or round the corner?

"Mr. Lee, I'm here."

The voice came from behind him and, in his present state, caused him to start.

She had managed to secrete herself behind the open oak front door, which had a porthole window through which she could see right down the hotel drive.

"You okay?" Rollo whispered, hoping that no one would notice he appeared to be talking to himself.

"Everything under control," the big cat keeper replied reassuringly; she feared little from mere humans. "And you?"

"Oh, I'm fine," Rollo assured her. "Half an hour then . . ."

He walked backwards through the front door and skipped deftly back up the stairs. Had he lingered for five more seconds outside he would have seen a large grey Mercedes turning through the hotel entrance, with a man wearing a broad-brimmed Australian hat at the wheel.

". . . and, as Stephen Hawking has pointed out, in order to understand what you would see if you were watching a star collapse to form a black hole, one has to remember that in the theory of relativity . . ."

Rollo stood at the bedroom door, almost too astounded to speak. Had this man simply failed to notice that he had left the room, or was he in such an advanced state of schizophrenia that he was actually able to engage himself in conversation? Either way, he was mad. And, despite his previous assurances, he was still fiddling with the second microphone on the leg of the telephone table.

Rollo decided to shock him. "Will you hurry up!" he barked.

But Bugsy seemed blissfully unfazed. "May I point out . . .," he began as he slowly turned round.

"No!" Rollo strode into the room. "Is the microphone fixed?"

"Yes," said Bugsy.

Downstairs, behind the door, Cub's hands flew to her mouth in panic. She had often seen actresses do this in films or on television and had always thought it to be an overdramatic gesture, but now she found herself doing it involuntarily as she watched the welcoming committee of Vince, the hotel manager, undermanager, and senior receptionist, plus two porters, move swiftly past her and line up outside the door as if they were expecting visiting royalty.

Vince broke ranks to guide the arriving Mercedes into pride of place in front of the hotel, in the manner of someone bringing an aircraft into its final mooring position. He then fell down on one knee in front of the car, like a bullfighter, in a form of salutation. Cub needed no more evidence as to the identity of the large grey-haired figure who now began to emerge from the backseat, even though he was partially obscured by the obsequious hotel manager. She fled up the stairs.

"If they're both fixed, let's get in there and close the door." Rollo, towering over the still-kneeling Bugsy in the middle of the Churchill Suite, indicated the bedroom he had booked.

Bugsy rose reluctantly to his feet. "I'd just like to make the point . . ."

"I don't care." Rollo grabbed him by the arm. "I just want you to be quiet."

Bugsy stopped to explain. "I know my loquacity sometimes . . ."

"Look"—Rollo wondered if the man might provoke him into violence—"will you just can it for once! Are you aware what a complete windbag you are? You are completely incapable of—"

"Sssh!" Bugsy put his finger to his lips to silence the man who had spent so much of the evening doing exactly the same to him, with little success.

This was too much. Rollo decided that he would cuff the impudent ant keeper. And then he, too, heard a soft knock at the door of the Churchill Suite.

Obviously it wouldn't be Vince or his father, since they would have a key, or more likely, a flunky with a key. "It could be Cub," Rollo suggested hopefully, making to open the door.

Bugsy restrained him. "It might be the maid," he warned. They weren't meant to be in the main room.

There followed another knock, more urgent. The two men remained frozen under the rose in the middle of the room,

167

hoping whoever it was would go away. For several seconds there was a chilling silence.

"Let's check." Bugsy now took the initiative and gingerly opened the door. Rollo peered over his shoulder as they glanced both up and down the corridor. Whoever it had been had gone away. For the moment the coast seemed clear.

"They're here!" It was a woman's voice, and one in a considerable state of panic.

Rollo and Bugsy spun round in simultaneous alarm.

Cub was at the bedroom door, looking very beckoning in a deep-cut cashmere buttoned top and black silk skirt and, unusual for her, dainty high heels at the end of her elegant brown legs. Indeed, she was beckoning—anxiously beckoning them to come to the bedroom she was in, for their own good.

"What!" cried Rollo.

Cub entered the suite to reiterate the news. "They're here." As she walked in, she knocked into the waste bin that Rollo had placed to keep the door open, and it slowly began to close behind her.

"They can't be." Bugsy fumbled for his fob watch.

"They are. Quick!" implored the comely cat keeper.

But, alas, it was too late. As the three of them made for the bedroom door, it clicked closed. And, claw as they might, there was no way of opening it from within the suite. As they changed direction with alacrity to effect an exit via the door of the suite, their route was just as surely barred by the ominous noise of approaching voices.

At the sound of a key being inserted into the lock, Bugsy made for the opposite bedroom while Cub swiftly slid back the door of a large, louvred cupboard on the corridor side of the suite and dragged Rollo hastily in behind her.

Their escape was made not so much *in* as just *after* the nick of time but, fortunately for them, the fawning behaviour attendant on the entry into the suite of Rod McCain diverted all attention from anyone but him.

The manager ushered the great man into the room, followed by the rock-hard shape of Neville, still in his broad-brimmed hat, two assistant managers, and a waiter carrying champagne in a bucket of ice, which he proceeded to place on the low table by the fruit.

Vince, in the vanguard, smiling his appreciation at the arrival of his father, went to open the bottle.

McCain glanced round the suite, showing no signs of appreciation or pleasure. His eye took in the reproduction antique furniture, the anodyne yellow wallpaper and sofas and chairs with their fleur-de-lys patterns. It was the sort of place designed not to offend anybody—or to impress anybody, either. He was glad he wasn't staying overnight.

"It is said that Sir Winston once graced this very room"—the hotel manager put the tips of his fingers together—"as the guest of Sir John Marwood when it was a private home. Sir John was a very well-connected man, you know, and his philanthropy—"

The word made McCain feel uncomfortable. He cast a cold eye on the manager and then glanced at Neville.

The manager took the hint and began to exit backwards, his head slightly bowed. "Enjoy your stay, although it is so short. If there's anything at all you need, please just—"

A telephone began to ring on the small table on the far side of the louvred cupboard. Neville immediately strode across to it and lifted the receiver.

"Yep." The henchman wasted little time on the niceties of conversation. He put his hand over the mouthpiece and, in a fashion that managed to communicate to the welcoming committee that they had outstayed their own welcome, announced: "Rod, it's Melbourne."

169

McCain growled a form of apology to the manager and his staff. "Ah, gentlemen, ladies, if you'll excuse me I have a rather important call."

"Of course. Thank you. Thank you very much." As the party turned to leave they were joined, unnoticed, by an additional waiter from the adjoining bedroom with a thin white linen towel over his left arm, carrying a bowl of fruit. Bugsy had almost engineered an ingenious exit when he found his path blocked by the substantial back of Neville, who was in the doorway, making quite sure the hotel staff were well out of the room and thus out of earshot.

To his utter horror he was spotted by McCain, who was by now on the phone. The media mogul indicated he should come over to him. Bugsy did so, with extreme trepidation. He had blown it. He straightened his bow tie and approached his doom with solemn steps.

McCain's left arm shot out in his direction—and greedily removed the entire bunch of grapes from the top of the fruit bowl. He pressed some into his mouth, still talking all the while, and managed to indicate to the supposed waiter that he should make himself scarce. This Bugsy did with rapid relief, only to hear as he approached the door the sound of Neville returning from down the hallway. As he stood, caught between the Scylla and Charybdis of these two massive Antipodeans, the louvred door of the cupboard slid swiftly open, and a hand grabbed the back of his collar and dragged him into temporary safety. Rollo managed to slide the door closed a millisecond before Neville swept into the room. Throughout all of this, fortunately for them, Vince had been preoccupied with trying to unravel the tightly twisted wire that covered the cork of the bottle of vintage champagne he had ordered.

"And what'd be the cost of a plant in Papua New Guinea?" McCain's voice, low and gruff though it sounded,

170

was terrifyingly close to the louvred cupboard. Cub and Rollo stood like waxworks as they listened. Bugsy celebrated his narrow escape by offering them a piece of fruit. Looks, on this occasion, were able to kill any thought he might have had of saying anything.

"Well, they should have thought of that before they made the demand." McCain was in full flow. A large element in the secret of his success was to break up the unions in whatever asset or company he acquired, thereby arrogating to himself unchallenged power. It had been a foolish and unpardonable weakness of most employers in the late twentieth century, he had reasoned, even to countenance the idea of a union that could hold management for ransom; and, indeed, many employers in the late twentieth century had followed his lead in dismantling them.

"So, keep negotiations going while we move the plant to Papua. And then give them our standard termination speech." McCain was making notes on a pad by the phone all the time he was talking.

The Octopus manager at the other end was obviously trying to suggest a less harsh alternative, but it made no impression on his boss. "Forget it," snapped McCain. "They shouldn't be so greedy."

He slammed down the phone, ripped the top page off the pad, and handed it to Neville, who was by his side. "Fax this to Atlanta."

Neville took it and, in exchange, took a folded yellow sheet of foolscap from his inside pocket and handed it to Rod. "Talking of termination,"—he smiled conspiratorially—"you might want to leave this with him."

As he left the room, he looked with undisguised contempt at Vince, who had mastered the coiled wire and now proudly popped the cork of the champagne bottle.

The sound sent shock waves to the three inside the cupboard, who were all in a state of understandable tension and unable to see very much of what was happening in the room.

Bugsy took the noise as a cue to break his unaccustomed silence. "Nobody turned on the Revox. It's not being recorded," he whispered to Rollo.

"I know." Rollo pointed to his ear and glared at Bugsy. "That's why I'm trying to listen to what they're saying. So shut up."

"Well now, Vince, what do you want to talk to me about?" McCain offered no thanks as he accepted the glass of champagne from his son and slumped down on the sofa.

"Dad, it's very good of you to accommodate me schedulewise, Dad." Vince sat nervously on the edge of the opposite sofa. "And flesh-and-bloodwise. It means a lot."

"Cut the crap," his father retorted, taking a slug of champagne. "It was on my way."

"The zoo's going real well." Vince was either oblivious or used to the austere lack of paternal response.

"So?" McCain seemed unimpressed.

"So what I wanted to ask you—," Vince began.

"Gimme the sponsorship figures," his father interrupted.

Vince eagerly opened his briefcase. "You won't believe what I've put together here, Dad," he said with pride.

"Probably not" was the dry response as McCain stuck out his hand to accept the documents.

Outside, in the corridor, Pip could hear their muffled voices as she crept by, still carrying her lamb. Being in the bar on back-window watch, she had not been aware of McCain's arrival, and Cub had not had time to inform her. But eventually a buzz went round the hotel that somebody very important had arrived, and she had managed to get the information confirmed by Sydney's mistress at reception.

She tiptoed past the Churchill Suite, fearful that somebody might come out—although she was committing no crime—and tried the door to the bedroom Rollo had booked. It was unlocked—but nobody was there. Where were Rollo and Bugsy, and where was Cub? Something had gone wrong. The voices from next door were clearer now: she could certainly make out Vince's. But the tape recorder on the bed wasn't working—she could tell that because the giant reels were static. She knew that the plan had been to use radio microphones to pick up the conversation, which was even now under way.

Using her initiative, Pip plonked the lamb on the bed and lifted the heavy Revox down onto the floor by the wall so that she could plug it in. She scanned the buttons beneath the reels. Even on Bugsy's Stone Age machine they weren't that different from those on her CD-cassette player. She pressed "play" and "record" simultaneously. Nothing happened. Shit! There must be another button somewhere, she thought. Then she realised she had forgotten to switch on the power supply at the wall. Hooray! The ten-and-a-half-inch reels began to turn.

Crawling closer to the door, she decided to live dangerously, reaching up to turn the handle and edge it open an inch. There was Vince, sitting in anticipation like somebody awaiting his exam reports, and there was the thick grey mane of hair which she presumed belonged to his father.

"Only fifty thousand from Schweppes?" Rod sounded disappointed.

"I'm going to talk 'em up. No worries." Vince radiated a less than convincing air of confidence. "I've done well, haven't I, Dad? So what I really wanted to ask—"

But his desires were put on hold by the rearrival of Neville. He burst through the door with glee. "Rod, the Hong Kong call is coming through."

McCain got up immediately, the pages of Vince's sponsorship statistics discarded at his feet.

Neville indicated the door to the adjoining bedroom. "Vince, I think he'd like to take this one alone."

Pretending to be happy to oblige, Vince took the hint and made towards the room. "Oh good, I needed to visit the john." But once he shut the door behind him he struck the wall with his fist in painful anger at again being thwarted in his game plan.

Inside the cupboard Rollo and Cub stood taut with anticipation at what this important call could be. But Bugsy was otherwise engaged. He was searching for something in his side pockets, and when he couldn't find it, he crouched down and started patting the carpet.

"Right . . . Done . . . Agreed . . . You have my word." McCain was triumphant as he put down the phone. "Yes, yes, yes, yes, YES!"

"The public executions?" Neville inquired eagerly.

"The Chinese are seriously interested," McCain nodded. "They'll give us world rights."

"How often?"

"Weekly!"

"No!" Neville yelled in disbelief. "Bloody beauty!"

"Hit me!" his employer instructed and, in disbelief, Rollo and Cub—Bugsy was now crawling round the cupboard floor and had definitely lost interest in what was happening in the suite—heard the sound of a sheep-shearer-size fist thwacking into a solid stomach.

"At least five guys a week." McCain was exultant. "Do you realise what this is worth?"

"We'll get a lot of liberal whingeing, Rod," Neville warned.

"We'll just show them in Asia to begin with." McCain was furiously making calculations on a pad. "My God. Executions. This is totally cross-cultural. This is what television was invented for." He tore off the top sheet and slipped it into his inside pocket. "But no documentation. Not yet."

Back inside the cupboard, Rollo feared that Bugsy had suffered an attack of tarantism or something; he was scrambling round the floor like a spider.

"What is it?" he hissed.

"Terry's escaped," Bugsy hissed back.

"*Who's* escaped?" Rollo was bewildered. The man was mad; no doubt about it.

"Terry."

"Terry who?"

Bugsy clambered back on his feet, indicating an empty side pocket.

"My tarantula."

Rollo's elongated body assumed an upright state of rigor mortis as he emitted a low moan of desperation.

"What?" Cub was on his other side.

"His tarantula's loose."

"Oh shit!" Cub knew exactly what to do in this situation and, after brushing down both shoulders, began to take off her top to see if the creature was secreted in her clothing. Rollo immediately followed suit. But not Bugsy. "He's harmless," he tried to assure them—but to no avail.

"Sorry about that, Vince," McCain uncharacteristically apologised as Neville let his son out of the bedroom. "When's Willa due?"

"In about ten minutes," Vince replied sullenly.

So, what's on your mind?" Heady with the Chinese deal, McCain was prepared to grant his son that amount of time—

or at least part of it. The sound of a knock came from near the door. Neville went to answer it, but there was no one there. "I'll be in the car," he said as he left.

"I told you I'd kick ass here, Dad." Vince was happy to have the field clear to himself; he rarely felt comfortable in Neville's presence. "Chip off the old block, eh?"

"Time is money, son. What's your point?" came the icy reply.

Vince looked at his feet and spread out his hands in a nervous gesture of explanation. "Dad, I feel really close to you in these last . . . er . . . moments . . . er . . . Can I have a raise?"

"Out of the question," McCain snapped back before giving himself time to even consider the request.

"Dad!" whined Vince.

"I don't have the money," his father explained. There was another noise, from what sounded like the cupboard. McCain walked towards it. Inside Rollo and Cub stood trapped in double jeopardy—a tarantula on the loose and Rod McCain about to expose them, with Rollo in his boxer shorts and shirt and Cub only in bra and pants.

"You've got six billion dollars!" Vince wailed.

"Seven," McCain corrected him. "But things are tight at the moment."

Rollo and then Cub could see his shadow approaching and, at that very moment, became aware of the tarantula prowling along the shelf by their heads where the extra pillows were kept.

But Rod walked past them and opened the door of the suite to find nobody there.

"Dad, all right." Vince was not giving up. "How about a small advance against my inheritance?"

"What inheritance?" Rod grabbed some more grapes from another bowl and walked back towards the window.

"I'm your son," Vince reminded him. "You've got to leave me something."

"Why?" his father demanded combatively.

"You screwed up my childhood."

"How could I?" Rod was rather enjoying this. "I wasn't even there." He pushed a handful of grapes into his mouth. "Anyway, I'm not going anywhere."

"What do you mean?" Vince's humiliation was now compounded by anger.

"The moment I become seriously ill, I'm being cryogenically frozen until they find a cure. Everything goes into a trust until I'm back."

" 'Back'?" Vince echoed. "You mean you're not going to die?"

"You're goddam right I'm not." He finished the rest of the grapes as he looked out the window at the darkening sky. "Bad news, eh?" he said with a chuckle.

Just at that moment Terry the Tarantula decided to use the top of Cub's head as a springboard to a safe exit between the slats of the cupboard. The big cat keeper half-stifled a high-pitched scream.

"Get ahold of yourself!" Rod said as he turned to his son, contemptuous of him for this pusillanimous response.

Before Vince could seek an explanation for what his father had just told him, out of the blue there came the sound of a sheep bleating, not once but twice.

McCain spun back to the window. "That was a sheep," he said.

"Can't have been," said Vince.

"I grew up in New Zealand," his father pointed out, "and I know a sheep when I hear one."

But Vince only had ears for his recently revealed reversal of fortune. "You mean you're going to be immortal?"

"Now you've got it. Mind you, this cryogenics stuff isn't cheap. It's costing me an arm and a leg."

Vince snatched a sharply pointed fruit knife from the bowl. He had half a mind to plunge it into his father's back. Or should he slit his own wrists? he wondered.

"Sheep are just like people, you know," McCain ruminated as he looked out the open window. "Give them a couple of meals a day and they just stand there quietly till you eat them."

He turned back unexpectedly. Vince, caught in mid-mime with the knife, plunged it accidentally into his own thigh.

"Christ!" exclaimed McCain.

"What?" His son whipped the knife out of his leg, hoping his father hadn't noticed.

McCain indicated the sofa in front of the cupboard. "It's the biggest goddam spider I've ever seen."

"That's probably what was making the bleating noise," Vince suggested, relieved that Rod seemed not to be looking at the wound he was desperately trying to cover with his right hand.

"I don't like spiders—kill it!" McCain ordered.

Vince limped over to where the creature had been. "It's terminated, Dad," he cried, bringing his bad foot down on the spot the creature had crawled to. As he doubled over in agony, neither he nor his father noticed the cupboard door being slid open, with Bugsy attempting to come out and rescue his pet, only to be pulled in by the collar once more.

"Now listen to me," McCain growled. "You may have to close down the zoo on twenty-four hours' notice."

"What?" Vince was still in agony and still searching by the sofa for the errant insect.

Not twelve inches away from his left ear, in the cupboard, was a frozen tableau of a distinguished man in boxer shorts and a nearly naked woman in black underwear, pinioning a

178

man in a bow tie to the floor, with their hands tightly clamped over his mouth.

"Yeah," said McCain. "Some Japanese may make me a big offer to turn it into a golf course."

"But, Dad," Vince pleaded, fearing the loss of future revenue in sponsorship and other shady deals he had planned, "you'd have to shoot all the animals."

"That's a public relations problem," said McCain, shrugging. "We just get some tame vet to say there was a dangerous disease, some virus spreading among them. So, if I decide to sell it, when you're firing the keepers just read this out."

He handed Vince the yellow sheet of paper that Neville had earlier given him.

"Read it out?" Vince repeated lamely as he glanced at the document.

"It's what we always say." McCain pointed to the other side of the sofa. "Look, there's the spider. Quick! Kill it!"

As Vince tried once more and just as unsuccessfully to stamp on the tarantula, Bugsy hammered on the door of the cupboard in an attempt to break free. McCain walked smartly to the bedroom door and flung it open, anxious to get out of this place, and there, on the other side, giving herself some last-minute makeup touches preparatory to knocking, was Willa. She looked drop-dead beautiful in her strapless Thierry Mugler evening gown, slim necklace, and diamond earrings.

"Oh, hello, Mr. McCain," she smiled.

"Rod," he insisted, taking her outstretched hand.

"Am I early?" she asked.

"Let's get some dinner," he answered. "It's good to see you. How's business?"

"It's really exciting. We—" she started to say, but Rod was already moving past her.

179

"Good. I'm hungry," he pronounced as he continued down the hall.

Willa was nonplussed by this lack of reaction to her looks. In their past encounters Rod had shown himself at least appreciative of, if not vulnerable to, her allure. And she had taken a lot of trouble tonight. She saw Vince standing on the sofa, his hand on his thigh, and entered the room to check her makeup at the mirror by the door.

"Do I look all right?" she asked.

"Great," came the reply.

Somehow his voice didn't ring as airy as usual. She glanced at him and noticed an expression of concealed agony on his face. She could see blood suppurating between the fingers of his right hand.

"What's wrong with your leg?"

"A spider stung me," Vince explained stoically, stumbling off the sofa and limping towards the door. "It's nothing."

"How did the meeting go?" she continued, adjusting a smudge in her eyeliner.

"Never better," Vince insisted as he shuffled past her and hobbled down the hall. "Just give me two minutes more. I've almost got him where I want him."

Willa looked at herself again in the mirror. Was it too much makeup? Maybe, she thought, she should take a little off the eyes. She pulled out the room key which Neville had left inserted in the lock and, slamming the door shut, followed in pursuit of Rod and Vince.

Immediately, the cupboard door slid open and Bugsy leapt out. He scuttled round the room on all fours, his incessant chatter now replaced by a lachrymose wailing, in anticipation of finding the squashed remains of his many-legged friend.

Cub and Rollo emerged more tentatively, checking to make quite sure that the coast was clear. They looked as if

180

they had stepped out of a sauna. She was still in her underwear and the sweat glistened on her bare shoulders and
stomach. Rollo's hair was wildly awry; his shirt open and
unbuttoned, his boxer shorts rumpled, and his black socks
round his ankles.

"My God," he breathed, seeking refuge on the sofa.

Cub, more alert, saw that Vince, in his distress, had left
behind the yellow sheet of firing instructions. She was in the
process of lifting it from the side table when they heard the
distinct sound of a key being inserted in the door.

Cub looked at the mirror and could see Willa's Prada bag
on the table below it.

"Her handbag," she whispered, galvanising Rollo out of
his recumbent position and back into the cupboard.

"*There* you are! They couldn't stamp you out, could they.
They're a million evolutionary years behind . . ." Bugsy,
over by the window, had evidently recovered Terry.

"Shut up. The door," Rollo hissed.

Bugsy could see it opening and prudently prostrated himself behind the second sofa, cupping Terry in his palms like
someone who had just scored a try at rugby.

It was Willa; she *had* forgotten her Prada bag. She
whipped it off the table, apparently oblivious to the flurry of
activity that had preceded her return but not to her own
looks. Holding the door open with her left hand, she again
assessed her appearance in the wall mirror. Was the strapless
Thierry Mugler too much? The earrings too expensive? The
hair—she'd shown photographs to the woman in the salon
in the local town. No, it must be the makeup. Worth a couple of minutes—men, even those as powerful as Rod, were
always respectful of the privacy of the powder room.

She let the door slam closed and searched her bag for a
damp tissue to make the necessary adjustments.

But she could hardly believe her eyes as she looked up into the mirror to decide where to begin. She must be seeing things, she told herself. For behind her head she witnessed the unmistakable figure of Rollo Lee in an open shirt step out of the closet.

"Oh dear. Please God. Never again. Please," she heard the figure moan.

Willa swirled round on one heel. Half-clad and breathing heavily, he had flopped down on the sofa in a state of post-orgasmic exhaustion.

Rollo closed his eyes to help him exterminate the memory of the ordeal, and when he opened them Willa was standing in front of him.

"Hi!" she said, quite calmly. Cub, who had crept back behind the cover of the closed side of the cupboard, had been unable to communicate any warning to him.

"Hi!" he replied, automatically bringing his knees together in modesty.

"What are you doing here?" she inquired.

"Ah"—Rollo started patting the sofa and lifting the cushions on either side of it,—"contact lens. Once you lose the dratted things you can't see to find them again. Beats me why opticians or—what do you Americans call them?—ophthalmsomethingorother don't figure out—"

"No," Willa repeated, "what are you doing here?"

He rose and clapped his hands together. "Well, to cut a long story short, em—"

"No," Willa interrupted, "let's have the whole thing."

Rollo began rubbing his hands furiously together. "Ah . . . well . . . last April . . . hah! . . . joke . . . No, the thing is . . ."

"Go on." Willa adopted the tone of a village schoolteacher addressing a penitent five-year-old.

Terry chose this ill-timed moment to escape from Bugsy's grasp and scuttle towards Willa's foot. At the same time Pip, who had intermittently been observing all of this from the crack in the bedroom door, finally managed to catch Cub's attention and, while Willa's back was turned and Rollo commanded her attention, the lion keeper dashed from cupboard to bedroom, leaving her dress behind her.

"Well, you see, I took the room next door for the evening," Rollo started hesitantly, "and, not three minutes ago, I found the connecting door was unlocked. So I kind of wandered in here, kind of out of curiosity . . ."

He was finding it very hard to keep going—as hard as it was not to watch the tarantula approaching Willa's foot from the side of the sofa. His relief when Bugsy's hand snaked out and snatched it was palpable.

". . . and, to my absolute astonishment," Rollo went on, "you walked in and I . . . er . . . panicked."

"You took the room next door for the evening." Willa spelled out the words slowly and in a considered fashion, like a judge weighing evidence.

"Just wanted a bit of peace and quiet." Rollo pulled his shirt around his stomach protectively as he backed towards the bedroom. "Haven't been sleeping too well—the hyenas have been playing up a bit recently. So I—I do this frequently; well, when possible—rented a room, where I could take my tape recorder and listen to a little music. Do you like Purcell?"

By now he was standing guard in front of the connecting door. Willa indicated to him to step aside. She marched forward and flung it open.

There, four-footed on the bed, was a baby lamb. It looked up at Rollo, and Willa turned round to look at him, too. Her personnel director was transferring his weight from foot to foot and staring fixedly at the ceiling.

Willa turned her attention back to the bedroom. Cub, the lion keeper, scantily clad in black underwear, with Pip, the teenager from the mammal house, clinging on to her back, were both cowering behind a chest of drawers.

Willa smiled a knowing smile and looked back at the lanky, kinky, sexual athlete of an Englishman in his boxer shorts and black socks.

He looked round the room and began to whistle.

"Purcell," he explained.

CHAPTER
11

Willa glanced blankly at the screen of her computer. She found it impossible to concentrate due to an uncomfortable feeling in her stomach that matters were going to go from bad to worse. She had joined the others at last night's dinner in an understandable state of bewilderment. Of course, she had read about things like that before, but she'd never witnessed them with her own eyes. The Englishman was undeniably attractive, still, he had always seemed so . . . upright . . . so proper.

But she had no intention of mentioning anything she had seen to the three men guzzling large whiskies and being fawned over by the maitre d'. Not that anyone had even talked about the zoo; the subject had never been mentioned, as if it were the black sheep of the Octopus family. No, the distaste that Rod had for his son—something that had begun to become apparent in Atlanta—had been made more manifest by the fact that he virtually ignored him, addressing all his remarks to her or Neville. He seemed to have a debased view of his staff as well and, after a few drinks, began to quote Napoleon: "The surprising fact is not that each man has his price, but how low it is."

Neville, despite doubtless having heard this from his boss many times before, purred with laughter. And then the two of them reminisced about the way Rod had ignored the decisions of Senate committees, succeeded in changing FCC rulings to acquire TV stations, managed to take over newspaper chains with the promise of setting up independent boards of directors which he never convened, and generally bullied even the most senior members of his staff with the threat that he could pull the rug from under them whenever he liked.

"When one of my executives or editors gets too big for his boots and thinks it's him and not me who's running the station or the paper, what I do, Willa," he confided after a few more drinks, "is not sack him, but offer him the job of his dreams—they all want to be as rich and famous and powerful as me. And when they fail—and they always do, because they need me to back them up—and resign, it only costs me a million bucks or so, which is less than I would have had to have paid in redundancy. And they've learnt that without Rod McCain they're just another statistic looking for a job. Right, Neville?"

"Bloody right," Neville had agreed, his fawning deference undoubtedly accounting for his own longevity at Octopus.

Did she really want to work for a man like McCain? He appeared to have no other ambition than ambition, understandable in a young executive in his twenties but not a sixty-something-year-old who should be thinking about Florida and golf courses and grandchildren. His life seemed to consist of seeing off any potential rivals—even if it cost him and his shareholders dearly—and manipulating governments in as many countries as he could by tweaking them at both ends: influencing the governed with his commanding media presence and influencing the governors by reminding them of this power. It worked. There were few governments anywhere in the world that would dare prevent an acquisition by Rod McCain. Yet didn't they see that all he did was to debase standards? If he could double the profit of any asset—newspapers, television, zoos, anything—by halving its quality, he would do so without a second thought. People didn't matter much to Rod; not as much as power.

Willa glanced at her watch. Ten to seven. Vince said he had a surprise for her in the old llama cage. She shuddered at the thought as she switched off her computer.

The keepers had all received an officious memo from Vince McCain ordering them to report immediately after work that day to the zoo office and collect yet another set of new uniforms. After that, at seven o'clock precisely, they were to assemble at the old llama cage, where Vince had promised them a spectacular announcement.

Neither Chaucer's *Parlement of Fowles* nor Lewis Carroll's Caucus Race in *Alice in Wonderland* could match the sight of the crowd of miserable humans that grouped round the newly tented cage that evening. Their expressions may have been as dull as the overcast sky, but their costumes were a kaleidoscope of colours, as bright as they were humiliating.

Old Fred was garbed entirely in pink, dressed as a flamingo with webbed feet and a giant beak above his head. Sydney was a porcupine, the look of evil on his face as sharp as the bristles on his back. Bugsy was a giant bee with four proboscises, and balls wobbling from the antennae on his head that made him look more like a creature from another planet. Beside him Ant looked suitably morose as a turtle, as much because of the weight of the giant shell on his back as the absurdity of the outfit.

Little Reggie was zipped into a grey one-piece sea lion outfit, with flippers so closely sewn together that it made it virtually impossible for him to walk; he could only wobble. Sky towered over him, a collation of scarab green and azure blue, her peacock outfit featuring an overflowing fan that spread across her back. Hugh Primates filled his gorilla outfit, but he filled it with sorrow.

Cub, it had to be said, looked extremely sexy, her body-clinging black jaguar suit, tights, and boots reminding people of Michelle Pfeiffer as Catwoman in *Batman Returns*—it was the image that Vince had in mind. Pip looked cuddly and fetching as a little lemur with her tail tucked under her arm. But Gerry, his giraffe neck and head sticking a full seven feet into the air above him, was the picture of mottled discontent. Among other sorry humans were a panda, a buffalo, and, worst of all, poor Jenni garbed as a pink octopus—the hideous symbol of a theme park.

In the middle of this miserable assembly stood Rollo Lee, dressed as a kangaroo with his head under his arm and a murderous expression on his face.

Vince, natty as ever in a loose-fitting fawn Armani suit and charcoal shirt buttoned to the neck with no tie, was wholly oblivious to the invisible rays of sheer hatred that were targeted at him from every direction.

"The good news is that the customer pull-through is way up and the feedback has been sensational. I want to personally thank you one and all for your terrific enthusiasm vis-à-vis our latest new innovative initiative. You look great."

He seemed to think he was Henry V addressing his troops on the eve of Agincourt, little realising that he was getting the unspoken response the king might have received had he been addressing the French army instead of the British one.

"You're no longer smelly, run-of-the-mill animal handlers," he went blithely on, "you are hands-on-zoo-visitation-enhancement facilitators. Now remember, this is *your* zoo."

"No it's not," Sydney whispered to Pip. But Vince didn't hear.

"It's your party"—Vince was intoxicated by his own adrenaline—"and you have to make those bozos feel like they're guests of honour. So kiss a little ass and get those wallets out there in the clean fresh air where they belong."

"What does he mean?" Reggie's all-encompassing grey sea lion head made it difficult for him to look up at Sky.

And she had difficulty bending down, so constricted was she by her outsize wand of peacock feathers. "I think he wants us to get the visitors to spend more money," she suggested.

Vince had now moved in front of a tassel hanging from the vast sheet that was covering the cage. An announcement was imminent.

"Now the really important news, the big one." He could hardly restrain himself in his excitement. "The coup de zoo! I challenge you, fellow conversationalists, to guess what is behind the screen."

The weight of the long neck above his head had made Gerry more impatient for this to end than anyone else. "Is it giraffes tap-dancing?" he asked exasperatedly.

"No," said Vince, while taking the idea on board, it might prove quite an attraction, he decided. "Write that down," he ordered Di. But the zoo secretary made no effort to open her notebook.

Hugh—Primates by nickname and primate now in costume—had been studying the large pantechnicon with European plates that had brought this new monstrosity to the zoo. "Is it a machine for firing keepers?" he inquired in a deliberately double-edged way.

189

"Firing keepers? You mean into nets?" Vince was incapable of absorbing irony. "Nice try, but wrong."

"Is it a supermarket with all the assistants dressed as complete idiots?" There was little doubt where the arachnoid Bugsy got the inspiration for his question from.

"Way off." Vince was delighted to prove the know-all wrong.

Sydney, even deeper in depression than when he had heard Rollo's five shots, and wishing he could smash the quills on his back into Vince's smug face, cleared his throat so that all could hear his thoughts. "Is it a place where people can go when they want to commit suicide?"

"No! You lose!" Vince, wholly impervious to the significance of the remark, was, once again, a winner. "It's only the biggest draw in the entire zoo spectrum."

A roll of drums and a fanfare of music blared out of the zoo's public-address system and, in keeping with this circuslike atmosphere, Vince, in his role as ringmaster-cum-illusionist, tugged the tassel. As the white sheets hiding the contents of the cage fell to the ground, the keepers could not disguise their curiosity. They stepped forward to see what new indignity could be nesting behind the low bushes of this pleasingly grassy enclosure. And there, to their utter amazement, it was.

Ailuropoda melanoleuca. Three hundred pounds of one of the rarest and most endangered species in the world. The giant panda. Found only in the forests of south-central China at an altitude of more than eight thousand feet. And in a very few zoos around the world which desperately tried to mate the ones in captivity to ensure the survival of the species. There were none in England. This, indeed, was the biggest draw any zoo could possess.

The remarkable creature, the black patches surrounding its eyes making it look sempiternally mournful, was duly sitting on a bamboo tree, using its forefeet to wrench off shoots and carry them to its mouth. Most of the keepers knew that the animal had to eat all day—or, in its natural habitat, from twilight to dawn—to feed itself sufficiently on its chosen diet. It took no notice of them as it continued to chew bamboo.

"A panda?" Hugh couldn't believe it.

"That's incredible." Gerry was in awe.

Sydney glanced again at the truck. "How did you get it?" he asked suspiciously.

"It wasn't easy." Vince had known he was going to impress them and relished his triumphant trump card.

"It's beautiful," he said as he opened the cage door and made his way to the munching animal.

"Don't go in there. Stop. They're dangerous. It'll kill you. Listen to us. Get the guns. They rip you to pieces. Get back. The blowpipe, quick. Stop, for God's sake."

The keepers tried to keep pace with Vince as they ran along either side of the cage. Sydney, followed by Hugh and Gerry, boldly followed him in, but the giraffe costume caused the ungulate keeper to topple over, then bring down the other two with him in a sprawling mess on the ground.

When they looked up it was to see a grinning Vince sitting on the panda's neck going rhythmically up and down as the great creature continued to chew bamboo.

"You diabolical bastard," screamed Sydney.

"Pity it wasn't a real one." From the right side of the cage Rollo had realised at the same time that they were dealing with a working model, albeit an incredibly lifelike one.

"You can't put an animatronic animal in a zoo." Bugsy, on the opposite side of the cage, waved his insect feet in agitation.

"Why not?" Vince said with a smile.

"It's not real," Reggie stuttered.

Vince held out his hands like a used car salesman. "So what? It fooled you and your keepers."

"You . . . you . . ." Pip, the little lemur, couldn't get out her words for anger. "You . . . can't do this."

"Why not?" Vince repeated. "What's the problem?"

"It's a model!" Sydney exploded.

"So what?" Vince was all smiles. "It gave you all a thrill. Look, thousands of people from all round the world who have never seen a panda before in their miserable lives are going to come here and have the experience of a lifetime."

"Are you going to say it's not real?" asked Reggie.

"What? And spoil the whole experience?" Vince pretended to be insulted.

"But that's dishonest." The feline Cub, hands on hips, spoke for all the keepers, who echoed their agreement.

"I don't believe this." Vince climbed off the panda's neck and came forward to address them. "You want to take this incredible thrill away from people who've paid good money to see it? *That's* dishonest."

"Why have a panda at all? Why not just say it's inside sleeping?" The irony was coming from the insect.

Vince spun towards Bugsy and pointed an accusing finger. "Who's being dishonest now? Because, my idiot friend, that won't give them a thrill."

"But it's not a *real* thrill," Sydney tried to point out to him. "It's artificial."

"Having pandas in England is artificial," Vince retorted with venom. "What do you want me to do? Put everyone on a plane and fly them to Africa?"

The keepers looked at one another in bewilderment. "To Africa?" they repeated.

It was left to Bugsy to explain to their ignoramus director. "They come from China."

"Not this baby," Vince shot back. "I don't want some cheap Chinese panda here. This panda was handmade in Belgium. I accept nothing but the best. This is quality."

His remarks were greeted by a wall of silence. Vince ripped off one of his Gucci loafers in anger and brandished them. "Look at my shoes. Four hundred dollars. That's quality. Quality. You may even make enough money to appreciate it one day—though I doubt it."

The carnival of animals had by now turned their backs on him and were disappearing into the dusk.

"All right, I'll break his neck," the kangaroo confided to the lemur, none too quietly.

"What's the matter with you?" Vince shouted at his departing staff. "Are you the Britons who built Hadrian's Wall? I cannot stand all this negativity."

He turned back to his panda, who was contentedly consuming more bamboo.

However, just outside the bars, he could see Willa, standing there with her arms folded. She looked less than content.

CHAPTER
12

"What does it take to get appreciated round here? This is a hit zoo, and it's all thanks to me."

Vince strode angrily back to the office along the path by the gorilla enclosure, with Willa struggling to keep up with him. She wished she wasn't wearing her Jimmy Choo high heels.

"Vince, just listen," she pleaded, slightly out of breath. "When people come here, they can feel their connection with nature—where they came from, what they're still part of. You don't get that from electric pandas."

Vince stopped, swung round, and glared at her. Had she joined the enemy?

"And you don't get it from billboards, either." She indicated the vast green Gordon's Gin sign behind her bearing the slogan VISIT GORDON THE GORILLA. "It's madness: the gorilla's name is not Gordon. It's Jambo."

"But the punters don't know that." Vince was taken aback by her naivety. "Look, we're giving them what they want."

Willa refused to be swept aside by his phony logic. "But what about the quality of their experience?"

Vince moved hastily on, anxious not to get into a row with her. "Quality has never worked for Rod," he said.

"That's right." She caught up with him again. "Everything he touches gets tackier."

Vince stopped again, turned on his heel, and regarded her patronisingly. "That's the price of success."

"Vince." she had his attention and she did not intend to let this opportunity slip. "I know you didn't major in sensitivity, but if I can share something with you, maybe you'll understand where I'm coming from—"

"Two Trees, Georgia, isn't it?" he interrupted, happy to remind her that she was a small-town girl.

Willa ignored him. "I had an extraordinary experience today. I . . ."

Again she was finding it very hard to articulate what had happened, especially to Vince.

"What sort of experience?" His voice was curt and impatient.

Although it had been an overcast day with no evening sun, Jambo was sitting as usual on his familiar mound, barely moving but undoubtedly observing them.

Willa pointed to the gorilla. "With him!"

"With him?" Vince's voice moved up a register into a high-pitched sneer.

Willa composed her features to be as serious as possible. "Yes, a sort of contact."

Vince could hardly believe his ears. He stared uncomprehendingly at her, as if she'd gone completely insane. "What?"

She read his expression only too well. "You don't know what I'm talking about, do you?"

"I think I do." Nobody ever got the better of Vince McCain. "I know *exactly* what you're talking about. You've gone cold on me; I no longer turn you on. But you've got the hots for a gorilla."

He indicated the animal derisively. Jambo remained motionless.

Willa hated this. She wanted to put the record straight. "No, Vince, it's much more than that. I—"

His ears were closed to her entreaties. "Great! So that big ape is more attractive than I am, right?"

"You said it, I didn't." She wasn't prepared to let him mock her.

"Well, let me just ask you something." Vince was on a roll. "How much does he earn? Just tell me that, will you? How much does Mr. Gorilla take home after tax every week, eh? Come on, impress me." He moved closer to her and formed a circle with his fingers which he thrust in front of her face. "I'll tell you. Zero. Zip. Zilch."

Willa backed away. "Are you serious?"

"Are you?" he countered. "Do you know what I'm worth? Do you? Do you know what I've made so far since I've been at this stinking zoo? One point two million dollars." He turned pointedly to Jambo and screamed the sum at him. "One point two million bucks."

"What are you talking about?" Willa was genuinely mystified.

"You don't believe me? I've made nearly eight hundred thousand dollars in sponsorship deals, in cash. Plus consultancy fees. Plus commission on animal futures. Have you any idea how much rhinoceros horn is worth?"

"You've been stealing?" Willa wasn't at all sure whether he was just lying to impress her; it wouldn't have been the first time.

" 'Stealing'?" The word seemed to come as a surprise to Vince.

"Stealing." Her tone was solemn and accusatory.

Vince shook his head in dismay. "No matter what I do, no matter what I wear, I never impress you. You're just like my father."

"You stole," she repeated.

"All right, I stole," he acknowledged. "So what? How do you think the big players get so rich? By playing by the rules? You know what Balzac wrote: 'Behind every great fortune lies a crime.' "

"You've never read any Balzac," she snapped back disdainfully.

"You're wrong. It's in *The Godfather*. First page." Nobody got the better of Vince. "So don't start lecturing *me* on morals when *you're* trying to figure out what you're going to wear for your next hot date with hair boy." Vince gave the gorilla the finger, not for the first time. One day he'd get that boneheaded primate.

Willa was appalled. "This is going to close the zoo, Vince."

"So what? Screw the zoo. You and me, we make two million and move on. The place closes—what a shame. The Japs buy it and, 'Fore!' " He swung an imaginary golf club in the manner of Johnny Carson leading into the first commercial on the old *Tonight Show*.

For the first time Willa could see him for what he was: a pathetic con man; the failed son of morally moribund father. She shook her head. "I never realised just how far down the food chain you come, Vince. Do you know what you are? You're pronoid."

"Pronoid?"

"Let me explain the word to you. You've heard of 'paranoid,' right? It means you think that everybody's out to get you. Well, 'pronoid' is precisely the opposite. It means that, contrary to all evidence, you think that everyone you meet likes and admires you. Your perception of life is that it is one long benefit dinner where everyone cheers you on and wants you to win everything. This is an irrational delusion, wholly at odds with the facts. You think you're the prince, Vince. Well, you're not. Are you listening to me, your highness? Let me tell you something: you're going to put every last cent back in the zoo account by ten o'clock tomorrow morning."

"Or what?" he countered defensively.

Willa adopted a mock Southern accent as she walked past him. "Or I'm going to call your daddy and tell on you."

And she was gone.

He knew that she meant it.

CHAPTER
13

When the Americans had first arrived at the zoo, Willa hadn't moved into the director's office. It was small and cramped, and now it was filled with the mass of marketing paraphernalia that Vince had accumulated. She had been genuine in her desire for more open consultation with the keepers and, anticipating a series of seminars, had installed herself in the adjoining boardroom. In fact, due to the warmth of that summer, what meetings had taken place had been held outside, usually on the canteen terrace.

But Willa welcomed the airy space of the room and had put her desk, along with a mainframe computer bounded by files on either side, in a position where she could overlook the lawns and the old elm tree, which still wore its unwelcome burden of a vast inflatable rubber octopus. In her high-backed leather chair she could easily turn back into the room and address whoever had come to see her.

Returning from that fateful encounter with Vince, she flung open the door in white-hot anger and slammed it behind her with equal vehemence. What was she going to do?

Too much had happened too quickly. She felt desperately alone, and she needed help and consolation and guidance. She picked up the phone to ring her analyst in Atlanta but then plunged the receiver down. How could he help? This wasn't a psychological problem that related to childhood— not hers, anyway; this was a fully blown crisis in which she needed all the courage she could muster. How could Vince do this to her? It was one thing to be a congenital idiot who worshipped at the feet of the great god Marketing; it was another to be an out-and-out criminal.

She fell into her chair and swivelled round towards the open window. Through it came the smells and sounds of a summer evening, and in the distance she could hear the grunts and hoots of the mountain gorillas as they played their bedtime games.

It was more than she could bear. She folded her arms on her desk, put her brow upon them, and let loose all the pent-up anger and sorrow in an outburst of sobbing that she hadn't allowed herself since she was a schoolgirl. At the very moment when some meaning had begun to enter her life, it had been cruelly whipped away from her.

And at that very moment there came a knock on the door. She couldn't hear it: she was crying too copiously. Nor did she hear it the second time. Nor did she hear the door ease slowly open.

"Hello."

She was aware of someone in the office, but she didn't care.

"I was just checking about our dinner date tonight," came the tentative inquiry.

Willa raised her head from the desk but didn't turn. She just closed her eyes and shook her tresses in a gesture of despair. At that moment she could neither think straight nor communicate.

"Fine, fine." The attempt by the English voice to sound carefree sounded more than a little artificial. "Let's leave it."

Rollo Lee decided that a strategic exit might be the order of the day. Maybe he had got her message terribly muddled. Then he realised: of course! Why hadn't he thought of it— the unfortunate incident at the Marwood Arms. She must be waiting for an explanation. He approached her chair with caution.

"Look, perhaps I should explain why I didn't have any trousers on the other night."

She didn't turn, but merely shook her head. "It doesn't matter" was all she said.

"Right." Rollo rubbed his hands together. Something was troubling her, he knew that. "I suppose you were wondering why the girls didn't have any kit on either."

"No!" she cried, still not turning.

"There is a perfectly simple explanation," he persisted. "What was it they used to say? 'Strange but true.' "

"No, no." Her head went down on the desk again and he could see she was completely distraught.

"Look, I'm sorry." Rollo didn't know what to do with his hands, whether to try and comfort her or to merely extend them in apology. "I don't know what I've done to offend you."

"It's not you." At last she turned round to face him, her cheeks bearing their watery burden.

"Oh, good." He took a step back, relieved to be let off.

She looked at him. He had put on his best suit for dinner and was standing like a nervous sophomore on his first date. Was this the trick that pulled all these women? He seemed unfathomable. On an impulse she decided to tell him the truth. She had to tell someone.

"It's not you. It's Vince. He's been stealing from the zoo. Ever since we came here. Sponsorship money, animal futures, consultancy fees, rhino horn—you name it, he took it."

"How?" asked Rollo.

"Damned if I know. All I know is I love this zoo, Rollo. And if McCain finds out—and he will—he's going to close the place down."

Rollo thought for a moment, took off his jacket, and, changing his body language completely, authoritatively pulled up a chair beside her and switched on the computer.

"Do you think I don't love it, too?" he said as he punched the relevant keys to call up the accounts documents. "It's pretty well the first home I've had since my parents sent me to boarding school at the age of eight."

The confession surprised her, and he even surprised himself with it. But it was true.

"Right." He loosened his tie and drummed his fingers on the desk. "Let's see how obvious the stealing is to Atlanta. First we have to check if the bank reconciliation figures and the cash flow tie up."

He reached to the right and took a ledger from the shelf.

Willa got up and moved behind him, impressed. "How do you know about all this?" she asked.

"Well, I was in the police for twenty years." He could feel the warmth of her admiration. "And it's not just hitting people on the heads with truncheons."

She wiped her face with her hand and managed a grin.

He put the book back on the shelf and tapped further into the computer. "Damn. He's got to have an account that no one else can access. Do you remember Nick Leeson, that Singapore trader who brought down Barings?"

"Vaguely."

"Not a very impressive criminal. He wanted to be caught. The bank had their eyes closed. Ah, here we are . . . Our friend Vince has got a file all of his own, and I shall be very surprised if it doesn't contain a bank account none of us has ever heard of."

Willa was standing beside him now. "But it's password-protected."

"Of course it is," said Rollo confidently. "But not for long. Let's try . . . 'Braves,' is it? They usually choose a sports team. No. Right. Mother's name?"

"Mary," said Willa eagerly.

He typed it in. "Mary. No. Maybe a few animals: elephant, tiger, gorilla. No. I doubt if he's heard of any others."

"Panda," screamed Willa. "Try Panda."

Rollo tried it. "Yes. Very good. Here we are. It's pretty obvious if you know what to look for. He's using one of the old favourites. The account's in the name of the Marwood Zoom Lens Company."

"I don't follow," she said.

"Simple. He gets them to make out cheques to Marwood Zoo and then adds on the other words later. So, let's just try and reconcile . . ."

His right hand shot out for the ledger but instead landed plumb on Willa's left breast.

"Oh, I do apologise."

She held it where it was. "Don't" was all she said.

He rose slowly from his chair, and as he did so her lips came down to meet his.

He knew he was dreaming, and his first instinct was to will himself to remain asleep. Never in his life had he experienced such a sensation. The tender cushion of her mouth transported him into some sublime territory he had long ago given up any hope of ever entering. It was as if all her femininity and passion were channelled into this luxuriant embrace and feeding themselves into his receptive system.

He was standing now, and he opened his eyes. She was there, her sapphire eyes gazing into his with unflinching ardour.

To ask why would be to destroy the moment, he knew. He grabbed hold of her, and her body became weightless and compliant in his arms. And then he kissed her, aware that he needed to restrain the relentlessness of his desire as all the fire and testosterone built up over his hermit years seized his system like an unbidden fever.

Her tongue slipped into his mouth, a silken serpent, the temptation of Eve. To his embarrassment, he got an erection. There was no hiding it, so firmly were they entwined as it dug into her stomach.

"Now!" she cried, and began—-with some expertise he couldn't help noting—to pull his shirt out of his trousers while still embracing him with mounting ferocity.

He knew that he must match like with like, and reciprocated, pulling up her cashmere sweater to uncover her breasts. Never in his life had he seen a purer definition of the word "perfection."

"Do what I tell you," she instructed him as her hand dropped to his flies.

She manoeuvred him round and, hoisting herself up, lay on her back on the boardroom table, then drew his eager body down on top of her.

"Now," she repeated as he heard the sound of her unzipping her slacks, "Now, now, now!"

"All right, all right. I'll put it back."

Neither of them heard the words, so heavily were they breathing and so desperately were they pulling at each other's clothing.

"I'll put it all back. Every damn dollar. Every devalued pound."

Vince McCain, an oversized suitcase brimming with paper money in his arms, had had to back into the room in order to navigate his way through the door.

"I wasn't serious. You knew that. I just sometimes get overcome by these inexplicable . . . It's hereditary."

He staggered across to the sofa by the office safe and put down his burden, then pirouetted round and spreading his arms wide.

"There it is. Every last dime accounted for . . . What the hell!"

Vince took an involuntary step back as he was confronted with the unmistakable six foot five inches of the personnel director spread across the boardroom table with an indistinguishable female shape beneath him.

The sheer effrontery of this sex maniac literally took the wind out of his system, and he sat down on the sofa by his money to try and recover his breath. "Rollo, are you at it again? In the Marwood boardroom—Miss Weston's office—hallowed ground."

He stood up and approached the elongated figure, who was struggling to put his clothes back in some sort of order. "I'm going to call the zoo vet and get you fixed," ranted Vince. "Get out of here, and get that bimbo out of here."

The words had hardly left his lips when he realised to his horror who the bimbo was. "Oh my God! Not *you*! Not with Mr. Disgusting. You have got to be joking."

Willa sat up and with as much dignity as she could muster pulled her jersey down over her breasts.

"Vince . . ." she began.

But Vince was showing all the signs of a panic attack as he held his chest with one hand and staggered around the room. "This does not compute. Did he drug you? Do you owe him money? Is it a dare?"

She zipped up her trousers and tried to regain her composure. "He excites me, Vince."

Rollo had hastily tried to dress and was standing beside the table thinking he had managed to reassemble his clothing in a respectable shape, but in fact his shirt was hanging out below his jacket at both the front and back.

Vince stared at this lanky, officious idiot. "I must be going mad," he wailed.

Willa swung her legs down from the table. "Ask any of the girls," she suggested as a form of justification.

"What?" Rollo was mystified by her remark, but given the circumstances they found themselves in, he was not about to ask her to amplify it.

"Look at his clothes." Vince laughed, indicating a suit that would not be allowed through the doors of Emporio Armani. "You must be desperate."

"Don't speak to her like that." Rollo took a step towards him. This cad could chuck all the insults he liked at him, but Rollo would be damned if he'd let him get away with insulting a lady.

"Oh, engaged, are we?" Vince adopted a mocking, contrite tone. "I must say you broke up with that sheep pretty quick." Delighted with his own wit, he jumped up on the sofa beside the stolen money. "Who's the lucky girl next week? The warthog?" His hand went dramatically to his brow. "The level of morality in this place—"

Willa broke in to indicate the not forgotten gains at his feet. "Speaking of morality, Vince . . ."

He jumped down from the sofa with alacrity. "I'm putting it back! All of it," he said, adding by way of explanation to Rollo, "I'm repaying a corporate loan."

Rollo Lee did what he had been wanting to do ever since the day Vince had arrived at the zoo, and laughed derisively in his face.

Vince had no time to retaliate. He grabbed hold of the bag and placed it in front of the safe. He deftly punched in the combination numbers and, with the air of a man who had done this many times before, spun the handle to open the door. And then commenced to shovel currency from assorted sources—French francs, deutsche marks, yen, lire, pounds, and dollars, Canadian, Australian, and American—out of the suitcase and into the safe.

As he did so he kept up a nonstop diatribe to Willa about her inexplicable escapade. "Tell me, what *is* the attraction? I mean, just take a look at him. I could even understand the gorilla compared to that . . . but two-timing me with the Creature from the Black Lagoon . . ."

"I'm not even *one*-timing you, Vince," she corrected him curtly.

Willa and Rollo were not the only audience for Vince's invective. Unobserved by any of the three of them, they had quietly been joined by a bee, a sea lion, and a lemur, who stood solemnly at the open door.

"What's he got that I haven't got?" Vince continued.

"He's sexy," Willa snapped back. "He tells the truth. He doesn't steal. And he likes animals."

"He doesn't just *like* them"—Vince was on his feet in anger—"he fu—"

At this point he became aware of the group of animals who had edged inside the door.

"He f-finds them very attractive," Vince hastily amended his vocabulary, at the same time directing his ire at the intruders. "What the hell are you doing here? Can't you see we're in the middle of a board meeting?"

Adrian "Bugsy" Malone, still attired as the black and yellow bee he had become at the panda cage—rather like that man in Kafka who becomes an insect, he had told his assembled and wholly disinterested colleagues—stepped forward and prepared to hold forth. "We have been delegated by an emergency meeting of the Keepers' Committee to ask you—"

"What emergency?" Willa was genuinely perplexed.

The sea lion shuffled forward and pointed to Vince. "Last night Rod McCain told him that if we aren't making twenty percent by the end of next month he's going to turn us into a golf course. That's an emergency."

Willa glared at Vince, who shook his head with a look of sheepish denial.

"Next *month*?" she queried.

Vince shrugged his shoulders. "No he didn't. The man's a liar. Would you believe anyone dressed like that?"

Bugsy looked down at his absurd fuzzy bee suit, four long proboscises swinging demeaningly in front of him. "If I may remind you, Mr. McCain, this apparel was your idea. Would anyone believe a man who dressed his staff in these circus outfits?" He indicated the sea lion and the lemur. "Not only was I in the closet of the Marwood Arms listening to you and your charming pater, but we have prima facie evidence of our conversation thanks to the Revox A 77."

The lemur waved a large reel of tape she was carrying in her paw.

Vince was incredulous. "Wait a minute. You were in the closet at the Marwood Arms?"

Bugsy pointed his proboscises at Rollo. "He was with me."

"I can vouch for that." Willa stepped forward.

"Were you porking in there as well? I mean, how long have you two been at it?" Vince adopted his prosecuting counsel mode. "The closet, the boardroom—how about the kangaroo enclosure on the next bank holiday. Should improve the customer pull-through."

"We don't have any kangaroos—not real ones," Rollo remarked pointedly. "And I think you owe this lady an apology."

"Belt up, big boy," Vince snarled back. "You're fired. I want your cage cleared by nine o'clock tomorrow morning."

"You're not in a position to fire anybody"—Willa indicated his bag of loot—"and you never were. Why didn't you tell me your father was about to close down the zoo?"

"Because you were too busy with Don Giovanni," Vince shot back. "I was waiting for you to come up for air."

Willa ignored the insult. She turned to the keepers. "Look, I think things are going to be all right. I think we *are* making twenty percent."

"We are?" Pip and Reggie clung to each other in relief and exhilaration.

She had an instinct that to let word of Vince's stealing get out would ultimately be detrimental to the zoo. "Yes, we discovered an accounting error. So—"

"Good." She was saved from any further invented explanation by the voluble Bugsy. "But I'd still like to make three points."

Willa held up a hand to restrain him. Time was not on their side. She needed to get the money back in the safe and, more important, to get Rollo back on the computer to empty the Panda account back into the system before anybody in Atlanta found out. If they hadn't already.

"First," said Bugsy, undeterred, "this zoo provides a valuable amenity in this catchment area . . ."

CHAPTER
14

But, unfortunately, they had already—had accessed the Panda file. So Rod McCain, who had only dropped in to see his son at Marwood Zoo because it had been a marginal detour on his route to Dover, where he was about to buy the ships of a defunct ferry company (which had been put out of business by the Channel Tunnel) and convert them into cruise liners for use in the Caribbean, decided to drop in on him again.

And the large grey Octopus Mercedes, with Neville in his familiar broad-brimmed Australian hat at the wheel, was silently snaking through the Kent country lanes heading back for the zoo.

When the fax had arrived from the chief accountant in Georgia that there were irregularities in the zoo accounts, it had come as little surprise to Rod. He had known his son would rip him off as soon as he was out of his sight; the only surprise was that he had done it so quickly. And ineptly.

"I wouldn't have minded if the little shit had worked out a decent cover-up, but he's too pathetic to manage even that," he mumbled from behind the edition of the *International Herald Tribune* he was reading—or rather, checking, for the all-important numbers in the NYSE listings. Octopus was down two cents. That always put him in a bad mood.

"He couldn't manage to piss straight at the porcelain without his nanny holding his pecker." Neville was always happy for any opportunity to dump on Vince, and there were many metaphors in his Australian vocabulary to help him express his distaste.

"The stupid little fart," said Rod. "Didn't he realise he could go to court and walk away with the income of half of my estate—that'll be about fifteen billion by the time they freeze me. Instead he's going to court on a major fraud charge and he won't see a dime."

"You're going to press charges, Rod?" Neville's voice fell. "You don't want me to just rough him up a little?"

McCain lowered his paper. "I warned him last time that if he ever did it again, especially using my signature, he'd end up inside—and, as you know, Neville, I'm a man of my word."

"True," his sidekick admiringly acknowledged.

"Frank said he must have a stash of cash somewhere, or some offshore bank account. Let's see what the limey cops can do."

"Probably tick him off and tell him not to do it again." Neville was upset at the loss of an opportunity for some thuggery.

McCain laughed, his gold tooth glinting. "Not if I have a word with the home secretary he fucking won't."

Neville joined in the laughter. "What are you going to do about the zoo?" he asked.

"Close it," came the terse reply.

"There could be demonstrations, boss."

"You know our system, Neville. We never tell the work-force when we're going to close down a plant. We do it overnight."

"What about the animals?"

"Shoot them," said McCain in a matter-of-fact manner.

"Won't that get us some adverse publicity, Rod?" Neville was always a couple of steps behind his master: that was why he remained in the job.

"No problem. We get a tame vet to say some contagious virus had broken out. Dangerous to domestic animals in the neighborhood. The English care more for their pets than they do for their wives."

Oblivious—as were the others—to this impending arrival, Bugsy remained determined to get his points across.

"Any attempt to close it down would bring local opposition . . ."

"Do you think McCain worries about that?" Willa countered. "He doesn't even worry about *national* opposition. Or international opposition. He loves it."

". . . and very unfavourable publicity," Bugsy continued, as if she had never spoken.

"Listen to her," Rollo pleaded.

Vince was stomping round the room like a man with a bee in his brain. "Stow it, will you?" he yelled.

"Secondly . . ." Bugsy went on.

"I can't think!" screamed Vince, putting his hands to his ears.

"Please!" Willa implored.

". . . it takes at least eighteen months . . ."

"Be quiet!" insisted Rollo.

"Shut up!" Vince seemed about to resort to violence, but this did nothing to faze the insect keeper.

". . . to close down a zoo . . ."

212

Vince looked around him for a blunt instrument. This madman had to be culled. "My life is falling apart," he cried.

". . . as homes have to be found for . . ."

"He won't stop talking," Vince wailed to himself and to nobody in particular just as a cabinet on the wall caught his eye.

". . . all the animals."

"Bugsy!" Even the imperturbable Willa was becoming exasperated.

"Shut the fuck up!" cried Vince as he marched across to the object of his desire.

But he wouldn't. Not for Vince. Not for Willa. Not for Rollo. Not for any living person. "And thirdly . . . ," he began.

"Right!" Vince was unlocking a cabinet on the far wall opposite the window.

". . . this zoo is playing an absolutely vital role . . ."

"Please . . ." Rollo was virtually down on his knees.

". . . in both conservation and ecological education."

And then the most remarkable sound filled the boardroom, so remarkable that Vince and Willa stared at one another and then at Bugsy in amazement.

Silence.

Bugsy looked back at them uncomprehendingly. "I've finished" was all he said.

Willa took advantage of this lull in the unceasing storm of words to try and get her point across. "Bugsy, here's the problem," she began to explain quietly and carefully. "We all want to run this zoo properly, right? But—"

"That may mean that income may fall below twenty percent." He was off again.

"Listen to her!" Rollo ordered in his most stentorian voice.

"But what is so sacred about twenty percent?" The reedy whine of the autodidact probed like a dental instrument. "That's the question I tried to ask when he was in charge."

He turned round to look for Vince and found, to his considerable surprise, an old but what he knew to be a perfectly serviceable revolver pointing at his padded stomach.

"Shut up or I'll shoot," Vince warned with enough menace in his tone to make all of those present quite certain that he meant it.

"Careful!" Rollo had been in situations like this before, and knew that when tempers ran high the ratio of accidents rose in direct proportion.

Bugsy, however, seemed wholly unconcerned by the threat. "Oh! So this is the latest Harvard Business School management technique, is it?" he taunted Vince.

The American was in no mood for games. "I'm warning you."

"Or is it part of your policy of consultation?" The warning clearly had had no impact whatever.

Vince approached Bugsy like an old-fashioned gangster, the gun still levelled at his ample belly. "You'd rather talk than live, wouldn't you?" he suggested with extreme menace.

"Oh, you won't shoot me," the bee replied airily.

"Oh, won't I?" Vince's intonation left neither Willa nor Rollo in any doubt that he meant business.

"No, you won't." Bugsy seemed to think it was a party game.

"Why not?" demanded Vince chillingly.

"Because you've got the safety catch on."

Vince looked down at the revolver, and at the same time both Bugsy and Reggie dived for it, the former, being nearer, managing to whip it out of Vince's hand. But he was not going to give up without a fight, and the three men be-

214

came interlocked as they tried to wrestle the gun from one another.

As this bizarre scrum was beginning, the sleek grey Merc drew up outside the zoo administration block. Rod McCain emerged, ominous in the black overcoat he was wearing despite the benign evening weather. Neville remained at the wheel. He pressed the button to lower the electric window. "I'd like to come in there with you, Rod."

McCain adjusted his tinted glasses as he looked around. The place seemed deserted. "Nah. You do as we agreed. Listen, I don't want some greenhorn sergeant on duty. I want the top man, even if you have to get him from his home."

"Understood." Neville nodded obediently. "But you're sure you don't need some help to begin with?"

McCain started to move away from the car to the main entrance. "No. I'd like a little word with Vince on my own before the police take him away. Be quick, though. And get the number one man."

"Yes sir." Neville said, falling back into his servile mode. He gunned the powerful car and whipped up gravel in his wake.

Rod McCain had never been to Marwood Zoo before—merely to the hotel—and had never expected to come back to Tenterden again. He had read that Hitler had spent only one day in Paris, despite occupying the city for nearly five years. He had merely been driven to the Palais de Chaillot early one morning in 1940 where he could look across to the Eiffel Tower and down on the city. That had been enough. He had ordered both monuments, indeed all the monuments, to be blown up when the Germans were forced to evacuate the city in 1944. But his garrison commander, Dietrich von Cholitz, had disobeyed him. That's the sort of thing that happens, thought Rod as he marched through the hall, when you put the wrong man in the job. Now, if he'd had a tough Australian . . .

But his musings came to an abrupt conclusion when he threw open the door to the boardroom. The sight that assailed his eyes was not one that he'd expected, to say the least.

There was his son trying to get up from the floor, embroiled in a fight with a man dressed as a bee and another wearing some kind of seal costume with a little girl in a rodent outfit pulling at his leg. And beside them, there was Willa, looking equally dishevelled, next to some tall character with his shirt hanging out and his arm around her.

"What in God's name is going on here?" he bellowed.

The fight froze at the sound of this thunderbolt, and the participants looked across to the imposing figure at the door.

"Hi, Dad!" Vince brushed down his ruffled Armani suit as if nothing had happened. "Great to see you."

McCain ignored this greeting, his gaze fixing on the three keepers in animal costumes who were sheepishly rising to their feet.

"Get these freaks out of here!" He shouted the order to no one in particular but with the air of a man who expected to be obeyed.

Surprisingly, he wasn't entirely. Pip and Reggie beat an expedient retreat past him through the open door, but Adrian "Bugsy" Malone saw this as the God-sent chance he had been waiting for. His four proboscises dangling in front of him, he walked up to the owner, founder, and creator of Octopus Inc. in the expectation that the man at the top might be able to follow his reasoning where others, most notably his son, had failed.

"Ah, Mr. McCain," he began quite nervelessly. "I'd like to take this opportunity to make three points about the zoo."

216

His face could have been no more than two feet away from the media mogul, who spat back with utter disdain: "Go away!"

But Bugsy didn't. It was not in his nature. He was determined to get his message across. "First, it provides an important amenity . . ."

However, that was as far as he got or was likely to get. He doubled over in extreme pain, McCain's granite fist having caught him in the centre of the stomach with a lethal punch which was as powerful as it was low.

The sad bee stumbled and fell breathlessly to the floor while the others looked on in helpless shock.

McCain addressed his attention to his son, who was beginning to look more than a little apprehensive. He knew the moods that overtook his father.

"You've been stealing from me," barked McCain.

"That's not so," Vince began, indicating Willa and Rollo. "I have witnesses . . ."

But Rod McCain had no time for explanations. "Neville's fetching the police," he said, smiling.

"The police?" Vince felt his body go cold and his legs weaken.

"Remember what I said last time when you forged my signature." McCain was in no mood for mercy; that anyone, even his own son, should have the temerity to fake something that so intimately belonged to him was, in his eyes, an act of high treason.

"But Dad, I haven't stolen," Vince pleaded.

By this time Willa and Rollo were looking concernedly at the open safe with the suitcase half-full of banknotes beneath it.

"My God," McCain exploded as he, too, saw it. "I've caught you red-handed!"

"Dad, you don't understand"—Vince's laugh was piping and artificial and desperate—"I was putting the money back. That's the reverse of stealing."

He looked to Rollo and Willa, as if for confirmation of this fact.

"Putting it back?" Rod McCain sneered at his son. "I see your suitcase two-thirds full of cash in front of the office safe, with the rest about to be shovelled into it—and it looks to me that you're moving into the high zeroes there—and you expect me to believe that you were putting it back! It's bad enough that you're ripping off the company, but to treat me as some kind of idiot is to add insult to perjury."

"He was, Mr. McCain," Willa interceded, but the boss of Octopus Inc. had already made his mind undeviatingly up. He knew Vince, he knew his past history, and he knew the evidence of his own eyes.

He pointed menacingly at his son. "You're going to jail."

"Oh no, Dad. Please no!" Vince was reduced to rubble; the striding, confident entrepreneur who had gulled so many innocent investors and sponsors into parting with their money on the basis of his vaulting vision of the zoo now looked like a schoolboy who had been caught smoking behind the bicycle shed.

"Yes, you are." McCain meant it.

"Dad, you can't do this to me. I'm your son."

"They'll probably take that into account—and double the sentence." Rod laughed. "And I'm going to close this dump as well."

Vince began to twist his body into an inhuman shape like a drawing by Daumier and let loose a series of yelps and howls, sounding like a hound that had been shut out of his master's house.

Willa's mind had been racing at triple speed during this exchange, intent on saving not Vince but her beloved zoo.

She approached McCain boldly, exuding her assured sexuality. "Rod, you can't close this place. It's precious."

"It's worth precious little to me, darling. It's a mere blip on the UK balance sheet, and one that fails to give us a twenty percent yield. You'll be okay, Willa. I bought back WOCT for two-thirds of what I sold it for. Certainly pissed off Rupert, but I knew the FCC would never let him keep the stations. You can run them now. You've got your old job back."

"I never had it." She looked him in the eye. "And I don't want it. I want to run this place. It matters."

"Not to me."

"Can't you see?" She gestured to the suitcase by the safe. "No money has left the zoo. It's solvent and it's making more than twenty percent."

"We've located the Panda account as well—" Rollo began, but McCain cut him off dismissively.

"Shut up, you."

"I just wanted to substantiate Miss Weston's fig—"

"I said shut up," snarled McCain. "Who the hell are you, anyway?"

"He's Rollo Lee," Willa explained eagerly.

McCain eyed the six-foot-five Englishman with the loose shirttails and looked him up and down. "Lee. Lee's a hard-nosed little Chinese bastard. This man's a fraud, Willa. The police will deal with him as well."

"I can vouch for him, Rod. Just as I can vouch for this zoo. We will make money. And the publicity attendant on closing down a place that is vital for your ecological image in England would be disastrous."

Rod McCain thought quickly; he didn't want any goddam demonstrations. "Okay. You've got twelve months' remission," he lied, and then turned his attention to Vince. "Unlike you, you little shit."

His eyes feel on the hunched back of his son, still shaking with despair. But, always the author of the unexpected, Vince twirled round and confronted his father with the revolver that had been the centre of the earlier struggle. Deliberately he clicked off the safety catch.

"Promise me you won't have me arrested or I'll kill you." His voice was a touch unstable, as was his mind.

McCain didn't move a muscle. "You won't shoot me."

"I will too. Oh yes . . ." Vince was growing in confidence; the possession of a weapon made him master once more.

"Vince!" It was Rollo who moved towards him. He sensed that disaster was in the air.

"Get back!" Vince warned, temporarily directing the revolver at him.

"Go on, then." McCain moved threateningly towards his son. "Go on and pull the trigger."

Faced with his father, Vince McCain was caught in an intractable dilemma. If he killed him, with witnesses present—hostile witnesses, he noted, as Reggie and Pip peeped back round the door—he would almost certainly go to prison for life or even be hanged or whatever it was they did to people who committed patricide in this godforsaken part of England. If he didn't get an amnesty out of him, he was going to go inside anyway for larceny and, considering the sum involved, that would be a stiff sentence, too. He knew that Big Rod was reading his mind precisely.

"See? You haven't got the guts to shoot your own father," McCain taunted him. "You're no son of mine."

Vince's hand began to tremble. Okay, so his father knew he would never kill him. But how about if he killed himself? How would that look in the newspapers if the great Rod McCain had pressured his own son into suicide? He brought the gun up and rested it against his temple.

"Yes, do it." Rod snarled with contempt. "Give us all a good laugh, you wuss."

"I'm not a wuss," Vince cried.

"Wuss, wuss, wuss," continued McCain, metaphorically trampling all over him as he had for his entire life.

"I hate you," yelled Vince, casting the revolver down to the floor. It skidded across the polished surface and was fielded by Bugsy, who was still on his knees as a result of McCain's stomach punch.

Vince now joined Bugsy on the floor, lying flat on his back like a truculent three-year-old and screaming: "Not prison. Not prison."

"Give it to me." Rod McCain nodded towards the weapon at the end of Bugsy's upper right proboscis.

"Certainly," replied the insect keeper. "And may I just say on behalf of all the other keepers how delighted we are that you have decided to keep the zoo open."

As he was delivering this paean of praise, he wobbled forward—still unsteady as he recovered from the blow to his gut—with the gun in his padded pincer to give it to McCain.

However, accidentally, it went off.

The neat red hole in the centre of the tycoon's forehead looked as if it had been put there by an expert marksman. A Siberian silence descended on the room.

"You're fired," growled McCain as he slumped to the floor.

Bugsy stood there aghast, the smoking weapon still in his possession. Vince stared at the prostrate body in utter incredulity. Reggie and Pip now felt liberated to enter the room. Willa, for perhaps the first time in her life, had no immediate idea of what to do.

But Rollo did. He stepped forward, kneeled over the body, dabbed the seeping hole in McCain's forehead with his fingers, and tasted the blood. Willa and Vince exchanged suspicious glances; this was where they had come in. But it was real, all right. Then he expertly checked the tycoon's breathing and heartbeat. There were none.

Taking a deep breath, he raised himself up and rounded on Bugsy.

"Oh, great. Terrific! The most powerful man in the world decided to keep our zoo open, so you kill him. Brilliant. Thank you so very much, especially for shooting him right between the eyes so that it doesn't look like an accident. Because everyone at Octopus knew he came here to close us down—hence, our motive for murdering him. Stunning! As an ex-cop, I'm telling you that not even the O. J. Simpson jury would acquit us of this one. Well, Mr. Brain of Britain, what are we going to say to the police, who are already on their way here—another example of the thoroughness of your planning."

Adrian "Bugsy" Malone stood staring at the corpse in a state of advanced trauma. He opened his mouth to try to formulate some explanation, but none was forthcoming. He became as wordless as the bee which he was dressed up as.

"So what's the plan?" Rollo was as surprised by this state of silence as Bugsy himself was. "Yes? What?" He cupped his hand to his ear. "Sorry, we didn't quite catch it."

But all they continued to catch was a mute and dumbfounded arachnid.

"Ice! Ice!"

It was Vince who suddenly broke the silence.

"What?" demanded Willa.

"Send out for ice. Quick!" Vince repeated.

"Ice?" Willa wondered what devious scheme Vince now had in mind. She didn't have to wait long to find out.

"Yes. He's got to be cryogenically frozen till they find a cure." He looked round at the assorted animals. "Call a bar!"

"A cure?" Willa was incredulous. Vince had clearly lost what was left of his mind.

"Don't worry, Dad." He was down on one knee reassuring his dead father.

Willa walked round to the other side of the corpse and hunkered down so that Vince was straight in her eyeline. She indicated the hole in Rod's forehead. The blood had started to congeal. "He's got a bullet in the brain," she said.

Vince appeared not to hear her. "Can we put him in the freezer?"

Like the young Prince Hamlet, he had clearly lost his mind in his grief, Willa realised. She took pity on him and put an arm round his shoulders. "Vince, this isn't an illness like cancer or motor neurone disease which they might find a cure for in the distant future. This is a bullet in the brain. There isn't any cure for a bullet in the brain. There never will be. It's very fatal."

Vince closed his eyes to assimilate this information. "You mean . . . he's not coming back?"

Everyone in the room solemnly shook their heads—although he couldn't see them.

"He's . . . dead?" Vince seemed to need final reassurance of the fact.

Willa tightened her grip on his shoulder, afraid he might collapse with grief. "I'm afraid so, Vince."

He stared at his father's corpse for several seconds, and then the light shone into his mind as he rose up, casting off Willa's arm and embarking on what looked like a ritual dance.

"Oh, I'm so happy. This is the moment I've been waiting for all my life. You're dead, you bastard." He looked up at the heavens. "Oh thank you, God, thank you, God. Life begins."

Rollo, embarrassed by this display, looked anxiously at his watch and then at Willa. "The police are going to be here any minute. What are we going to do?"

She shrugged. They knew they were helpless.

"Why don't we take his body and feed it to the big cats? We've done it before."

The suggestion came from Pip. Rollo looked at her innocent, angelic face. "Done it before?" he asked.

"It's a good idea but it wouldn't work," Willa intervened more practically. "Neville must have dropped him off here. He's probably on his way back with the cops right now."

"I'll never have to listen to you again saying"—and here Vince went into an approximation of his father's antipodean accent—" 'You're no son of mine, you miserable little worm. You disgust me.' "

It came to Willa in a flash, like a message being infiltrated into her brain from some source way, way out in the universe. It was the sort of thing that can happen to a human once in a lifetime or, more likely, never in a lifetime. But it had happened to her.

"Say that again," she said very quietly and very firmly.

Vince looked at her and obliged, his Southern twang all the higher from the state of ecstasy he was in. "You're no son of mine, you—"

"No!" Willa interrupted him. "In your father's voice . . ."

Vince eyed her suspiciously but, once again, was only too pleased to play along. He was only too pleased to do anything. He was free. Free to be himself at last. He looked at the body on the ground and cleared his throat, this time coming closer to the dismissive growl of his late father. "You're no son of mine, you miserable little worm. You disgust me."

Willa looked at Rollo and Rollo looked at Willa.

Rollo's eyes scanned the room desperately. "What about the moustache?" he asked.

Willa had been looking around, too. "What about yours?" she suggested.

Three minutes later Vince was sitting on the lavatory seat looking at himself in the mirror of the administration block toilet. He was clad entirely in his late father's clothes, right down to the socks. Reggie was furiously inserting rolled-up newspaper and broken-up cardboard padding into the shoulders of his jacket to give him Rod's girth. Willa had coloured his hair with talcum powder to add age and now was using her Bobbi Brown makeup kit to wither his skin as subtly as possible.

Pip had the hardest task of all. Having carefully measured Vince's upper lip, she had created a three-and-a-half-inch length of double-sided tape. With nail scissors she had almost finished removing Rollo's proud military moustache and transferred it to the sticky surface. As she put the final hairs in place, Willa added more talcum powder to match his hair.

"G'day, gentlemen. I'll tell you why I called you here . . ." Vince sat like a rapidly ageing Anzac actor running his lines in front of the mirror.

"Bit more white," Pip instructed Willa.

Bugsy was seated at the computer in Willa's office, typing furiously, a legal-looking tome by his side.

"You finished?" Rollo demanded urgently, running his forefinger across his unfamiliarly naked top lip. He hadn't felt it in thirty years.

Bugsy nodded responsively but silently and punched the printout button. Rollo moved swiftly across the room to inspect the document as it emerged from the whirring printer. Eventually he ripped it out and brought it back to Willa.

"What do you think?" he asked.

"You're the lawman," she replied flirtatiously.

"It'll stand up in court," he assured her in a cautiously confident fashion. He pointed at the document. "This is the bit that matters: "I leave Marwood Zoo together with all animals equipment and property on which it stands to be held in trust by the directors (Rollo Ernest Lee, Willa Ethel Weston, and their assigns) of the said zoo for the continuing research conservation and preservation of species and animals."

"Do you have to include the Ethel?" she grimaced.

"How do you think I feel about Ernest?" Rollo replied. "It's legalese. There's always the danger there might be another Willa Weston somewhere in the world." He looked at her lovingly. "Not that there could be."

"You haven't stitched me up?" Vince had reverted to his native accent in the accusation.

"An Englishman's word is his bond," Rollo enunciated very carefully.

"Oh really? Tell me about Lloyd's." The American laughed.

"Here." Rollo handed him the document. "Read it yourself."

"And read it in Rod's voice," Willa demanded. "I can't understand why the cops aren't here already. Pip rang the station and they left twelve minutes ago."

By now, Vince looked very like his father and spoke quite like him. "Subject as aforesaid and to the payment of my funeral and testamentary expenses and debts I give all the remainder of my real and personal estate wheresoever and whatsoever to my son Vincent Colin McCain." He lowered the document and reverted to his own voice. "Do we have to include the Colin?"

"Its legalese," Willa assured him.

"It's straight out of the book." Rollo pointed to the legal volume in Bugsy's claw. The muted insect keeper nodded his head eagerly, rather in the manner of Harpo Marx—the silent brother.

Willa was worried. "It's very short."

"The simpler it is, the more watertight," Rollo reassured her as Bugsy continued to nod furiously.

"Okay." She sounded far from reassured, but there was hardly time to engage a firm of lawyers. She turned her attention to Vince. "What do you think, Rollo?"

"Excellent moustache," said the Englishman. "Do you think I could have it back when he's finished?"

"There's no time for joking. Will they believe it? Pip said they were sending three policemen, one of them an inspector."

"You could put a rhino in Rod's clothes and fool most of the bobbies round here." Rollo had little respect for the local Kent force.

"Be sensible!" she pleaded.

"He looks fine. They've only ever seen him in the papers or on television."

"Neville," said Vince nervously. "What about Neville?"

"We've got to keep him on the other side of the room." Rollo became decisive. "And Vince, you must try to stay out of any direct light—for a change." The insult sailed over Vince's head.

"Keep practising the voice," Willa pressed him. "It's not right."

Vince picked up the will and attempted a closer approximation of his father's growled and flattened vowels. "I Roderick Genghis McCain of Octopus Inc. Atlanta being of sound mind . . ."

"Let's compare them," suggested Willa.

". . . hereby revoke all former wills made by me . . ."

Bugsy and Reggie lifted up the dead body of Rod McCain from which they had taken the clothes and placed his face just behind and to the side of Vince's so they could contrast them in the lavatory mirror.

". . . and declare this to be my last will and test—" Vince nearly leapt out of his seat at the sight of his father. "Jesus Christ Almighty. Dad, I didn't do it! It was the fucking anteater. Him, the one with the tentacles—"

Willa pressed a hand on his shoulder. "Calm down. Your father's dead. We're just comparing you."

"Very good," pronounced Rollo.

"Earlobes?" Pip was a perfectionist, and indeed Big Rod's pendulous lobes were noticeably missing from the fake face of his son.

"No time," snapped Willa. "Let's get this body through to Vince's office. Where's the coat, by the way?"

"We left it in there," Reggie replied.

Once they were clear of the lavatory, Vince indicated to Rollo that he should close the door and beckoned him over.

He indicated the will on the shelf in front of the mirror. "Rollo, I have a problem with this."

"What are you talking about? How can you have a problem? You get Octopus—the entire empire. What more do you want—the presidency of the United States? Mount Rushmore? The Great Pyramids of Giza?"

"No." Vince seemed lost in thought. "You see, you get to run the zoo with Willa."

"That is correct."

Vince looked up at him with as much sincerity as he was capable of. "I think I love her, Rollo."

"You think you love her," Rollo repeated slowly. "Watch my lips. This is the equation. I get her and the zoo. You get seven billion dollars."

Vince thought for a second. "Okay, it's a deal."

CHAPTER
15

As he followed the police car's blaring siren and flashing blue light through the winding byways of Kent, Neville Coltrane pressed his foot on the throttle with a sense of excitement. His face had abandoned its usual fierce expression for a look of joyous anticipation. Neville had been waiting for this moment for a long time—a very long time. It had taken him more than twenty-five years in Octopus Inc. to reach the inner sanctum and the unofficial position of Rod McCain's right-hand man. The job was one that he was born to perform: the daily intoxicant of power, the pride of walking in the footsteps of one of the world's legendary figures, and the delight in doing dirty work when it was allocated to him.

But one thorn had repeatedly pierced his flesh: Vince. The court jester of Octopus was allowed a long leash solely because he was the boss's son. Not that Rod didn't treat him like shit, but Vince was too obtuse to notice this. Nev could put the fear of God into every living servant of the corporation except this cretinous creature whom Rod, in order not to upset his ex-wife, permitted to think that he was a vice president of marketing.

And when, four years ago, the golden opportunity to kick him out had presented itself after Neville had caught him red-handed forging his father's signature on a check, Rod had exercised unusual restraint. Vince had had the fright of his life when his father had threatened that he was going to bring in the cops, but then Rod had discovered that the account on which the check was drawn was not one that had ever been made public, especially to the IRS, and so the whole incident had had to be hushed up.

But not this time. Neville's craggy Australian features broke into a smile at the prospect of what was in store. Vince's charmed life had about two minutes to run. The full might of Scotland Yard or whatever these guys in front were called was about to descend on the petty con man and put him inside for a long time. A million bucks might be loose change to Rod McCain but, as the inspector had told him at the station, it was considered major larceny when weighed upon the scales of English justice.

The cars swept into the forecourt of the zoo and the three policemen—two sergeants and the inspector—leapt out, looking to Neville for guidance as to where they should go. In truth, he realised as he levered his bulky frame out of the Merc, he had no idea himself.

But, waiting on the steps of what he presumed to be the main entrance, there was Willa, more beautiful than any woman had any right to be. She spread her arms wide and offered a devastating smile as she came down the steps, like a society hostess greeting new arrivals for a weekend in the country.

"Good evening, gentlemen. Thank you for coming."

The police stopped in their tracks and one of the sergeants removed his helmet.

"Neville!"

The stout Australian was rooted to the spot and could feel his already florid cheeks redden further as she came towards him and planted a less than social kiss lingeringly on his cheek.

"You look great," she said, standing back to appraise him. "Have you lost weight?"

"Er . . ." Neville had been thrown completely off track by this greeting; she had never treated him like this before.

Willa now turned her charm on the inspector and introduced herself with an outstretched arm. "Willa Weston," she said with a dazzling smile.

"Er . . . Inspector Masefield," he replied with a questioning sidelong glance at Neville.

"I'm so glad you could come at such short notice," she said.

Neville had recovered his composure. "We'd better get in there. Make sure the boss is all right."

"Can I take your coats?"

The four men looked up at the main doorway, and there, standing upright and clean-shaven, was a tall man who could have been taken for the perfect butler were it not for the fact that his shirt was hanging down below his jacket.

Inside the boardroom the atmosphere had reached fever pitch. Nobody could decide which was the most obscure place to put Vince. Pip and Reggie favoured a spot beside the window so that the light would semisilhouette him. But Bugsy was pointing furiously to a chair behind a desk in a darker corner of the room where the ceiling was at its lowest. The sound of voices in the courtyard made them go with Bugsy's option, largely because a petrified Vince was sitting there when they heard them.

"Good luck!" said Reggie, patting him on the shoulder.

The three of them then bundled themselves into Vince's old office but, just as Pip was closing the door, Bugsy began to poke his finger like a jackhammer at Vince and then at his own face.

She got it immediately. "Glasses!"

But where were they? The three of them started to scour the room as the sound of the approaching voices grew closer and closer. Vince seemed to be in too much a state of stasis to be able to do anything for himself other than to mutter "G'day" under his breath like some waxwork figure.

Pip searched furiously through the pockets of Rod McCain's overcoat and jacket, but to little avail. Reggie staggered and hopped around the room, the sewn-together costume that tailed down to his flipper acting like a leg iron, and looked under tables and among the files by Willa's desk.

Bugsy may have lost his power of speech, but not of reasoning. He went to the most obvious place. Yes, they were still on the face of the corpse of Big Rod. The insect disrespectfully whipped them off and crashed into the others, who were dashing back into Vince's office as he came charging out.

There was now the sound of footsteps outside and, as Bugsy plonked Rod's darkened spectacles in his son's hand, he realised he had no time to get back to Vince's office. In desperation he dived under the desk, hoping it would provide him with a safe harbour until the police departed.

"Rod, the police are here," Willa announced as she tentatively opened the door, making sure that she could check that things were in order before anybody else could see anything.

"Rod" was clumsily fiddling with his glasses. "G'day," he mumbled as he attempted to fit them behind his ears.

Having appraised the situation, she threw the door open wider. "This is Inspector Masefield."

The inspector made as if to walk across the room to shake the great man by the hand, but "Rod" signalled him to keep his distance. "Terrible flu." He coughed. "Bloody British climate. Not your fault, though. Nice to see you."

The inspector affected a semisalute. "It's a great honour to have you here, Mr. McCain."

"Exactly," "Rod" agreed. "Hello, Neville."

His sidekick cut through the pleasantries. "Have you spoken to Vince?"

"Rod" nodded sagely. "Yep."

"Shall we arrest him now, sir?" the inspector inquired. The two sergeants were erectly behind him in the room and made motions of looking for the errant son.

"Rod" held up a restraining hand and, after a hidden gesture from Willa, quickly brought it down again. His flesh looked far too young for a man of sixty-five. But he shook his head in a sombre fashion.

"No. I have to tell you I've changed my mind, gentlemen."

"Changed your mind?" Neville's voice went up two octaves as he echoed his master's statement.

"Rod" ignored the interruption and, pushing his glasses farther up the bridge of his nose, fixed the policeman with a sincere stare.

"Do you have a son, Inspector?"

The officer was taken aback. "I do, sir. Two."

"Fine boys?" asked "Rod" in a man-to-manly sort of way.

"Fine boys, sir," the inspector warily agreed.

"So's mine," said "Rod."

All three policemen glanced at Neville, who exuded a blend of extreme embarrassment and increasing incredulity.

"It's a long time since Vince and I had a really long talk," "Rod" went on, "but we did today. Between ourselves, it was quite emotional."

Neville felt himself about to explode, and did. "Rod, you haven't killed him, have you?"

"No, you moron," "Rod" snapped back at him. "What I'm saying is: we've had a reconciliation."

This was more than Neville could take. The boss, he felt certain, must be having some kind of seizure. He needed help. The portly Australian began to make his way to the desk where "Rod" was sitting.

"Isn't it wonderful, Neville. Aren't you thrilled?" Willa adroitly managed to interpose herself between the backs of the chairs at the conference table and the wall so that Neville's passage towards Rod was effectively blocked.

"A reconciliation?" Neville steamed.

"That's right, Neville." "Rod" assumed a bedside tone to try and calm the man down. "I've misjudged the boy badly. I'm proud of him."

Anxious to get a clearer view of the expression on his boss's face, Neville tried to push past Willa, but she succeeded in giving way only a little without appearing in any manner to be acting as a barrier.

"You *are* joking, Rod, aren't you?" he queried.

The inspector was uneasy. Something in this situation wasn't right. He had a nose for this sort of thing. He scanned the room. It was just possible that the son was somewhere aiming a gun at his father in order to obtain this extraordinary volte-face. "Do I gather that you're not pressing charges, Mr. McCain?" he asked.

"No, no charges," said "Rod." "But there is something you gentlemen of the law *can* do for me, and it's the reason I didn't call Neville on the car phone and tell him there was no need for your presence. There it is."

He picked up a document from the desk and waved it at them. "I've just drawn up a new will, and it needs to be witnessed by persons of the utmost probity and respectability. None better than officers of the law."

"A new will?" In an effort to get a look at it, Neville once more tried to get past Willa. She kissed him for the second time on the cheek, saying calmly: "Don't worry."

Rollo came up from behind and put a very firm arm around his shoulders. "It's a momentous day, Neville."

"Momentous indeed," said "Rod," signing the document with a flourish. "As result of our talk I've decided to leave Octopus to Vince. Now if two of you gentlemen would be kind enough to witness this . . ."

Willa almost snatched the will and pen from the desk and presented them to the inspector, who dutifully did as he was bid.

This was not the man he had driven to the zoo; Neville was certain of that. Had they drugged him? Something was amiss. "But Rod . . . ," he began.

"What?" his boss snarled back.

"You said, not half an hour ago, that every time you look at him he just makes you want to throw up."

"How can you say that?" "Rod" rose from his desk.

"You called him a waste of sperm," his henchman yelled.

"No I didn't." "Rod" came round the desk towards him. The police sergeant who was adding his signature to the will looked up in surprise. Willa deftly removed the document from him.

"Yes you did. Are you going out of your mind?" Neville was certainly close to leaving his. "You're always saying what a complete wuss he is."

"No I'm not . . . ," yelled Vince, completely forgetting to put on his father's voice as he thumped Neville in the stomach. The three policemen stared in mute amazement. Nothing like this had ever happened in Tenterden before.

"No I'm not . . ." "Rod" regained the right vowels—"going to let you say that about him."

His vowels may have come back, but in the attack he had dislodged one side of his artificial moustache, which now drooped down over the centre of his mouth.

Neville rose to his feet, holding no grudge; this playful thumping was part of their language. But the man who had hit him was not Rod. The blow was too soft, for one thing. And he spoke American.

"Rod, are you all right?"

"I told you," "Rod" replied, "I'm a little emotional."

"But your voice . . . ," Neville went on. "And there's something wrong with your moustache."

Vince had sensed something tickling his lower lip and now, as his hand flew up to it, he realised to his horror that half his moustache had come off. Neville had certainly spotted it, but what about the cops? There was a fair-to-even chance that they were far enough away to have been more diverted by the extraordinary behaviour of Neville and him than to have paid much attention to details. But they certainly knew that something was amiss. It could only be a matter of seconds now before they rumbled him.

Willa realised this simultaneously and, quick as a flash, pulled a handkerchief from her pocket and ran across and thrust it into his face.

She rounded on Neville in anger. "He's very upset, Neville. And very depressed."

"Yes," "Rod" mumbled from behind the handkerchief, which now covered his fallen moustache. "I'm very depressed."

Neville turned imploringly to the police. "This isn't like Rod, Inspector. Didn't you see—"

"You're right." Willa placed herself between Neville and the approaching policemen. "But isn't it wonderful to see a man getting in touch with his feelings?"

"That may be all very well and good," Neville conceded, "but the man you see is not—"

"Gentlemen. You're going to have to excuse me." "Rod," handkerchief to face, tearfully stumbled towards the closed door of Vince's office. "I need to be alone. I'm feeling so depressed-slash-suicidal."

"What?" The inspector came after him.

"Rod" stayed his progress with a raised hand. "I've behaved disgracefully to my son in the past. I don't know if I can live with that. Good-bye!"

He threw open the door of the office, seeing to his relief that neither Pip nor Reggie was in sight, and staggered in, locking the door behind him.

"That's not Rod McCain," Neville bellowed at the police officers. "You're going to have to arrest him."

"Of course it's Rod," Willa countered, like the counsel for the defence in a court case. "Look at this signature. Get a document out of your case, Neville, and compare it."

Neville was taken aback by this. He picked up his case from the floor and opened it, confident that he would be able to prove precisely the reverse.

"Oh, the agony! The sheer agony!" "Rod" wailed from the other side of the door. "To think how badly I've treated my beloved boy. How I undervalued his talent. His extraordinary charm. His dress sense. How I ignored him. How I never came to my birthday parties, the bastard—"

He was given a sharp nudge by Pip, who was undressing him as fast as she could. Reggie had propped up Rod's corpse against a table leg and had embarked on the difficult task of dressing a dead man while Vince's soliloquy masked most of the noise they were making. Time was of the essence. If the police believed Neville they would have the door down in a matter of seconds.

"Oh, I'm so ashamed to be me," "Rod" continued.

"Is he all right?" the inspector asked Willa. The three policemen were lined up by the door listening to the tirade. Neville, meanwhile, was thumbing through his files to try and find something that Rod had signed.

"It's one of his black moods," she explained.

Neville looked up. "What black moods?"

"He's probably never allowed you to see him like this," Willa shot back. "Ask Vince about them."

On the other side of the door Vince was down to his underwear and peeling off the rest of his moustache as he watched Pip and Reggie trying to do up the tie on the dead body of his father.

"Oh, Vince, how can you forgive me?" He was beginning to run out of words. "No, I can't face it. I can't live with myself any longer."

"My God." On the board room side of the door Willa threw her hands to her mouth. "Has he got the gun?"

"What gun?" demanded the inspector.

Rollo rushed to the desk where "Rod" had been sitting and pulled open the top drawer. "It's gone!" he exclaimed in despair.

"This is the end of the road," "Rod" cried from the other side of the door, waving the gun out of the window. "I'm going to finish it now."

But he couldn't finish it just yet, as some of the padding that had been used to fill out his body had spilled over the floor. Pip and Reggie scuttled around to pick it up. Their task was not made easier by the sound of the police battering on the door.

"I think so, anyway . . . ," Vince improvised feverishly. "It's certainly on the cards. I'll make my mind up in a moment."

Willa watched helplessly as the police tried to force the locked door open. Fortunately, they didn't have any implements to hand.

"Use the desk," instructed the inspector.

The sergeants sped across the room and struggled to lift up the desk. As they did so a man-sized bee shot out from under it. Completely startled, they immediately dropped it, hitting one of them on the foot.

At the same time, on the other side of the door, Reggie was holding out Rod's right hand as Vince pointed the gun out the window. "With a final cry of "No, I'm going to end it all. Forgive me, Vince" he let off a shot and passed the revolver to Pip, who polished off his prints with a duster and passed it on to Reggie, who squeezed it into Rod's palm.

Vince leapt through the ground-floor window, with the other two following suit just as the desk crashed the office door to the ground.

The inspector was the first in, immediately removing a plastic glove from his pocket as he bent over to check the prone body of Rod McCain for life.

Rollo and Willa followed with trepidation. As soon as they were in the room, Rollo placed a hand over Willa's eyes with the injunction: "Don't look!"

"I can take it," she said, brushing his hand away. "Is he dead, Inspector?"

"Very dead," Masefield replied. He gingerly removed the revolver from Rod's right hand and gave it to one of the sergeants. "Take this to forensics."

"Poor Rod." Willa began to cry.

"I'm sorry, ma'am," the inspector apologised.

"We should have seen what was going to happen," Rollo added remorsefully.

Through her tears Willa betrayed signs of anger. "Why were your men so slow?"

The inspector rose to his feet. "We just didn't realise. We had no idea that—"

"I don't think you have to apologise, Inspector." A burly figure had entered the room and taken up a position between Rollo and Willa and the body on the floor.

"Neville!" Willa warned him. "Show some respect in the presence of the dead."

"This man may be dead"—Neville knelt down by the body—"but he is certainly not Rod McCain."

"What are you talking about?" demanded Inspector Masefield.

Neville turned round to confront the three inquiring faces. "This man is an impostor. And I can prove it. Nobody except me noticed that he was wearing a false moustache."

He turned back to McCain's body, gripped hold of the left end of the dead man's moustache between his forefinger and thumb, and tugged it with a flourish, hoping the whole thing to come away in his hand.

It didn't.

Neville tried again, and still it didn't. "Listen, I could have sworn. I don't know what the fuck's going on here, but I saw with my own eyes—"

"I know what's going on." The inspector put a severe hand on his shoulder. "You are interfering with Crown evidence, which the Home Office pathologist will view with the greatest concern. Don't you realise that we are dealing with one of the most powerful men in the world?"

"Do you think I don't know that?" Neville was utterly bewildered. "It's just that in that other room, a few minutes ago, I saw with my very own eyes . . . or, I thought I saw . . ."

"What's happened?" A familiar American voice floated through from the next room. "What's everybody doing in my office?"

Vince appeared at the door, casually dressed in a Ralph Lauren tracksuit as if he had just been for a run, with an Atlanta Braves baseball hat on his head. "Police? Has there been a robbery?"

"It's worse than that, Vince." Willa went up to him and embraced him. As she did so she managed to push under his cap a shank of powdered white hair. "Your father."

"Somebody robbed my father? After our loving talk I wandered down to the gorilla compound and I heard something that sounded like a shot. Did you get the burglar?"

Then he affected to catch sight of the corpse on the floor. "Father!" he cried, going down dramatically on one knee beside it. Hamlet could not have been more upset over Ophelia.

"I'm afraid he's dead, Vince." Rollo put a sympathetic hand on his shoulder.

"Dad dead? No, no, no. It's not possible. He can't be."

"He shot himself, Vince," Willa solemnly informed him.

"Why?" Vince turned to her in despair. "Was he in one of his black moods?"

"How come I never—," Neville began, but Willa was quick to interrupt him.

"He couldn't live with what he'd done to you," she said.

Vince, still on his knees, held out his arms penitentially. "But I'd forgiven him."

Placing his head beside that of his father, he wailed: "Oh Dad, Dad, Dad."

Even the three policemen, senior officers who had seen it all in their time, were moved close to tears by this display of filial affection.

It was Rollo who broke the respectful silence. "There's something you should know, Vince."

"What?"

"In his last act—the last thing he did on this earth before he took his life—he made out a new will leaving everything to you. The whole of Octopus."

Vince blinked his eyes to absorb this information. "Do you know, more than the money—most of which I shall give to charity, of course—is the thought. You see, it proves he did love me after all."

The two police sergeants, still deeply affected by this display of grief, were somewhat startled to find themselves standing beside a sea lion and a lemur.

"Everything but the zoo," Willa remarked.

CHAPTER
16

Marwood Zoo,
Tenterden,
Cranbrook,
Kent TN17 4AA

8th November 1996

Dear Archie,

You must think me an absolute shit (excuse my French) for taking so long to reply to your letter of 8th April. But I have had rather an eventful summer and personal correspondence, as you know, always seems to get shoved to the bottom of the pile.

I've been rereading your letter and I can see I owe you a succession of apologies. First the change of name—Lee. Yes, well, I sort of hoped it might help in the Hong Kong force—the whole place was throwing off the colonial mantle and giving preferment to the locals but, in truth, it didn't do much good since the moment they saw me any claim of

Chinese ancestry went out the window. Evidently there's no such thing as a six-foot-five Chinaman, or Chinese man as they prefer to be known these days.

And, as you can see from the above address, even if you had been able to find me through the Hong Kong directory it wouldn't have done you much good today, since they don't include too many Kent telephone numbers (joke!). Come to think of it, if I were to put my name in the Tenterden telephone directory I'd probably be the only Lee, although there is rather a good Chinese restaurant run by a chap called Tang who might have a cousin of that name working for him.

Listen, I'm sorry about your continuing exile and having to eat all those awful meals with Ronnie Biggs—isn't there any way you can lure him to an offshore island where they do have an extradition treaty with Blighty and tip off that Slipper of the Yard as to where he is? Or has Slipper retired? In truth, I don't think the British public are that interested in the great train robbers any longer, if they remember them at all. They've got that West man who chopped up half of the women in Gloucester starting with his own daughter, or the exceptionally innocent Mr. O. J. Simpson.

After I sent my letter, I realised I should have contacted you a long time ago, but pretended to myself I didn't know where to write—but more important, I didn't know *what* to write. I'd always looked up to you, Archie: Cambridge, the bar, Wendy, the Jaguar, the horse, Portia and all that, and it came as a bit of a surprise when you chucked it all in and went off with that American gangster. It just shows how you can misread people—even those close to you—if you don't really know what's going on inside their minds.

It seemed to me that all that success was exactly what our parents had planned for us, and I felt for a long while that I was a total failure. But then in Hong Kong, in the police force, I began to sense that I had a role to play: to serve my country, to uphold the rule of law, to try and establish a sense of fair play, and, especially, to export British values so that other people could see how the old system worked. And it was enough; I didn't need loads of cash or children or, indeed, women for the most part.

So I was happy—or, let's say, I was content. I'd established a way of life that was not opulent, but not impoverished, either. And there was such comforting camaraderie in the force. But then it was indicated to me that after twenty-something years it was time for colonials like me to retire, and that was when I was lucky enough—or thought I was lucky enough—to pick up a well-paid job working for Octopus Inc., where you tracked me down.

I hated it. It consisted of watching the management acquire new assets—mainly in the media—and then me being brought in to fire people and negotiate their redundancy terms. For some reason, wholly undeserved, perhaps because of my police background, I got the reputation of being hard-nosed. That was why I was sent to England.

I suspect that if you manage to read the New York Times or even the Tijuca Echo, or maybe you're wired to CNN, you will have made the connection between the address at the top of this notepaper and the late Mr. Rod McCain. Yes, he really did commit suicide here at the zoo, before our very eyes. Well, not quite before our very eyes, but in an adjoining room we had seen him enter a mere two minutes earlier. In a most remarkable piece of behaviour he kissed and made up with his estranged son, Vince, and then called the local police to witness a new will, leaving Octopus to the son and the zoo as an independent trust.

Not greatly mourned, I'm afraid. I suppose if you run your companies by fear one of the things you have to fear yourself is that no one will give a toss when you shuffle off this mortal coil. And they didn't. I went to the memorial service at St. Columba's Presbyterian Church in Pont Street, London—McCain, being of Scottish descent, was a "press button B"—and it was full of greedy insincere men paying lengthy insincere tributes.

I mean, get a load of this; it was actually in the order of service, and I quote: "A mere handful of men in the modern world have really seized the rich opportunities that life can offer us. Rod McCain was a true visionary. He used his unquenchable energy, his bold leadership, and his unerring eye for an asset that was undervalued to acquire slackly run corporations and companies where misplaced philanthropy and employee welfare had pared down the profits, to make them lean and fit, and to feed them to the ever-hungry Octopus Inc., which spread its tentacles to every corner of the globe."

Unbelievable, isn't it? His widow, Megan, couldn't even be bothered to turn up—which might indicate something about the state of their marriage. I understand—from a confidential source—that Rod, who sent videos of himself to everyone in Octopus telling us what to do, was in the habit of even sending them to his wife on birthdays and anniversaries, with the text written by one of the copywriting staff in the (ugh!) marketing department. I also know—from an even more confidential source—that it was his intention in his previous will to have himself cryogenically frozen when he died and his assets put into a trust fund until they could find a way of taking him out of the deep freeze and curing him. Well, the wife ignored all that. So she didn't make it to the memorial service but sent a video in the Almighty Rod tradition. We got ahold of a copy for the zoo. It's a hoot. She spends most of her time talking like a lawyer about the court case she has embarked on to try and wrest control of the company from her stepson, Vince. (Fortunately she has not challenged the Marwood Zoo Trust—not enough dollars in that, I suspect, for it to matter.)

In the few weeks that he was here this summer (very hot, incidentally) Vince McCain had tried to turn this place into some fucking fun-fair (excuse my French again, but I become apoplectic at the thought of it). What had been a haven of animal care and conservation was beginning to be despoiled by the graffiti of his crude and addled imagination. We had all manner of sleazy sideshows, clockwork animals (and probably clockwork keepers, too, if he stayed long enough), and ghastly blowups of international personalities that were meant to attract people to compounds where noble animals were living in near-natural habitats.

It gave me exceptional pleasure to watch these being turned into a series of bonfires that lit the way for Vince to accompany the coffin of his late and unlamented father out of the place, which was rapidly restored to normal.

Anyway, I have resumed my duties as director of the zoo—I had to stand down temporarily after some ghastly smears in the local press calling me a "Vampire Gunman." Utterly without foundation, and if you'd still been practising here I'd have had them in the High Court before you could say Jeffrey Archer. I'm codirector, actually, with Miss Willa Weston, a young executive from Atlanta. We have a polite but distant relationship.

I wish you could come here and see this place, Archie. You know, when I would go home on furlough from Honkers, I'd find a country that was more and more alien from the one of my birth. But here at Marwood, by some miracle, I really have rediscovered England's green and pleasant land. It's something of a time warp—the grounds are so pleasing and peaceful; despite very little money, the zookeepers have a total commitment to their vocations and retain a terrific sense of humour; and even the customers are polite and well-mannered, the way families used to be. A lot of single dads come with little ones at the weekends, so we've put in a petting paddock for them to enjoy themselves. They even named it the Lee Compound after me— the keepers know I love the little brown jobs. And sometimes, in the evening after the zoo has closed, we sit by the flamingo pool and just . . .

Ah. I was going to cross that bit out. But then I read your letter again. You've been candid with me, so I may as well be candid with you. Miss Weston and I have entered into a relationship. It didn't go too well at first. Her mind must have been poisoned against me by the odious Vince, because she kept asking me what sort of things I did with three or four women in a bed, as if I'd written the Kamabloodysutra. On the evidence so far, I'm pleased to say, she appears far more likely to have been its author than me.

And, do you know, judging from the newspaper cuttings, Willa looks a lot like Wanda. I enclose a photograph of us taken the night we were runners-up in the darts competition. Of course she has never—to my knowledge—organised a jewellery robbery. But she has stolen something far more valuable.

My heart.

Your affectionate brother,

Rollo